BURDEN
OF
TOMORROW

Dr S.C. Narula completed his undergraduate studies in Physics and Astronomy, followed by a postgraduate degree in English Literature. He went on to earn his PhD from Delhi University. His doctoral dissertation focused on Christopher Fry and was later published as the *Theocentric World of Fry's Drama*. His work on Milton was published as the *Milton Handbook: Analysing Poetry in the Context of the Pulpit & the Ludlow Masque*, along with several shorter poems. The chapters comprising this work originated as presentations at academic conferences and Milton Seminars, garnering global recognition for him.

Having extensively travelled, he has contributed numerous research articles to distinguished international literary journals. His initial venture beyond academia was *The Third Passenger*, a collection of poems published in 2016, which has now entered its second printing. In the same year, he published his second compilation of poetry, titled *Inheritors of Broken Sky*. Furthermore, he has penned several volumes of short stories, a novella titled *Damyanti: Woman of Substance* and a novel, *The Ranas of Solan*.

Dr Narula has earned acclaim for his skill in translating Urdu, Punjabi and Hindi poetry into English, a role he undertook for the esteemed Sahitya Akademi (India's National Academy of Letters) and Rupa Publications. He is also honoured with the Dhaka Translation Fest (2018) Lifetime Literary Award.

Also by Subhash Chandra Narula

The Ranas of Solan

BURDEN OF TOMORROW

SUBHASH CHANDRA NARULA

RUPA

Published by
Rupa Publications India Pvt. Ltd 2024
7/16, Ansari Road, Daryaganj
New Delhi 110002

Sales centres:
Bengaluru Chennai
Hyderabad Jaipur Kathmandu
Kolkata Mumbai Prayagraj

Copyright © Subhash Chandra Narula 2024

All rights reserved.
No part of this publication may be reproduced, transmitted
or stored in a retrieval system, in any form or by any means,
electronic, mechanical, photocopying, recording or otherwise,
without the prior permission of the publisher.

This is a work of fiction. Names, characters, places and incidents are either the
product of the author's imagination or are used fictitiously and any resemblance
to any actual person, living or dead, events or locales is entirely coincidental.

P-ISBN: 978-93-5702-628-4
E-ISBN: 978-93-5702-707-6

First impression 2024

10 9 8 7 6 5 4 3 2 1

The moral right of the author has been asserted.

Printed in India

This book is sold subject to the condition that it shall not,
by way of trade or otherwise, be lent, resold, hired out or otherwise
circulated, without the publisher's prior consent, in any form of binding or
cover other than that in which it is published.

To
Abha

Contents

Part One / 1

Part Two / 83

Part Three / 97

Part Four / 135

Epilogue / 245

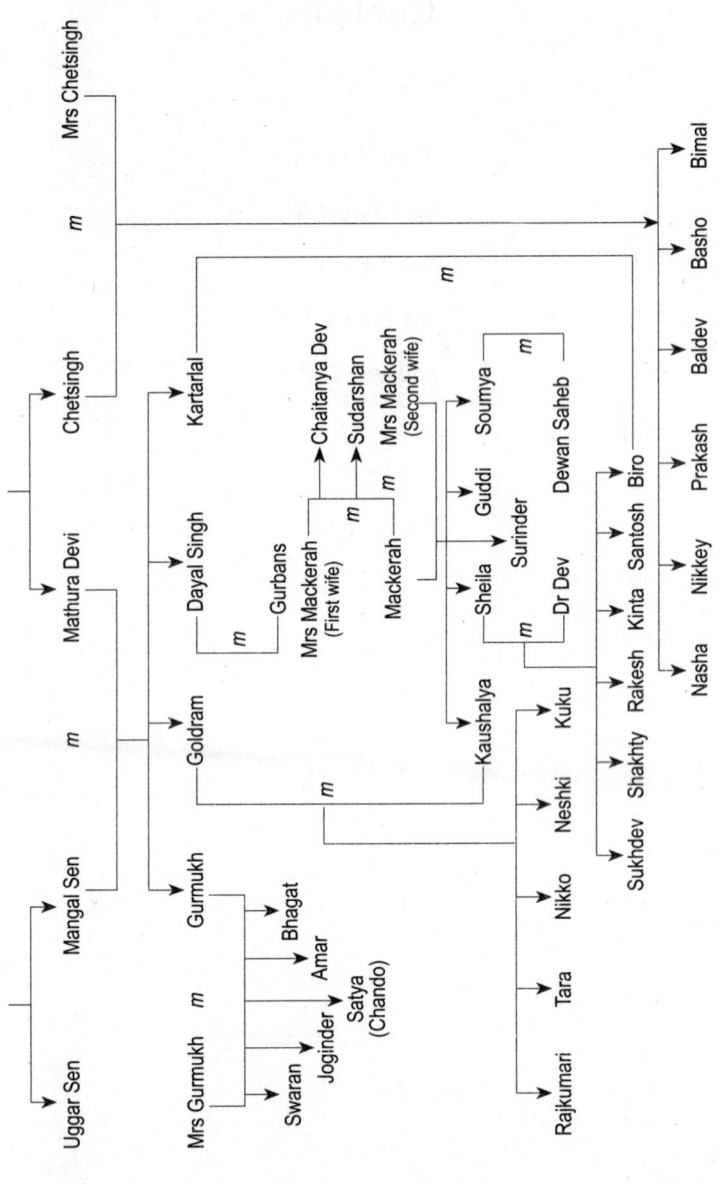

Part One

1

Unless detained by his duties at the desk, wanted by his chief or working late on the exclusive responsibilities entrusted to him, his team of draftsmen and the chief estimator by Sir Rolland—the chief engineer of Burma Railways—Goldram reached home promptly by six in the evening. This project was the latest and most ambitious of the colonial projects in Burma to be undertaken by railway engineers, involving the laying of a railway line from Lashio in north Burma across the border into China under a recently signed commercial treaty between the two governments.

1935-1940

The sociopolitical condition in north and north-west Burma was of violence and terror, fomented by rebel groups of the Karen people. But it was not deterrent enough for the government in Burma to alter the projected plans. For the first survey of the terrain, someone had been sent by the chief engineer to the border areas for eight weeks. Based on this reconnoitre, the later theodolite survey was conducted and blueprints were prepared under the general supervision of the chief engineer and his trusted right-hand man, Goldram.

During the preliminary processes of drawing up plans and estimates for the project, Sir Rolland had been closely watching Goldram and couldn't help but admire his quiet, methodical and level-headed contributions. Goldram smiled to himself with satisfaction to find all was being executed with immaculate precision—the best the chief could expect from his trusted staff.

On a late afternoon, when other members of staff were winding up their day's work to knock off, Sir Rolland approached Goldram and signalled him to his cabin. He offered him a seat across the table and sat with a beatific smile.

'After you've tied up your files in those red cords and are ready to leave, I wish you to have a cup of tea here in my office today. There's something I know I can talk to you about. You have referred to the *Bhagavad Gita* often in our casual conversations and it was a pleasure to hear the precise words and turn of phrases with which you put across your comments and chiselled the idea into a finely cut precious stone.'

Goldram, though taken by surprise, said, 'Oh sure, Sir, it would be my pleasure to share with you whatever my views and ideas are about what I make of the profundity of the message in the verses of the *Gita*. I'll see you later as you desire.' Goldram smiled to himself as he made his way back to his huge table. On it was a drawing board upon which several big and small drawing sheets were pinned up, with erasers and sharpeners strewn over them (and some more in the adjacent stationery tray). Also present was a collection of leaf-green pencils with curvy golden lines running across, sloping downwards or upwards, depending upon the end from which you looked at them—the standpoint does matter.

A little after five, when the rest of the staff had left or were in the process of leaving, Goldram wound his way round his table, straight to the entrance of his chief's cabin.

He saw the chief's liveried attendant laying down tea on the side table near the corner by the wall. The table was covered with an elegant red and white chequered tablecloth.

'Do come in, Goldram, and sit down,' Sir Rolland said. He

walked up to the opposite side of the table to join Goldram with a handshake and then settled down on his side of the table, waiting for his guest to make himself comfortable in the chair. 'I have been reading about the presentation that Vivekananda delivered in Chicago on 11 September 1893 during the inauguration of the World Parliament of Religions. Following his oration, I consulted the *Bhagavad Gita* to clarify some ideas that confused me. I found the reading of the second canto very rewarding and enlightening, but even there I couldn't clearly sort out the concept and exposition of dualism assayed by Sankhya; the duality that exists in the whole creation. I'm sure you have read the *Gita*, and with your clear-headed approach to this native text of yours, you would be able to make things intelligible about the duality of such a worldview for someone alien to oriental thinking, such as me.'

Goldram said, 'I have no claim to make any specialized study of the original Sanskrit text of the *Gita*. But like you rightly said about the text being native to me, there's an element of inherent response to what it says. The *Gita* is something to which we belong, and it belongs to us, like the air and water on which we subsist; though we remain quite unaware of the value of the freely available elixir. The ingrained inward-looking tentacles of both faith and reason draw easily on these abstractions of the *Gita*'s subtle philosophical observations, which make the abstractions acceptable and simple to take in.

'I shall invoke one of the greatest English poets to put across my understanding of Sankhya's exposition on dualism. Without denying the Christian doctrine, Milton's worldview can be simplified, not without awareness of its nuances, into two distinct parts—Nature, in all its multitudinous sensuous splendour, is the manifest world given to eternal flux and mutation; and Grace, which breathes and pulsates in all sentient and non-sentient beings of Nature. That is life, which, too, ultimately shall be redeemed, even in its ugliest manifestation called the fallen state. So almost akin to it is Sankhya's dualist view of the world. All elements in Nature have their distinct attributes.'

'Just wait, Goldram, I'll need to take down a few notes. I'll get a pencil and my notebook.' Rolland went and fetched his writing materials. 'I'm sorry for the interruption, but please go on.'

'As I was saying, every element is distinctly different, but they are all innately gifted with the flexibility to be able to combine with one or more elements to mutate and form multiple new ones, or they exist either inertly or stirring live. It would be helpful to remember, Sir, that for both Milton and Sankhya, Nature and Grace, or Jeevatman and Grace, are considered by stipulation eternal and indestructible.

'Even a creation as complex as a human being is compounded of such elements in naturally right proportions. But for a creation to be sentient and intelligent, the living being must possess a latent mind and spirit, or soul. The soul is untainted and the purest form of motive force for all matter or material combinations. But all matter, in its utmost refined form, creates a repository, which we term as the "mind". The memories stored in the mind are vital to any action, for all action takes shape as an idea or thought in the mind, deduced and decided upon as a conclusion from the consideration of memories. This mind, subjoined to the soul, is what Sankhya calls "Jeevatman" in a human being; the rest is gross matter driven by its elemental attributes. But Jeevatman permeates all else and, by its volition, is awakened by the jolt of disenchantment of the jaded and repetitive experiences of the vicissitudes of life, working out man's salvation.' Goldram exhaled a long breath and, yes, he smiled his broad and candid smile while looking up at his chief.

Sir Rolland was beaming with joy, not only because of the discourse he had just enjoyed listening to but also because his choice of man to repose his trust in had turned out to be better than his own estimation. He was glad that he had entrusted the job of the latest government project of laying railway lines across the Burma–China border to Goldram and his team. His current experience doubly assured him of the successful completion of the project.

Indeed it was Sir Rolland who, having observed Goldram's overall devotion and the quality and quantum of work he left behind on his desk at the end of the day, had assigned the project to Goldram. He also urged Goldram to prepare for a diploma in advanced bridge construction from the London Institute of Engineering. This was particularly in line with his far-sighted view of providing Goldram's intelligent mind with a deeper understanding of the theoretical aspects and the practical work he wanted to entrust on the ground.

~

Goldram left the office and reached home in exactly forty minutes, the time it took for the local train to travel from Pagoda Road to Gyogon. In all, there were eight brief wayside stops at intervening stations—one almost at every mile. The terminus for the local running from Rangoon was Insein, from where it started its journey back to Rangoon. Add a five-minute walk (from the station, down Cohen Road, to the turning into the empty lot and a two-house lane) and there was Goldram's house. On one of the two gateposts, over which a bougainvillea creeper arched abundantly, was inscribed Goldram's name in Urdu and on the other, in English, and on the smaller-lettered second line, the number of the house and the name of the road, Cohen Road.

Sometimes it took him longer to get home when he stopped to share a laugh with the boys flying kites. They knew him as the father of Nikko, their friend. The bunch of kids were from

Burmese, Anglo-Indian and British families—all residents of the well-manicured suburb.

It was, in fact, Frank Rose, smelling of fresh bread and butter, one of Nikko's friends, who, in his freckled playfulness, had asked Goldram for his name as he passed by the children playing on the green verge of the dark-pink gravel path while walking from the Gyogon station. And not having heard quite clearly the words 'Govind Ram', Frank called him 'Goldram'. Prancing forward in great joviality, he offered to shake hands with him.

'Let's be friends, Mr Goldram. My name is Frank. Nikko knows me and we like fishing and flying kites together. My house is on the lane behind your house,' he said and withdrew with a broad grin. Others, too, rushed and crowded around him, eager to shake hands and shout out their own names. And so, Goldram got his name, his second christening.

2

Cohen Road stretched beyond the turn that led to Goldram's house, moving further past an empty lot, which was used by the local boys to fly kites. Then the road turned left from a huge Victorian mansion, which belonged to a prosperous cloth merchant from Gujarat, where the subcontinent's western lands end at the Gulf of Kutch in India's Arabian Sea coastline. Young Bholanath Maneklal Shet had come to Rangoon with a dream of a booming prospective market during the first decade of the twentieth century. He continued to flourish there even after Burma had been granted the status of a separate entity under the Government of Burma Act 1935 and ceased to be a province of British India from 1 April 1937.

Following the east–west route, the well-treaded red gravel Cohen Road went around the northern end of the suburb, meandering lazily, bordered by trees of all tropical varieties with houses and bungalows on both sides, in the north–south direction. The neighbourhood was quite familiar to Nikko and he had free entry into almost every household. Towards Cohen Road's end, after it turned left from Mr Lawrence's house, at about two and a half kilometres it merged with the branch road, which then joined the main motorable road from Rangoon to the smaller— but strategically important—town of Prome, situated in the southern strip of Burma, tapering into the Bay of Bengal. The importance is emphasized by the fact that the fourth station on the local railway line from Rangoon to Insein is called Prome

Road, and a country road that finally joined the main road to Prome originated there.

It is at this arrowhead junction of the two roads that a bazaar springs up at around four in the afternoon, continuing late into the evening till around ten. The vending stalls, made of either a jute sheet or old tarpaulin (of about one and a half square metres), were put up with all kinds and varieties of wares and utility items of daily requirement, which were bought by the residents of both the eastern and the western side of Gyogon, as it was this crossing beyond which extended the other half of the locality. This was largely inhabited by the middle and working classes, like carpenters, blacksmiths, fishing net makers, dhobis, waiters, domestic workers and other such labourers. But they were not the only inhabitants; there were middle and lower-middle class people, the clerical and other such staff employed at government establishments.

Joining the eastern and western segments was a narrow lane with a slight climb starting from this bazaar junction. This lane made a T-junction with another red gravel road that went around the western part of the locality, which, indeed, was a self-contained township.

The first building on the left turn was a gurdwara. It was a place of worship, but not just for the Sikh community. All resident communities flocked together to pray and celebrate an occasion, such as Gurpurab, or other such festivals announced via handbills or a herald going round the streets with a drum (and sometimes even a megaphone), inviting one and all for the celebration filled with song, dance, fanfare and festoons of lights at night. Besides the three-day ongoing prayers, sessions of reading from the Sikh holy book—*Guru Granth Sahib*—were held, which was followed by *langar*. The Gurudwara Prabandhak Committee, under its tutelage, ran a free public school, which especially taught

Gurmukhi to enable the children of the neighbourhood to read the holy scripture. The classes extended to teaching Mathematics, English and Hindi.

The children were encouraged to come in the evenings as well to learn and sing hymns and devotional songs, accompanied by the harmonium and a pair of percussion instruments, the tabla. It was the same arrangement as the choir in the local Salvation Church. So during the first half of the day, the high-roofed building and the surroundings echoed with the lively din of such activity. At half past one in the afternoon, the children, thirsty and hungry, quickly packed their bags and scurried out of their classrooms in the gurdwara and into the freedom of the road outside. Through the winding lanes, the freed children shot homeward, back into the comforting smells of freshly cooked meals, which they couldn't wait to devour.

On the right side of the T-road was a sprawling half-open house. It had a low boundary wall with a spacious open yard that was dotted with two or three jacaranda trees and a cow shed, where some hens and goats strayed across. Another fixture at the main entrance to the house and facing the road was a guard dog, a mongrel flecked with white and brown. This sprawling house looked as though it had been transported from a Punjabi village. It was owned by a Sikh family of professional carpenters from Punjab. The family was popularly known in the neighbourhood as the 'Crowing Ones'. No one could have passed by the house without becoming aware of the high-pitched cacophony of voices talking to one another in the rustic language. The sound came from all directions of the house, home to, perhaps, two generations of the family.

There was a small workshop in one corner and a mound of rice bran covering blocks of ice on the other. Harjinder Singh's family ran the ice vending business, breaking the ice with an ice pick he made himself. Everyone knew that ice was not available anywhere else but at the Crowing Ones' house. There was a corner devoted to selling children's toys, which were designed, crafted and pigmented appropriately by the carpenter himself. The carpenter was now an old man with a flowing white beard and a tiny knot of sparse white hair on the top of his head. He tied his turban only when he went downtown or to the gurdwara next door for prayers. At home in his small workshop, he wrapped his head in a shorter version of a pagri called a patka, which was a little more than a metre-long cotton cloth, either yellow or blue in colour.

The house was walled in by a variety of things. A bucolic sort of odour wafted from the yard, and the passer-by could not help but be assailed by the pungency in the air, just as they were assailed by the loud cacophony of human voices.

To go further into the locality and then beyond it to meet the highway from Rangoon to Prome, one took the lane in front of the gurdwara into the western part of Gyogon, which was thickly populated. This lane, after a few houses lined on the left side, spread out into an open lot. The teenagers of the suburbs from both the east and the west sides of Gyogon had turned it into a cricket ground, and unofficially, the group called themselves the Gyogon Cricket Club. There was an abandoned hut, which they used as their all-purpose pavilion.

They pooled money to buy items like gloves, pads, balls and bats. When it had all started, there wasn't a fixed amount to be paid for subscription. By mutual understanding, they paid or bought stuff as and when necessary. For instance, Alan, the son of a rich man (popularly known as Baba as his Ayah had been calling him since his childhood until it was commonly adopted as his nickname), was generous when it came to pooling resources. He was the son of the owner of the Continental Confectioners of Frere Road, Rangoon. He did not stint on being liberal and paid for the shortfall of funds every time. The accounts were maintained by a Punjabi boy, Kartarlal, from eastern Gyogon. The boy was new to the locality, supposed to be outstanding in his mathematics class, and an honest fellow from the well-known family of our genial Goldram.

~

Kartarlal was Goldram's youngest brother. He was not very tall but was well-built, packed with muscular prowess and good stamina. He could remain steady for long hours at the crease. He had understood the basics of the game since his days in Daska and played like a true sportsman. To the delight of his teammates, he easily hit boundaries and his amazing shots, showing perfect coordination between sight and the movement of hands and feet, brought rounds of applause from all over the small ground.

It was Goldram who had gone to their native district in the mainland of India to fetch Kartarlal so that he could pursue higher studies in Rangoon and become an engineer. Towards the achievement of this aim and career, he showed ample promise at school and having played some cricket at the district level, Kartarlal had straightaway found acceptance and appreciation in the local Gyogon Cricket Club.

In the small town of Daska in the Sialkot district of the Punjab province (now in Pakistan), where Goldram's family hailed from, there was only one good school, run by a private trust called the DAV Trust. The school had the facility for local students to study till the tenth standard and prepare for their matriculation examinations for the state-level Punjab University. Going by the standards of teachers and teaching, it may be graded as a modest school, but it had a learned headmaster called Pandit Parmanand.

Pandit Parmanand combined his scholarship with rectitude in imposing discipline, not only for the boys' behaviour at school but also for inculcating its spirit to guide the formative lives of the young men who came to study there. By his very upright carriage and social communication with the local gentry, he had earned a well-deserved reputation and the respect and sobriquet of 'Guruji'. He usually wore a white pyjama and kurta and literally glowed in the pink of health. He sported a black cap with a light wrap around the shoulder in the summers and a shawl during the winters.

Goldram's family hailed from this part of the country. Kartarlal had been one of the bright students and was the recipient of three hundred rupees per annum as a school scholarship. This scholarship was to honour and encourage a student who showed proficiency, although he remained unaware of the honour. One day, soon after the exams were over and summer holidays were around the corner, Kartarlal, with Balkrishan and Mohan—his two good friends—had come to school to watch an inter-school football match against the local government school team and were ambling through the empty corridors along the classrooms.

As they turned towards the administrative block of the building, they saw the school accountant with his bulbous pink nose, his cracked, pink, jutting lower lip, and his loosely poised, smudged, horn-rimmed glasses. He was squinting over their rims at them. Having mentally confirmed that he had spotted right, he gave them a hard look and advanced towards the boys.

Kartarlal, in fact, was quite taken by surprise when he was asked by the accountant to follow him to the office and even more so when he was asked to sign on a register with a pink revenue stamp stuck on it. Across this stamp, he had to sign his name. He pocketed the envelope the accountant had given him.

The accountant also handed him a larger envelope containing a glazed Certificate of Meritorious Performance. Kartarlal's guess was correct that the envelope had some crisp currency notes. He felt so overwhelmed that he didn't even open the envelope and made a dash for the narrow lanes to reach his home, holding the certificate against his chest. He handed the envelopes to his father.

Mangal Sen, his father, a rich trader in the wholesale mandi of land produce, knew the value of money. Feeling the crisp banknotes inside the envelope, a broad smile appeared on his face. He was indeed very happy to learn from Kartarlal that he had been officially given the envelope of money by the accounts department of the school for his proficient performance. But it was only later, when Goldram came, that he told them that, in fact, the certificate was of much greater value than the money.

'The certificate shall vouchsafe his outstanding proficiency long after the money is spent,' he said. But as a good and loving father and as the head of the family, he made a gesture of encouragement and support for the achiever. He sent Sundar, the family's young employee for odd jobs, to get sweets and other goodies from the popular Mehru Halwai at the corner of the lane to add a glow to the pride of joy on everyone's faces.

Mangal Sen got his long locks trimmed in a straight line at neck-length and wore his turban with a supporting Kulla in an Afghan Pathan style along with a Pathani salwar. He even looked like a veritable Pathan with his fair and crimson complexion. He rose from the midst of the celebrating family and walked slowly away into the solitude of his room inside their haveli. Noticing the shadow of anxiety crossing his fair and pink mien, his wife, Mathura Devi, followed him, carrying a tumbler of water. Her assumption was correct. Mangal Sen was worried about Kartarlal's future.

Kartarlal was intent on going for higher studies at college and university levels and taking up engineering as his major. The first idea that came to Mangal Sen's mind was to send him to Rangoon to Goldram to pursue higher studies. After pondering over the issue, he concluded that sending him to Sialkot would involve worse hassles than just separation from the child. Even in ancient times, he thought, pupils stayed away from their parents for 10 to 15 years, but they were under the constant care of disciplinarians and highly learned gurus. The culture they absorbed during their stay at the gurukul in their formative years shaped them to become good human beings before they went forth to take up a vocation and be a man of the workaday world.

He knew Goldram's financial condition fairly well. Goldram had gotten his elder brother Gurmukh settled in Maymyo in Burma. From his provident funds, he had helped Gurmukh launch a small shop of daily provisions. But due to the latter's inexpert handling and general attitude of carelessness towards business, it ran into troubled waters within two years. Mangal Sen knew that Goldram had a good job with the railways, had a steady income and lived well in a house he had designed himself, which was built on a piece of land that he had bought a few years ago.

But at the same time, he was aware that other relatives had also ventured to Burma for jobs and better futures. They settled in smaller towns like Moulmein, Mandalay and Prome, either as practising physicians, in other positions in the government offices or with private companies and other such establishments, and had sent their children to Rangoon periodically. They had found it convenient to send their children to Goldram's home and assign the family to care for them. The truth is that they had taken the plunge and sailed across the Bay of Bengal because they were assured of temporary moorings with Goldram to tide over the difficulties of settling in a strange and foreign land. Goldram, devoted to the family's welfare, took on these developments in his stride. But Kaushalya, his wife, had to balance his conscience. She, with some firm authority of character, did have to pull the reins on her broad-shouldered husband's magnanimity and keep his generosity from running away with him. Yet later, it was she who willingly supported the idea of getting young Kartarlal over from Punjab so that he could strive under the better guidance of his big brother to attain his ambitions.

The families, of course, paid some amount towards the maintenance of their kids—a pittance, not entirely enough. It was more out of obligation to sustain the ties so that Goldram and his strong, broad-enough shoulders would take on the job of caring for the growing family without a twinge of hesitation. When he had lived in the family haveli in Daska, he had often heard his mother stress that the family must remain united. Whoever is capable and has the wherewithal of giving support, must give it unstintingly. And it would be a shame to let the family, especially his mother, down in times of adversity and need, and God had been kind to enable him with the means.

And besides, Goldram had grown up to be a man of sturdy faith. He often quoted some choice Sufi, Persian and Punjabi couplets to the family, which were never out of context. These pearls, as he called them, were based on the authority of the ancient wisdom of poets and scriptures, preaching ideologies like 'choosing what you get' and that the whole universe moves only by the will of the supreme creative power, called by different names by different people. 'Be, therefore, of good cheer and fare forward,' he would say.

Mangal Sen contemplated on these concerns, endeavouring to detach himself from the thoughts that appeared to weigh him down.

Kartarlal, searching for his father, strayed into the room. Mangal Sen, on seeing his son, brought back his smile and asked him if he'd like to go sailing on a steamship. Hearing his father and getting the hint, he snuggled close. A lump formed in his throat and his eyes reddened with gathering tears. Given a choice, he wouldn't have agreed to be separated from the family, ever.

Being the youngest in the family, Kartarlal held a special place in his mother's heart. Their bond was strong, and he, too, felt a deep attachment to her. He had a gnawing fear that no one on earth would give him such warm hugs or extra helpings of his favourite sweets. He had an inkling though that his father was worried about his education and had covertly mentioned to his mother that the only option he had was to send for Goldram to come and fetch his young brother.

And indeed, not wishing to delay matters, Mangal Sen had already dashed off a missive to Kartarlal's older and well-established brother in Rangoon soon after he learnt about the pre-matriculation results.

While waiting for Goldram's letter, Mangal Sen primed Kartarlal to mentally prepare for the journey and his stay in the new environs of a distant place. He mentioned how everything was going to be different, especially the people around him at home and outside, but with his elder brother there with him, he should not have any fears about adjusting to his environs. Also, he must never forget that his only purpose in leaving home was to acquire a good education and enough competence to get a respectable job that would later decide the kind of life he would live.

Kartarlal's consolation was that his separation would not last more than six years. The other seminal thing he had to remember was to always be respectful to his elder brother and listen to his advice if he found himself in doubt about anything. Not only was Goldram older than him, but having been in Burma for around ten years, he had the experience to guide and advise him on any matter at any time.

~

A different kind of activity kept Kartarlal engaged in this interim period as he waited for his future to unfold. Feeling both happy and sad, he began a round of visits to his friends—mostly to those who were close to him because of all the cricket they had played together for over four years.

The smell of grass, dust and the sweating young bodies all came back to him as he took to the streets of Daska, somewhat saturnine for his young age. He was gripped by a sudden pang as he stood outside the house of his closest friend—the wicketkeeper, Tej Prakash—Teji to all his friends. The faded pockmarks on Teji's lively face and his set of widely-spaced teeth added to his healthy charm and innate geniality. He came with a ready smile and laughter, much to the great joy of the circle of friends who all waited for the quaint jokes and funny one-liners (some verging on smut) that he used to tell from behind the stumps. He perhaps didn't know their full implication, nor did his listeners, and nor did he know their source. But it was all great fun to have a laugh together. Even in the most serious situations, he could come up with one-liners that produced a smile even on the opponent's face on the other side of the crease, in the more serious position of batting.

Having shared the information with Teji, Kartarlal suggested that they go and get the rest of their friends together. They could go for a swim in the canal a mile or so away and then eat together at the small, popular, unostentatious but affordable Sharma Restaurant, known for its good and tasty vegetarian fare. And so they did, going around giving Moorty, Chhotu, Kuddu and others a shout, taking along those who were available at home.

Though aware of the mist of melancholy surrounding them due to the forthcoming departure of their hearty friend, they still pranced along the familiar streets with its familiar shops and the friendly faces of the owners. They didn't know how long he was going to be away from them, and this brought a lump to their throats. All of this, though, lost its edge after their hour-long swim and gambol in the stream.

The sun was now high and it was getting really warm. The breezes dropped a little and mellowed towards the afternoon, and the birds went back into the shade of the foliage of the neems and poplars lining the canal. The boys got back into their clothes and were in good cheer at the prospect of the finger-licking meals at Sharma's. Indeed, the young chaps were hungry after their playful exercise in the running waters of the canal; some had even swum against the current. Prem was his usual, morbidly quiet and aloof self. Somewhat possessed by what was physically happening to him, he reached for his crotch and scratched violently. Teji was, as ever, bubbling with suppressed laughter even before he finished telling a joke about the Sanskrit teacher, Ram Suresh Pandey, and his loosely tied dhoti that the notorious Dhaka had once tried to tug off.

All this hilarity continued during their delicious meal. Kartarlal said that today was not his farewell and paid for them. This implicitly meant that he would wait until they all got together again to arrange a farewell for him.

It was late in the afternoon but pleasant enough to go for an enjoyable stroll along the banks of the canal. On both its sides, ripening corn fields spread out far into the horizon. They tried hard to remain cheery, especially buoyed by the wisecracks from Teji, because they found that as soon as there was a pause, a pallor of gloom enveloped them. When some women and girls carrying fuel wood passed by the open fields, they hardly noticed.

Otherwise, it wouldn't have been possible for Teji to check himself from a passing comment on the singing or the loud jewellery of the country damsels. Indeed, there was a giggle or two from the younger ones among them before the women passed. They continued their stroll for a long distance.

3

The end of March and the following month of April was the time for harvest to be collected, for which the farmers and labouring peasants arrived in the wee hours of the morning and remained busy with their sickles and hoes, reaping and gathering. By this time of the day, during the harvesting season, the sun drops in the west and the shadows of trees begin to lengthen. The tanned leathery skins of farmers are covered with sweat and dust and they look forward to calling it a day as they walk back homeward, chatting and laughing to shake off their fatigue.

~

There would be enough worries at home with the unwanted guests—his in-laws—and then Satya, lovingly called Chando, who was also of marriageable age, thought Gurmukh as he reached his doorstep. The buffalo gave out a subdued grunt as she saw her master return. The buffalo and a cow were tied to two separate pickets outside the door. A manger and water trough were running along the wall of the house that faced the street. To prevent them from straying far into the middle of the street, two thick iron rings were buried and plastered into the wall to which they were separately tethered for most of the day. On the other side of the entrance, as was customary in those days, was a shallow waste pit lined with bricks. Every house had one, and in the early hours of the morning, the street sweepers scavenged and cleaned up the pits. Not all streets were laid with pink-baked bricks, and those that were brick lain were worn, scarred and with time, had become uneven.

Like Gurmukh, his several other companions, with their own mental preoccupations, walked back home through the streets that were in need of repairs and cleaning, though children still played their harmless games like kho-kho or hopscotch on the street. The children of Lala Chuni Lal, the flourishing haberdasher in the market, and others who could afford it, rode their tricycles on the streets. It created a lot of nuisance for the pedestrians and the traffic of bullock carts and horse-driven carts (already loaded with hay, packets and huge parcels to be delivered at the parcel office of the railway station). The postman rode his bicycle, dressed in a khaki uniform with a red band on his turban. He always wore a broad smile as he pedalled along, greeting shopkeepers and acquaintances. He skilfully navigated the obstacles on the streets while making two daily mail deliveries.

~

Kartarlal and his friends decided to return to their homes in good cheer, promising to get together again. They parted to trudge back home. As Kartarlal took his turn, the others lingered slightly longer. They wanted to decide what kind of present they should get for Kartarlal and talked about the farewell arrangements they wanted to make for their dear friend. But for that, they would have to wait to be told of the date on which he would depart; his brother was yet to arrive from Rangoon.

Days and weeks rolled by as the family of Mangal Sen waited for Goldram to arrive. Then on a bright warm morning, the postman knocked at their door. It was Goldram's letter.

Mangal Sen, on his way back from the door in a flurry, couldn't wait and began opening the envelope without the slightest shake of his hands. He was a man of strong nerves and firm will.

Mathura Devi left the kitchen and the cooking midway, scurrying to her husband to find out what her son had written back. After Mangal Sen read the letter in silence, he looked up with a rather quizzical smile. He told his wife that Goldram wanted not only Kartarlal but also his parents to accompany him to Burma. It would be about a week from today that Goldram would arrive in Daska and stay a few days before they all left for Burma.

'He says we have enough time to put our things together and get ready for the journey and the stay there,' said Mangal Sen.

With the realization of having to leave, he suddenly felt hollow. He had left home before, whether to attend a ceremony or participate in a ritual at a neighbouring village, Eminabad, or for a trip to Gujranwala Town at some relative's request or to visit a close family friend, but it was always for a few days or a weekend. He always knew that in a couple of days he'd return and life would be back on track. Now he seemed to face a void. The uncertainty of where he was going and when he would be back in the seat of his shop, in the grains mandi, loomed ahead of him. He decided to have a chat with his very reliable younger brother, Uggar Sen, and sent Kartarlal to fetch him.

Uggar Sen lived with his family in another part of the house within the premises, and his living quarters were separated by a single door that almost always remained open. Kartarlal went with the message that his father would like to discuss a family matter with Uggar Sen and wanted him to come over as soon as he could. The Sen brothers together took care of the family business and the two hundred acres of arable family land. Through mutual understanding and without much trouble, every aspect of the work was taken care of by the brothers and their children. This had been going on for as long as one could remember. It happened like clockwork. They were prepared for all seasons, the quirks of the weather and the rise and fall of the rates in the stock market. And now, since Mangal Sen didn't know how long he would be away from Daska, he decided to let his younger brother know about how he was going to see an increase in the burden of work. Besides, Uggar Sen would also be saddled with the responsibility of the whole family.

A message from Uggar Sen's older brother would usually have him racing to his brother's. But he didn't want to further delay attending to the dressing of the sore on the right hind leg of the buffalo. The cleaning and dressing of the wound took more time than he thought it would.

After tending to the buffalo, Uggar Sen entered the room where his brother was waiting for him. He could smell the tempting pakoras that his sister-in-law was sifting out of the frying pan. The addition of chopped fenugreek gave her savouries a signature aroma. It was sort of a high tea that the brothers were being treated to, not all that rare. Over piping hot tea and savouries, Mangal Sen gradually broke the news of Goldram's letter and his impending arrival. He followed it up with details of the exigency the family had suddenly been confronted with. He then went on to tell his brother that he would try and make the trip as short as possible.

Uggar Sen understood every nuance of what his brother was trying to convey to him so earnestly. Having been brought up under the same roof, over the years, in the congeniality of family atmosphere, there was such understanding between them that everything was clearly conveyed and understood. Through it all, they continued to enjoy the snacks and tea.

When the serious aspect of the business was over with, they laughed and shook off the cloud that was yet on a distant horizon. Men of great faith, belonging to the old world, knew they would overcome all obstacles on the way and cross the bridges when they came to them. Yet, the gloom of the looming separation could be seen in the quiet that fell soon, their mouths still shining with the oil from the snacks, the taste of which lingered in their saliva. Yet, they felt they were out of the tunnel and in the open sun, and the world would fall into their normal immediate reality.

Other chores awaited him; so Uggar Sen got up with the intent to leave. Mangal Sen also got up and gave his brother a warm hug before he left for his quarters.

4

Goldram was happy returning to his home town, with all the congeniality of its atmosphere. It was quite unlike Rangoon, and the quiet and lazy pace of life here was like an affectionate hug from a friend. Moreover, you didn't have to strike up new acquaintances; everyone seemed to know everyone else. They had been together in festivities and grief of bereavement, and each met the other with a smile while passing by on the street or in the green ambience of fields. People leisurely went about their business and were not driven by the hurry of reaching a bus station or railway station on time to commute to work.

News of the establishment of some industry or a huge factory on the outskirts of the town had been circulating for some time. The arrival of a big industry may auger change in this lifestyle not a long time from now. Maybe it would happen gradually, but the prevailing attitude must undergo change. There would be a variety of jobs generated by the requirements of big industries, especially in the small towns, leading to the evolution of villages. The spreading of ideas and the influence of city life had been facilitated by the growing means of transportation. *Rangoon Gazette* was now available on the stands alongside *The Statesman* in Calcutta, and at the same time, the *Hindustan Times* with *The Tribune* at Lahore.

~

Goldram was not going to be in Daska for long. So he thought he must do what he had decided before leaving his place of birth and childhood. He must see his boyhood bosom friend, Habibullah. Theirs was a special relationship, and thereby hangs a tale worth going back to. Additionally, Habibullah's reappearance and the importance of his role in the yet-to-unfold life of Goldram needs this background tale. Besides his mother, uncle Uggar Sen and his father, only a few others knew about this episode.

The truth is that Goldram's innate detachment from the mundane world and his natural spiritual inclination were aspects few knew about. He was devoted to prayer, reading the *Granth Sahib* with such fervent devotion and intonation that he got totally swept and transported into another ethereal world accompanied by the Gurbani, as was the whole congregation present in the halls of the gurdwara. He was, therefore, specially invited during occasions of celebrations and festivals, or to offer seventy-two hours to read the *Granth Sahib*.

It is no wonder that he was drawn to a travelling group of monks and went to meet the sadhus sojourning in a deserted temple, slightly away from the limits of the town. He sat with them and discussed the essence of renunciation. They told him of the rudiments of renunciation—not something that was not already common knowledge. They tried to teach him that, in the initial stages, one has to try and loosen the bonds of all relationships. Adding to that, Goldram posited that renunciation can be achieved by understanding the relative value of all things, people and actions, 'within the framework of social and moral values that decide our priorities and make our journey to deliverance easier,' said he in his boyish hesitation.

Goldram, in his meditations, had delved deeper. He had pondered on these esoteric and subtle aspects in the light of having been a regular audience at Swami Ram Charanji's discourses on the *Bhagavad Gita* at the local Arya Samaj.

'All significance we attach to our relations and our possessions slowly begins to wear off. From the perspective of a man's journey towards his emancipation from human bondage, things will begin to appear in quite a different light. For comparison, death and emancipation must be placed side by side. Ordinarily, man considers all things from the value he attaches to them, which is self-centric. And then, through consistent practice of trying to concentrate the mind, we can affirm faith in a life devoted to developing an abstemious attitude. We can give up all attachments and distance ourselves from the whirlpool that tries to suck us into the workaday world of earning and spending, crying and laughing and yet forgetting or heaping it all up in the storages of memory to surface during after-dinner sleep.'

As he listened to their discourse, Goldram began to see himself as one of them. The repetitive rounds of human activity had always seemed to him of no value, not unless it was spiked with hope and ambition. Come to think of it, even ambition belonged to the realm of Sisyphus pushing the boulder up the hilltop.

The only difference, he had concluded, was that man was not under any curse. Man had a mind to think, and thinking may lead him to correct his course at any time in his life. Such freedom of will and judgement has been endowed to man. Yet being young and in a hurry to seek his own salvation, he thought it better to be in the company of those sadhus. They were mature, more experienced. Relationships of the world would always be lumber round the journeyman's neck. He was just around thirteen then.

And so, he left his whole family and the household; they grew frantic and were left harrowed and deeply anguished. They looked for him and from the neighbours' information it was learnt that he had been seen hobnobbing with a group of sadhus.

The sadhus had left without a trace, as they had done at every previous place of sojourn. The police had been informed and all others who were available joined the police search party.

Habibullah was Goldram's close friend and he was shocked and dumbfounded when he learnt of his friend's disappearance. He grew truly worried, especially after he saw the manner in which Goldram's tear-drenched mother, whom he called 'ammijaan', was shaken by this disaster and sunk into grief. She wept incessantly and was totally broken-hearted. Habib took an oath that he wouldn't come back home or eat anything until he brought the good news to the family that Goldram was back.

He informed his own mother and father as well that he was going to be away from home for a few days and told his mother about his mission. With a lump in his throat, he set out in search for his friend. He showed great grit and patience while going from pillar to post, working like a sleuth (with personal concern for the family uppermost in his mind). It was only after two days had elapsed that he was able to get a clue from a young loiterer in front of a sweetmeat shop in an adjacent village, Jangpura. The loiterer said that a group of sadhus were seen going in the direction of the village of Eminabad. Habib hurried and was able to locate the group in a remote and dilapidated mosque. Seeking his friend, Habib entered the mosque and saw Goldram.

The friends were glad to see each other.

Goldram began walking towards Habib who was entering the arched gate. The other members of the group were speechless; they did not know what to say and to whom. A few of them were still lying and lazing on their bedspreads; others, with their chillums or bidis going strong, were relaxed, seeming to have not a worry in the world. Making a beeline straight towards his friend, Habib took Goldram in his arms, hugged him warmly and took him outside to talk to him in private. He knew it was his privilege, for he considered himself to be family.

After they had seated themselves on a broken branch under a tree, a teary Habib began to speak to Goldram in soft and sombre tones. He told him all that had transpired at his home since he had stealthily disappeared into the night. People at home were able to guess that he had joined the group of wandering minstrels who called themselves yogis. He dwelt in detail on the situation at Goldram's home, and especially upon the condition of his mother, who was torn and broken, swooning under a mountain of grief. Her tears flowed and her eyes had swollen. Recalling the scene at home, Habib once again broke down.

Over the last four days in the company of these sadhus, Goldram, too, had noticed that none of the sadhus showed the true attributes of a sanyasi; none had severed their bonds and greed for the things of this world. On the contrary, he was struck by the rapacious desire and selfishness among them for all things. He did wonder at what exactly they could teach him and where indeed they could lead him to with such a stunted and blinkered view as they manifested in their conduct.

Habib reminded Goldram that it was he himself who had always said that the spirit of the Creator and Master pervades in all things equally; it is just a matter of man's heightened perception by which revelation becomes reality. Of course, the Guru is required for guidance, especially in early stages of pupilhood. But the Guru must be one who has risen above those enslaved by earthly bonds and indulgences of the senses and has, by his austere life and meditation, brought under his control the distractions caused by the wayward pursuit of the senses.

Thus reminded by his dear friend Habib, Goldram, who had been misled, swerved and stigmatized by the passing fogginess of his mind, felt the light shining again, bright and clear. He went back inside the old dilapidated mosque along with Habib and went straight to the leader of the group to declare his intention of leaving their company and going back with his friend who had come for him. He did not give any reasons or excuses for having taken this decision. He did not think it was necessary for him to explain. It was something that pertained to his personal life, and he had followed the guidance of his own mind, enlightened by a light within.

It is true, as he had felt, that there are moments in life where one is so engrossed in the affairs of existence that he becomes, in that dimmed light, without focus. People tend to stray away. His independence of will, to give direction to his life, may be exercised whenever he required. In life, it is never too late to revise one's decisions in the light of these ideas, make the right choice and correct one's course. Salvation is a matter of a moment or a few moments when the city is made new.

Habib was glad to have been able to redeem his word to himself. The family was happy to have their dear child back home safe. Gradually, life went back to business as usual. Goldram went back to his studies and friends. The whole episode faded away like a horrid dream. Goldram privately went up to his mother one evening and clung to her; she, in return, wrapped him in the fold of her arms and covered his face with kisses. After this, he ran to his father's room, hugged him, and in his childish way, expressed his regrets over what his gross ignorance had caused. Both father and son shed a few tears of love before Goldram parted from his father for the night and went to his bed with his favourite books. He had to regain the drift of work where he had felt it snap. He owed it to his dearest friend and the family.

~

After much time had passed, the wooden footbridge across the canal, the rendezvous of Goldram and Habib's leisurely days, had given way to a regular brick and mortar bridge. It was held up by pillars and arches of reinforced concrete, and indeed, so much water had flowed down the canal. Both friends were now in their mid-thirties. Goldram's strong urge to see his friend took over him just a day after he had arrived. He went towards the road that led to the local police station. There, in a by-lane, Rafiqulla, Habib's abbu, had a modest house. Facing the street, he also owned a good enough smithy shop, where a soft coke fire blazed almost all day, and bellows—out of breath and yet going on with its leathern lungs—kept the flames steady and bright. People passing by couldn't help but stop awhile and admiringly watch the synchronized movements of Rafiq's hand as he held his tongs and hammer to shape the red-hot sickle on his anvil.

In fact, he specialized in replacing steel rims on the wheels of carts and horse-driven carriages, proudly calling himself a wheelwright. Hanging on the pale smoky walls all around were tokens of his versatile skills—cooking irons or the tawas, kadhais, pliers, tongs and even some oversized sieves and ladles showcasing his manufacturing craftsmanship. In his work and production of assorted marketable commodities of domestic necessities, he was assisted by his sons, Habib and Naseem. He had trained both of them from their childhood. The noteworthy aspect of his training was that, he had not only groomed them in the skills of smithy, but taught them to have morality and honesty in all their dealings with their customers. They were also serving God, as Islamic scripture specifies that those who live by the precepts of morality and honesty serve Allah, the one God.

Goldram relished the aroma that wafted through the air as steam rose from the shallow tub of water infused with the tempering compound, permeating the entire vicinity, while Rafiq submerged the meticulously crafted red-hot sickle into it. It was the smell he associated with hard work, sweating bodies and heat-tanned shiny skin. After brief courtesies, Goldram realized that he was intruding upon Rafiq's work, so he went inside where Rafiq had told him Habib had gone to have tea with the family. He let himself in through the door connecting the inner quarters of the house and the storeroom of the workshop. Goldram and Habib's mutual joy was evident from the warmth with which they met and held each other long in their arms. Having spent about half an hour sharing snacks and tea with the family and updating them about his family in Gyogon, Rangoon, Goldram and Habib emerged on to the street from an exit on another side of the house.

They took to walking up to the canal side as a reflex. Goldram did not cease to wonder and comment upon the change in the topography of the area. Storeys had been added to the existing houses, and some new and grand houses had come up on almost all the streets. They walked perhaps a mile upstream, recounting and enjoying the memories of earlier days together. Habib was happy to update his friend on the latest happenings in town. After a while, they turned at a bend when at some distance, a high school building rose into view. They both had fond memories of the time when they had trudged their way to school day after day through the narrow streets of Daska. The thorn in their side was that Habib, for family reasons, had had to quit; he was an early dropout and didn't go beyond the eighth form. The school was just about a mile from the living quarters. Guided by something from within, they slowed down and then stopped, smiled at each other and started on their way back.

Finding in his friend a sympathetic and patient listener, Habib opened up about the tragic circumstances of how his marriage had had an abrupt ending. His wife, Zeenat, had gone to visit her parents during the month-long fast and prayers of Ramadan, and was returning for the celebration of the following Eid al-Fitr. She was on her way, travelling by rail on the Rawalpindi Express in a berth in the ladies' compartment. A few miles from the run-through wayside station of Raikot, the train had stopped in the middle of nowhere. It was dark all around but for some dim flicker of lights in the distant horizon from some village flung in the wilderness. A great uproar rose from the carriages just behind the one in which Zeenat was travelling. There was chaotic furore, and frantic screams rang out calling for help. People from other carriages came flocking to the area of trouble to be of help. In the milling crowd of jostling men and women, one could see some men in tight black outfits with tall, heavy bludgeons threatening the passengers. They broke a few skulls in the process of grabbing valuables and cash from helpless passengers. Once all their loot was transferred into plastic bags, it was loaded on the horses by the helpers standing ready alongside the rail tracks. They had also been acting as guards for the looters while they rampaged inside.

Some fair and young-looking women became the victims of rapacious assault, and were carried off on the goons' horses. Rapidly winding up their operation, the goons took to their mounts and zoomed out of the area around the train tracks on both sides. The Railway Police Force and other officials arrived half an hour too late. A thorough search was made; complaints of the people were deferred until later. When it was confirmed by the police force that there were no predators left in the carriages of the train, the train guard was given a 'go' signal. The engine driver went back to his cabin and his job, and the train slowly began to chug again.

Those who had lost their possessions or their women had to bear the grief and distress during the time that the train took to reach the next big city of Jhang. It was during this dacoity that Habib lost his wife Zeenat. In a month's time, that is coming June, it would be a year since the disaster overtook the family and left the life of the good young Habib in a rubble of memories.

5

Another memorable episode occurred during Goldram's stay, which caused a sensation around the neighbourhood and was a bit of fun.

Only the day before, a small group of young boys and girls had enjoyed playing kokla chappakki in the bright full moon night. The world seemed to be covered in a flimsy coat of whiteness, turning everything into a fairy landscape. Around noon the next day, a great hullabaloo was created a little distance from where Goldram's house was in Kucha Harnam Das.

People started coming out of their houses on to the street; some leaned out from their windows or narrow balconies out of curiosity. Their enquiries were loud and frantic. Mumblings of 'What's going on?' mingled with the words 'What has happened?' Some who had gone in the direction of the sounds of the gathering rabble seemed to be returning, out of breath. Going by the stray words shouted by the people running in every direction, it seemed that a young, not fully grown bull had been teased by a few street urchins. They were guffawing and enjoying themselves and had poked its sides and pudenda with sticks. Now it had started to run amok, with a lowered head and horns pointing forward, chasing the boys, who had continued to take swipes at its ribs whenever they could manage. Most people who had come out with staffs ran indoors, scared to death of the maddened wild beast. In a wild chase of the boys, it emerged from the street that opened on to an empty lot next to the standing crops. Here the boys began going round in circles, the bull foaming at mouth and kicking up dust trails.

Goldram, too, joined the crowd watching the bull-chase from the sides. He had come with a purpose in mind. His intent was to do something about the violent bull; it seemed to have been aroused into a rage and might harm someone. He, therefore, had left his turban at home so that it wouldn't become an encumbrance in his manoeuvres to get a hold on the furious bull. For a few moments, he stood and watched. He was on the left side of the beast, and then—seeing no other way to get hold of the mad racing bull—in a spontaneous manner, he came slightly forward as the bull closed in on him. He braced himself with a deep breath and gave it a full-blooded punch with his power-packed fist, making a full swing of the shoulder. And then, lo and behold, after a couple of wobbly steps, the wild animal fell down in a swoon. There was a stunned silence for moments and only the rustle of the foliage was heard, like a soothing shower of rain. The people who had gathered, seeing the high drama come to an abrupt end, moved lazily and began heading back home. Some remained, curious as to what was to be done for the fainted animal.

Goldram felt very guilty that he had killed a cow (considered holy, and such an assault was taken to be a heinous crime and a grievous unpardonable sin among Hindus). Going on a pilgrimage was necessary to atone for such a sin.

He rushed and brought a bucket of water from his home and sat down by the prostrate bull. He sprinkled some water from the bucket on its deadened face and eyes. A devoted Krishna bhakt, Goldram prayed to him to restore life to the bull—even if he were to pay with his own life for it. He sat there and began to fan the face of bull with a handkerchief. The whole exercise took around half an hour. Some neighbours and some of his friends, such as Habib, came round to be with him for moral support.

Soon, the bull blinked lazily and its breathing became regular. Goldram heaved a sigh of relief when he saw the bull standing firmly on all fours, jerking his grey and white coat. The bull shook its body as though it were a natural reflex and with its tail, whisked off the stray stubble and dust from his body. It started to walk leisurely towards the paddy fields, seemingly in a daze. Its overflowing energy was now calm, like the ocean's surface after a storm.

~

Dr Juneja, the dentist of the town of Daska, had been among the spectators (though he didn't share their enthusiasm). He was a solitary figure, as usual, his head drooping over his slightly stooped shoulders. With a leisurely pace, he made his way back towards his dental clinic located at the far end of the street, which formed a T-junction with the bustling market road of the town. Despite his slender frame and lanky limbs, his languid stride became a source of amusement for the mischievous boys in the neighbourhood, who wrongly assumed that he perpetually existed in a state of intoxication.

The dentist didn't have many patients. Few were conscious of their oral hygiene. Their food intake and lifestyle were naturally such that they hardly ever had problems with their gums or teeth. Only after a certain age, say fifty or so, was it understood natural to begin losing teeth or developing other physical or metabolic problems. That, for them, was the onset of middle age. Only the presence of an unusually foul or fetid breath, pointed out by sensitive and outspoken people, prompted someone to care to go to the doctor for a consultation. So the dentist had ample time on his hands to sit with someone familiar and of his own choice. Those who also had some leisure would have noticed the doctor idly turning the pages of a big fat book or newspaper.

Then the doctor would ensure a friendly neighbour would walk in to exchange a few words on topics of mutual interest—there is always something personal, local or political that made for an interesting topic of conversation and some discussion. It could even get heated among the intellectually inclined, and the doctor considered himself to lie within those ranks.

On that particular day, Goldram, after the eventful and physically strenuous morning, felt relaxed. Walking homeward, he fell in step with the dentist, with whom he had always been on very cordial terms. In a courteous and mannerly gesture, he enquired if it would be all right for him to spend some of his time with him. Upon being gladly welcomed by Dr Juneja, Goldram followed him into the office area of the clinic. After they had settled into their respective seats, Goldram began the conversation by telling him how life in Burma was generally quite different. The eating, dressing and going about of daily business of the Burmese conformed to the long-established conventions; it was conditioned and governed by the natural topography, weather conditions and, the most important thing, their religious faith, which regulated their life in society.

For instance, Goldram described to him how every morning the lady of the house stood out in front of the entrance door with a pot of freshly cooked rice for the passing monks, called 'phoungyis' in the local language, who came in a very orderly manner from their monastery to receive their alms for the day. They took them home generally for their companions too at the vihar (the small monastery of their sojourns). The monks went out in groups of about ten to different parts of the town to collect these alms. They returned by midday and stayed in until the next morning. Their vihar was invariably close to a regular Buddhist temple, in which they spent most of the day in prayers.

The common pursuits that sometimes ran in the family

from generation to generation was working with bamboo and cane. They were very fine artisans who manufactured almost all things of utility, from furniture to beautiful photo frames or decorative pieces. Others took up unskilled labour jobs at construction sites of buildings or railway lines and bridges. The educated class among them had begun to take up jobs in schools, government offices and some commercial establishments but were still considered among the lower rungs of employees.

Schools, colleges and universities had come up in Rangoon and in other bigger cities like Mandalay, Meiktila and Moulmein. In Maymyo, there was a college of dentistry and oral hygiene, a constituent of the university where Goldram's brother-in-law, Kaushalya's brother Sudarshan, was studying dental medicine and surgery. Their father was an excellent photographer, the finest in the town of northern Shan states, Taunggyi, and was patronized by the army cantonment. With the rise in the number of such institutions, the numbers of the educated and the competent in the employment market were steadily rising.

This development is noticeable in the increasing numbers of longyi and aingyi-clad men and women in the corridors of government offices, shopping enclaves and other public places, and also in good positions based on the strength of their education. Most Burmese men and women who go out to work spurn the anglicized dress code of a casual suit and necktie or skirts and jackets, and stick to the tradition of wearing their traditional headgear of a fine silk material supported by a round or slightly conical, fine-cane netting cap. The ladies, with their longyi belted slightly above the navel area and falling down to about six inches above the ankles, have a flower tucked in the bun or in a knot of hair at the back of their head.

Genetically, Burmese women, like Bengali or South Indian women, have long and lustrous black hair, which they are proud to display in a variety of hairdos. The most preferred hairstyle in high-end society was the elegant high and fine-finish coiffure; the modern preference though is for a shorter version of the mop, proper maintenance of which made their visits to the salons frequent. The fish protein in their diet and the use of coconut oil, used for both cooking and direct oiling of hair, give them such luxurious growth.

With the onset of modern work culture and the need to keep to a schedule, and also because of being outside the familiar and homely ambience among strange men folk, several shortcuts to women's make-up and hair styles have emerged. They preferred shoulder lengths, school-girl cuts or even bobbed ruffles, and sometimes the even tried perms, quite unsuited to their Mongoloid ovals but necessitated by the shrewd feminine adaptation to the new lifestyle.

Dr Juneja was so engrossed in Goldram's descriptions that he seemed to have been transported to all those places. Like a charmed tourist, he went along the trail of the fairy safari in the narrative Goldram had created and missed the last thing that was said. It was a casual light-hearted question that changed the course of their conversation.

'But how are things getting on with your domestic help, the cooking maid—or have you, in one of those fits of vexation, given her the marching orders?' Goldram asked.

From the Burmese fairyland of stretching green paddy fields, dotted with villages and groves of mango trees, bamboo orchards and waterbodies, the doctor was suddenly jolted back to his not-so-pleasant mundane reality. The harrowing caused by the dogged belligerence of his housemaid over trifles had been far, far away from his mind. Although it was in banter that Goldram had questioned him, Dr Juneja was now back in the middle of the slough of meaningless hair-splitting over how the gas lighter's button should be pushed to light the gas the very first time and how one should not go on clicking it and say, 'We have to have a new gas lighter; this one is gone and useless.'

The refrain of his lament was that his whole life was governed and steered by the whims of Sangita, the domestic help, a travesty of such description who's built and presence was akin to that of a boxer. Her trenchant voice and cantankerous mode, even in ordinary conversation, was of a pitch and volume that the people living in the neighbouring flats knew what the master was going to have for breakfast or what fare would be cooked for his midday meal. Let alone the loudmouth, because of which she had lost her husband and broken her home, she was narcissistically conscious of her fair and beautiful face and graceful form. She constantly stood in front of the full-length mirror of the mistress's dressing table several times during her working hours to admire herself and readily struck friendships with anyone she liked and had an easy smile for them. Coupled with her timbre of voice, her stout build made her formidable. The frail doctor was ready to give in to almost any of her quirky whims to be rid of her argumentative volleys if contradicted.

At night, the doctor usually walked up to Mehru Halwai's shop to have something with his glass of milk. The sweets and savouries were tempting, as always. It was his supper and dessert. What got his goat was the maid's diehard habit of coming late to work in the morning. During the early days of her employment with him, he had very diplomatically tried all kinds of things to bring her around to understand how his health was affected by her late hours. His regimen went all upside down if they started the day late, he would explain. If he finished his breakfast as late as eleven, when was he going to eat his midday meal? His dinner or supper, as he began to think of his last meal, was pushed to around midnight. Poor fretting old man! He was doomed to sniffing the foul breath of his patients reclined on the chair during the day and spend the nights on stale food.

He continued to explain this to the domestic help almost every day. His was a delicately balanced state of health, so it was important for him to follow the routine of his diet strictly. Not wanting to create unnecessary altercations, he was always as soft and persuasive as he possibly could be. Indeed, sometimes he lost his cool and flew off the handle. That made things still worse because, for the next few days, his domestic help came even later than usual and would linger over little things and took much longer to finish her chores. Besides, she went about her job with a surly look, ready to start a shouting match at the drop of a hat. For the doctor, these interactions were no less than walking on a tightrope across a gorge.

Once or twice, he seemed to have had enough and rang up the local policeman, Constable Ram Singh. He had been designated by the local police station to care for the seniors in the locality. His genial temperament made him a friend of the doctor, and sometimes, Ram Singh just called him up to have a cup of tea together. In fact, it was through Ram Singh that Dr Juneja had hired Sangita. He wanted Ram Singh to give her a dressing down.

Of course, there was never a complaint about the cooking. Having been a housewife, Sangita cooked quite well. Her idea of cleanliness though was a different matter altogether. The cleaning and dusting she did was just about perfunctory, passable. All these things, too, he condoned as he had himself created the pretexts to overlook her other shortcomings or lapses. He was aware that any new appointee, if he decided to hire one and chuck this one out, would have some other flaws in conduct, making her as much an irritant as the current domestic help. But his greatest resentment was that she did not keep any fixed schedules. That bound the doctor at home for longer hours, away from his clinic. Another irritant that the late hours led to was that he was always late in officially opening the clinic. He would take a while to sit down in his chair at a corner table to begin attending to the patients waiting for his arrival; the clinic was opened, swept and cleaned by the guard, who came early at his residence for the key, and his surgical tools were sterilized and kept ready for him by a male nurse named Dipu.

~

Dipu was a school dropout from Bihar. When he was in the eighth standard, he suddenly lost his father to plague and there was no support for him to continue his studies. His elder brother, Nand Kishor, worked with Oberoi and Company—the famous sports goods manufacturers in Sialkot. It was a decently paid job but his monthly wages were not enough to run the family and support his brother's education too.

This way, by taking up a small job and securing employment as a makeshift male nurse with the dentist, Dipu made sure that their mother, at least, didn't have to seek work outside home. The family also, within themselves, had recently and secretly been assailed by the fretting worry of a future event: the marriage of the fast-growing daughter, Mohini. In this part of the world, whether among Hindu or Muslim families, marrying off a girl soon after she has attained puberty is not only obligatory but reflects upon the honour of the family and the growing girl. Coming to the occasion and event, it is conceived of as something very elaborate and complicated, especially in terms of financial obligations that the parents must discharge. The birth of a girl child, therefore, after her umbilical cord is severed, is a lifelong cause of anxiety, leading to gnawing worry for the parents until the looming task is satisfactorily accomplished for all members of the families involved.

Adolescent girls always seem to grow faster, and even seem more mature in appearance and attitudes than boys of the same age. With their innocent heart, they fully identify themselves with the home and family. And then, suddenly one day, in the middle of spreading the washing on the line, the girl is called in and asked to get ready. Her beddings are already rolled up and her suitcases packed. Born with a fibre that is tough and enduring, she easily adapts to the family she hardly knew before; shall we say like is a duckling, just out of shell, is flung on to a vast open waterbody. There is no measure of the agony of the secret and private stream of tears. That remains wrapped in the several folds of mystery between her and what was her home and family. It is a mystery that has never been unravelled or understood. And so, getting the daughters settled in life leaves the parents older and leaner in every way, much before time.

Goldram was from a family where they believed they were under a curse that no girl child ever survived or would survive in their branch. So Mangal Sen remained deprived of the pious ceremony of 'kanyadaan' (giving away the daughter to a suitable husband under the stipulated sanctity of canon law). Goldram did have a sister, but she had died in the great upheaval of the earthquake in Quetta, where she had gone to visit an uncle. Goldram had seen the scene: mounds of rubble at the quake site from Rangoon to Quetta. He ended up unsuccessfully scraping up the debris, heaps and smithereens to which the town on the border of Afghanistan had been reduced to by the earthquake. Certain others like him were digging for their dead, injured and not-so dead, which added to the dismal scene around. The sky was swirling with vultures, crows and kites. After his labours, he came out of the heap wiping quiet tears with the extra length of cloth left hanging at the rear of his white turban.

His appearance, his rugged and stoic eyes were always

focused in the distance somewhere; they betrayed his sensitive temperament. His son had seen Goldram wipe his eyes in a similar fashion and, at times, even heard subduing sobs while he read the Punjabi epic poet Warris Shah's work, *Heer* or even the *Mahabharat*, both of which he kept next to his bed.

In his dealings though, Goldram was down to earth and very practical.

6

Goldram hadn't lost count of the days that he had been away from work in Rangoon, and the number of days of leave still left, even when he was engaged in pursuits of his heart in his home town. With a start, he realized that it was the weekend when he caught himself brooding over the prospect of returning to work. He had to depart on Tuesday and had been conscious of his mother making time to quietly put away clothing and other knick-knacks in the luggage to be taken along with them on the journey to Rangoon.

The early hours of Monday were busy, especially for young unmarried girls. They scurried along streets with a plate of offerings for Lord Shiva and asked for his blessing, hoping to secure an able-bodied good husband. It was a common belief that, for marriageable young girls, Monday was the auspicious day to worship Shiva for his boon. The rituals on Mondays were observed seriously. And so, the aspirant young girls, after an early bath and sometimes with their dripping hair covered with dupattas or saris, were seen heading towards the Shiva temple or a sacred peepul tree, beneath which would be a makeshift small alcove for a temple.

~

Kartarlal's friends, Teji and Moorty, were busy with something else. They were aware of the approaching date of their friend's departure. During a conclave of other close friends, mostly players of their cricket team, they had decided upon the gift they wanted to give Kartarlal and the time at which they should get together at Sharma Restaurant for a proper send-off party. Balkrishan went to his house after he had improvised and brought back long-stalked marigolds, roses, some narcissuses and tuberoses and tied the bouquet of flowers in auspicious red and yellow mouli threads. Kartarlal knew that his friends would come calling any time in the morning, and so it was he who ran to answer the knock at the panel. He was glad to see his dear friend, and indeed elated to be greeted with fresh flowers. Both of them went inside for a few moments. Kartarlal brought a glass tumbler with some water in it and tenderly arranged the precious flowers in that improvised vase. Then Kartarlal told his mother about the lunch he and his friends were going to have together. He would be back only in the afternoon, by three or four o' clock.

It was a little after eleven when they started towards the foliaged and umbrageous peepul waving in the cool breeze. Its leaves shimmered in the late morning sun. The boys were sitting and yapping under it as they waited for Kartarlal. Their laughter was interspersed with the inane, often-repeated jokes made by Teji. It didn't really matter what the jokes were, so long as they could all identify with the humour and burst out in guffaws—not a care even distantly touching their charmed and innocent world wherein every tomorrow was as enjoyable as yesterday and today. They all stood up and began to clap and dance—commonly known as luddi in Punjab, a rudimentary form of bhangra performed usually at the popular harvest season celebration. The dance truly embodies the spontaneous joy that pervades the whole countryside in its abandon with drums, song and the lilt of the musical accompaniments.

Then they saw Kartarlal and Balkrishan, arm in arm, arriving towards them but keeping time with each other. They were jumping and rhythmically skipping, repeating this over again, inventing a sort of tap dance. Then they all joined and gave out a loud shout of joy in unison, creating memories to cherish.

His friends had a surprise ready for Kartarlal. It was left to Teji to open the mysterious surprise. He pointed to the few packages they had tried to hide behind the wide bole—some food and fruit packages, a can of water and a glass and two dhurries rolled and tied. He went on to tell Kartarlal that they had decided not sit in the stuffy and smoky low-roofed hall of Sharma Restaurant, and instead had come to the small park, a little distance away from the Persian well. The soporific tinkling bell sound accompanied the constant groaning of a bullock, pulling the wooden lever to draw water from the well almost all day. You could sometimes catch the boy, who sat with a whip, goading the blinkered bullock on his winding journey, nodding into a nap—just short of rolling off his seat. The friends thought of having an impromptu picnic. It would allow them to have some extra space and time together, and perhaps to play a passing game, for which they had brought a football along. The park, too, was not a regularly maintained garden but an empty lot a bit away from the residential quarters. But there was grass, which kept it in a shade of green; the greenery was due to the canal flowing not far from it, and it attracted goats and cattle. Some neighbours had planted some floral hedges and trees, which they watered to prevent them from drying and wilting away. There were a few spreading shady trees too under which Teji and company had decided to spread out their dhurries and settle down for the time they were planning to spend together.

The sudden change in their programme brought good cheer all around. There was more open space and fresh air beneath the trees. The light and shade created patterns on the green below, which brought thrill and boosted their spirits as they began enjoying their time. They sat in separate groups, playing card games, ludo, snakes and ladders and even carom. Moorty, with his glasses on, looked more intellectual than the others; he had thought of carom and got the board and striker and all its parts. He had also thought of carrying along a cardboard chess board and simple wooden pawns. They all settled down to enjoy and have fun with different games and their partners. Their pleasure had no bounds, even more so because being close by, they were within earshot of one another and were able to go on with their wisecracks and share jokes while engaged in playing their different games. The ambience of general mirth and enjoyment was enriched by the music in the background. They heard a variety of birdsong—the symphony created by birds peopling the thick foliage and the passing migrant birds from the snowy lands in the north. Their guffaws of laughter created a general atmosphere of bonhomie, a harmony of luminous notes, which brought out curious faces from windows and balconies of neighbouring houses. Amused, the onlookers withdrew from the scene with a broad grin too.

To such fond memories one goes over again, perhaps not only seeking emotional warmth but also seeking to come out of the drudgery of day-after-day mundane chores. There too is the ache of never again having the occasion to create such heart-warming memories.

As the day advanced beyond noon, Balkrishan, the quiet and sedate fellow of the lot, made a suggestion. His observation was that they still had about half an hour before they would sit down to eat, and it would, therefore, not be a bad idea to have a stroll down by the canal and maybe some, who so desired, could have a swim to whet their appetite—though at their age they hardly needed any such thing as an appetizer. The young just needed to be out of the periphery of illness.

Balkrishan's idea was welcome for it allowed them to stretch the fun time they were having together. Moorty was quick to suggest that they better make arrangements for the safety of their foodstuff while they were going to be away, lest some stray dog may have a sumptuous luncheon and they go without their midday meal. He unfolded a sheet and tied all their smaller bundles and packets of things into a huge bundle and hung it to a branch high enough to prevent the leaping dogs from reaching it. Once satisfied that it was beyond the reach of the leaping dogs, they jumped into their shoes and headed for the canal banks, which was perhaps Kartarlal's last walk with his friends before they would be separated from him for an indefinite length of time. They all knew that Kartalal was going to Rangoon with his elder brother to study in an institution of higher studies in engineering—a constituent part of the university of Rangoon. Then he planned on joining the university for specialized studies and training in what was understood to be civil engineering. But such walks had been their frequent jaunts all through their conscious years of companionship, from school to the playfields.

They turned round from the point where, in the distance, the top of the school building came into view. Perhaps the awareness of the very short time left before Kartarlal's departure made the swaying of the trees along the banks of the canal seem like sighs of melancholy. The sunshine, too, seemed to have mellowed a shade as they walked back to their spot under the tree. Although there were a few dogs agitatedly barking there, they had failed to reach the bundle of food hanging. Their yelps and jumps were aimed at the line of three or four monkeys lined up just within the reach of the food bundle swinging from the branch. As soon as the boys, continuing with their loud chitchat, made their appearance on the scene, the naughty monkeys, true to their simian character, disappeared into the thick foliage. With shifty brown eyes, the canine clan scampered away with their tails tucked between hind legs, back into the streets whence they had come sniffing for food.

The main course was a sandwich of potatoes cooked in virgin mustard oil and flavoured with freshly ground spices, both dry and wet, and held between two fine flour dough patties. It was to be served with pickle or curd, both of which Moorty had thought of carrying along. By this time their appetite had peaked and all sat down to a hearty meal. They had one more course of cauliflower cooked the same way as the potato stuffing. The sun had warmed the surrounding atmosphere and they even sweated a little as they ate their favourite fare for lunch. To follow the spicy meal with something sweet and smooth, they had brought something that everyone liked—a sweet prepared from milk and sugar, commonly known as kalakand, added to which were grated nuts and currants. It is a favourite sweet among north Indians especially, but because of its sweet and soft texture, it is no wonder that it has won over the taste buds of people beyond the boundaries of Punjab. In other regions, they give it a slight local character by changing processes of preparations and adding a few ingredients to the recipe.

After the meal and the dessert, they quickly wound up their baggage to go to Sharma Restaurant and get a glass of whey with a little salt and pepper and some ice to chill it to wash down the spicy food they had just devoured. This drink is commonly called lassi, and most people like it sweetened. It is usually consumed after a sumptuous breakfast of bhatooras and chhole, or puris and aloobhaji (a potato preparation to go with the puris). Add to the menu some hot and spicy mint chutney, which is then followed by a welcome tall glass of sweet lassi.

The visit to the restaurant was inevitable for another reason. They had kept a parcel hidden under the running counter of

Sharmaji's seat. This was the gift that Kartarlal's friends had bought for him. They had got it wrapped and kept it ready to be given to him just before he would leave for the distant land. They all trooped into the restaurant and occupied their favourite corner in the dining hall. After they had had their glass of lassi, Balkrishan went up to Sharmaji's counter and slowly wound his way back with the parcel under his left arm. With a broad smile, he waved his right hand at his seated friends to signal that all was fine.

They had bought a cricket bat and batting gloves for Kartarlal, for they all knew of his love for the game and his proficiency in it. He was as good at it as he was at academics. They all clapped and there were smiles all around, even on faces of strangers at other tables who joined in the general joy of the moment. Kartarlal made a move to stand up to receive his gift from his comrades; he said thank you with a choked voice and his eyes were red with the welling tears of mixed emotions. Kartarlal waited for the clapping and sound of laughter to subside and resumed from where he had left off.

He truly wanted to say thank you to his friends for he was truly very fond of them, especially Balkrishan and Teji. He was aware that he would be away for a long time, away from the warmth of his friends. The most touching moment was when his friends got up from their seats and hugged Kartarlal one by one. Kartarlal brought out a slip of paper from his pocket and gave it to Balkrishan, saying, 'Here's my postal address in Rangoon. Share it with everyone and do please write to me. I shall miss you very much and wait for your letters. 'I shall write too and tell you about my journey and the new place that I'm going to.'

By this time, they had started moving out on the street. Not lingering too long over the painful parting, they looked deep into each other's eyes before turning away towards their homes. With one last look, a sweeping glance at his beloved Daska—the crisscrossing familiar streets, the sounds of lowing calves, bleating lambs and goats, the birds in the trees, air redolent of cow-dung cakes drying in the sun and the green crops waving in the open breezes—Kartarlal turned into the street leading to his home. He was followed by a light-brown street dog with its tail wagging.

His ears were still echoing with the sound of the distant temple bells and the heartache at the thought of his friends was receding already.

7

Uppermost in Kartarlal's mind now was the packing of his bags. He had to choose what all he just could not afford to carry with him besides, of course, the cricket bat and batting gloves he had received as a gift from his friends. The thought of them again brought up a lump in his throat. He would have plenty of time to grieve over the separation from his friends later during the long train and ship journey. Now he must concentrate on matters of immediate attention.

He went to his room, which he shared with his mother, and from beneath his cot, dragged out his suitcase and began emptying it out first. He would arrange and stack up the clothes and other things; he alone knew what his needs were and where they could find their right place in the valise. He found his mother also arranging and rearranging her clothes and other requirements for the journey and her protracted stay with Kaushalya, which made him happy for different reasons.

His mother, from the beginning of Goldram's marriage, had hit it off well with Kaushalya, getting along better with her than the other daughters-in-law. She had, therefore, especially gone to the Canary Bazaar to buy a fine Kanjivaram silk sari for her. She kept the original carry bag with its small beige print and bold brown lace border at the bottom of her large suitcase, not wanting it to disturb the folds before they reached their destination. She dabbed it with perfume as her added love. In her thoughtful preparations, she made sure to acquire tiny dresses and children's games for Goldram's sons and twin daughters—an extraordinary occurrence as they were the first girls in the family lineage to defy the prevailing curse. Despite the malevolent efforts of mankind, Mother Nature's power proved to be indomitable. Although she had yet to meet any of the children in person, the elders and wise individuals constantly emphasized that this was precisely how the family remained tightly bound together—through care and occasional sacrifices—and the same principle applied to all families and societies at large. These experienced elders, detached from trivial conflicts, possessed a profound understanding of the truth that guides one throughout their life.

By evening, all was packed and readied for the next day. As a last chore, Mathura Devi had to go out, scurrying to Mehru's shop to get an assortment of choice sweets packed. She bought a separate oil cloth bag to carry them so that nothing else in the portmanteau got soiled with the oozing ghee and oil with which the sweets had been made—she took every precaution she knew of that was useful when travelling. She could now lay back and relax, assured by the fact that both her husband and son, Goldram, would be able to put together whatever they felt was necessary for them.

Kartarlal, of course, meticulously went over each thing and detail before he thought he could lock his suitcase. He was a man unto himself. Being held as the front runner among his companions, he had begun to be aware of growing maturity, his confidence and his latent virtues of leadership. There was a long way he had to go, he knew. He was glad that he had launched on the path of discipline, beyond which if he were to ever reach even in thought, he knew it would be overreaching. It may even be an outright transgression of crossing over into uncharted and hallowed territory of the unknown and unseen.

In this aspect, he seemed to be taking after his older brother. Or was it a streak that ran in the family? More, perhaps, it was in the land and the rivers—and indeed, Punjab was known as the land of five rivers—well known for great sages and grammarians of the Vedic era, and devotional philosophers, like Nanak and Bulleh Shah.

Even an ordinary artisan or bicycle mechanic of Punjab comes up with a flash of transcendent observation in their day-to-day conversation with customers or chance passers-by. For instance, the man who mends punctured cycle tubes, without much ado, would, on hearing of the death of a young man of twenty while his father at fifty was still going about, say, 'Sir, the sins of parents visit the children', and take you by surprise. By implication, he meant to chastise the sinner, who, as the culprit, must atone by going through the pain of the loss of his progeny. The coordinates of virtues and fabric of values were found subtly ingrained in the common people of this ancient land of great poets and philosophers. It is not to say that life was lived always by such knowledge, for the deadliest infernal sin of 'parstrigaman' (adultery) was still committed every day. Such is human life, a compost of elements brought to order by self-imposed discipline alone. That, itself, was more than a job of a single lifetime.

~

The mail trains usually ran through Daska, a rather small station although it was on the main line. So to take the Frontier Mail, which made the shortest journey to Calcutta, Mangal Sen and family had to start early by a tonga, a single-horse fly to Sialkot, an hour's ride from their house. Since they had to catch the train at nine in the morning, which was also the time the train served breakfast to its first and second-class passengers, the family had to start early at around seven in the morning. By then, Mathura Devi, with the help of her sister-in-law—Uggar Sen's wife—had cooked enough food for the journey and for a quick breakfast at seven. They all got up at five in the morning and were up and about, fussing over the preparations of those who were travelling. Mangal Sen had sent Goldram to Ali, the tonga owner, the evening before. Ali maintained his tonga in top condition, the paint and polish done and, above all, he cared for his horse. In fact, it was a mare that he leased out during winters—the wedding season. When it was in hot demand, he took special care to give her a rub-down and a good feed of chickpeas after the day's labours when he brought her back to her trough of water. Goldram had the tonga booked for next morning to be at their doorstep by quarter to seven. They had to be on their way to board the Frontier in good time.

Come the morning of departure, the tonga arrived with its creaking leather trappings. The clip-clop of horse hooves slowing down echoed in the almost empty street. Ali was in the driver's seat. Looking smart, he came to a stop at their front door. There were tears and sobbing hugs all around; the haunting uncertainty of when the next reunion would be for the affectionately-bound family lingered in their hearts. But quickly, Mangal Sen and Goldram, deciding not to prolong and dally over the parting, got up into the tonga from the side and occupied the front seat. The few luggage pieces were shoved underneath the seats, and Mathura Devi and her favourite Kartarlal took the rear seat, separated from the front by the common backrest. Shama, the mare, snorted once and stomped her hooves. With Ali's sharp call, a tug at the reins and a crack of the whip, the tonga started to move and gained a brisk pace, meaning business.

~

They reached the harbour in Calcutta after a rather tiring, longish thirty-hour train journey across the north-western and central Indian districts, passing numerous big and small railway stations at different times of day and night. Late on the second day of the journey, they began to feel their train passing through the bright afternoon sun and saw stretching verdant green fields and vegetation interspersed with waterbodies. Within minutes, the chugging of the engine slowed and softened as they made it into the sprawling railway station of Howrah. The platform was teeming with passengers of all descriptions and dresses, like a conglomerate picture of this great land of diversity, all bound for a hundred different destinations. The cacophony, if patiently heard and analysed from closer quarters, revealed a variety of dialects of spoken languages from all four corners of the country. The family, aware of the prevalent situation, readily resorted to the convenience of English and the common spoken Hindustani, which they all spoke and understood when communicating across lingual regional boundaries. So the people thrived and went about their separate businesses, rubbing shoulders with one another, without as much as raising an eyebrow or an abrasion in the politically charged atmosphere. It was possible only because they all inherently respected the freedom of each individual's elbow room. Therefore, the fish odour, the smell of frying pakoras and jalebis, all commingled with the acrid smell of sweating bodies to create the familiar scent of humanity.

Hereon, the family had to take a steamer to Rangoon. They had more than two hours to spare before boarding the steamer at the harbour in Calcutta. For the onward journey, too, tickets had been bought and berths had been booked. The duration of the following journey was to be of three days and nights without any stops on the way. It was a short voyage across the Bay of Bengal but it gave Kartarlal the thrilling opportunity to sail across the wide heaving sea. Initially the sea appeared somewhat green and later changed to ultramarine blue in its deeper parts. It was all the magic of the reflection of light from the blue sky, Goldram had explained to Kartarlal. He would read about the Raman effect—the change of wavelength of the rays of light when reflected from a transparent medium, like the surface of the sea—in his lessons on light in his physics class. Kartarlal was sure to study physics, chemistry and mathematics since he had come mentally prepared to take up engineering as his subject of higher study at the university.

With the great love and regard that Kartarlal held for his elder brother since childhood, he enjoyed listening to the offhand pieces of learning and wisdom his brother shared. Though he didn't quite understand all of it, somewhere deep down within him was resentment for being patronized. And because he thought so, which was somewhat evil to think of his most revered brother, he snuffed it there and then, never to let such bad thoughts enter his mind again. Goldram was his elder brother, and even his father had advised Kartalal to listen to his advice carefully for Goldram was elder and wiser to him. He had to internalize the advice and act accordingly. Kartarlal was glad that he was naturally gifted with enough sense to take stock of what was going on in his mind and to divert such damaging thoughts when they possessed his mind, getting rid of them as quickly as possible. Imaginary spite would issue from imaginary rivalry, and the cycle would otherwise go on to pollute and then possess the mind with muck. He also realized that his mind was liable to be affected or stirred by even minor provocations from within. Innocent though he was, he could yet warn his mind to be chary of strangers, for a sniper assault may come from anywhere and at any time. He must, therefore, remain alert and take even small stirrings as a warning and put up his guard.

The example of his brother was there in front of him. Every single need or desire of their parents was attended to by Goldram. Even on small stations, where the stoppage was rather brief, he would run down on to the platform to get hot water or a cup of tea, or perhaps buy an aspirin or Combiflam for his father's aching knee joints. And at the end of every little mission, there would be a smile of satisfaction on his face when pride glowed on the faces of the parents. They seemed to be glad to be chaperoned by their able-bodied son whose conduct in little things was assurance enough of him being ready for any sacrifice for them during rainy days. Having seen the cavalcade of multifarious manifestations of life for more years than anyone else in the family, Goldram was always cautious to not be smug about his hopes and expectations and was inwardly ready to face adversity at any time.

~

Kartarlal knew Gurudayal, the president of the local panchayat of the neighbouring village, Naughara, about six kilometres away from Daska. His son, Sanju, for whom he had done everything he could to rear and educate, took tuition classes so that he may be among the top in school. Gurudayal then sent him to England to study law. He was ambitious and well aware that all those who rose in life and were among the eminent in the higher courts or political circles and corridors of power were graduates from Lincoln's Inn in England. But the sad part of his story was not that Sanju had belied his father's hopes; he had excelled. He passed with distinction but found work in England that lured him to demur on returning, and so he had stayed on there.

With scant regard for the increasing weakness in the wake of his father's advancing age and his obligation to be around him when they would most need him, Sanju wrote to his father in no uncertain terms—the more back-breaking for that matter—that he was not interested in returning to India. He would not claw his way up in sweat and grime when he could be, by all standards, comfortably placed without the toil and soot. He had been lured by his smooth and immediate break as an assistant in the law firm, Franco & Wickham, with an old man, eminent Sir Lindberg, as chief who was impressed by Sanju's knowledge of law and practice at the bar as an apprentice. Sanju also enjoyed the easy-going lifestyle. He thought he should do fairly well, even in competition with local whites. His hard work and methods gave him confidence, but at the end of it all, Gurudayal lost his son to his indulgent fondness and plans for an ambitious future. Regardless of the reasons and pretexts that may lead us to go back and forth, the sad experiences we accumulate ultimately teach us valuable lessons that enrich wisdom, albeit often too late to be of much use.

To Goldram, this realization came rather late in life and as it happens, only at the pretty heavy price of an emotional shock. It shook and left an assault on the roots of the organic bond of the family. However, regardless of the circumstances, things inevitably evolve over time. In the particular era being referenced, life was still guided by the principles of honesty and trust. Words spoken carried genuine meaning, devoid of hidden agendas or deceptive intentions, unlike the current arid landscape where the values that sustain life seem to be absent. Relationships, although they may sprout, often remain superficial, akin to mere brushwood. A certain order prevailed and was embraced by all, while only those with minds akin to electronic devices could detect the faint signals of impending danger—a demon lurking in camouflage, prompting the need for timely defence and countermeasures. In such hostile surroundings, society undergoes a transformation, both in outward appearance and in the prevailing atmosphere, ultimately reshaping the very essence of its existence and becoming the defining characteristic of that era. Life, it seems, possesses the intrinsic qualities of a hologram—intricate and multifaceted.

Even in the sacrosanct places, like temples held under venerated priests who dye their hair and beard, rapes are committed; it turns the holy precincts into centres of flesh trade. Besides, as history has recorded, they become hideouts for smugglers and bootleggers. These temples, at times, are a facade for dens of sin. The gold icons are gradually replaced with bronze ones and leave for foreign shores, leaving the pockets of the caretakers lined with thick, soiled banknotes. The overflowing coffers of donations and charity are scavenged by unclean and sinful hands and used for the purchase of narcotics and imported liquor, without any stripes of chagrin upon their hardened soul hides.

While these grim depictions of life's ever-changing hologram await their entrance at the appointed time, the mosques, temples and gurdwaras in Daska remain bustling with activity throughout most of the day. People from all religious faiths, without inhibition, went in to pray where they liked. Like devotees, no one ever took any notice of who entered and who left the portals of cleansing haloes. In a place of worship, it was understood there could only be a believer. This was long before some of these places became museums for tourists, celebrated for their decorative inscriptions and little alcoves with idols or frescoes along the walls.

Some young people, who had graduated in national history, chose to be a tourist guide. It was an opportune opening in an upcoming industry in the country, especially in areas, cities or towns where there were ancient monuments that had survived invasive marauders and plunderers. These places had their tortuous intrigues of princes and priests, rich and tragic stories to tell. Added to the fare of historical facts, the tourist guides sprinkled additional captivating myths to make their descriptive narrative scintillating enough to spread the word and attract more customers.

8

During the first two days of the journey, Kartarlal was slowly getting acclimatized to the balmy ocean breezes and the floating and rocking boat life. He did not venture out of their cabin much. He was aware of the open deck where another little world flourished. To explore that, the next afternoon, he climbed the narrow stairway to be under the wide-open blue sky. He was awestruck by the skyscape on which some grey and white cotton wool-like clouds appeared, sailing on the wind; they were like an artist's dabs on the canvas depicting clouds away in a distant horizon in the vast spreading of the sky.

Goldram's parents made the journey as going to Burma meant a chance to meet the long-parted family of their eldest son, Gurmukh Singh, in Maymyo, in the northern Shan states of Burma. Especially since the family had gone through the recent bereavement of having lost their daughter, Chando, only a few months ago. Of course, they were chiefly concerned about getting Kartarlal settled down with his studies before going ahead with other plans. Mangal Sen was rather impassive towards what sometimes excited Mathura Devi as much as young Kartarlal. She was the livelier participant in the conversation, which engaged the family. Goldram was on and off, bringing his parents up to date with the people at home. Mathura Devi's curiosity came with queries and doubts. Goldram didn't forget to mention how their daughter-in-law showed great patience and skill in managing seven to eight school-going children during certain periods of the year when the schools were on. She made sure that each one was properly washed and dressed in their school uniform, gobbling their breakfast and downing it with the ever-resented glass of milk, and out to take the 8.10 a.m. local to Rangoon.

There were smiles of mutual understanding between mother and son. She knew her son was trying to prepare her to be more tolerant towards her daughter-in-law, considering the usually accepted and infamous hostility between a mother-in-law and daughter-in-law. Mathura Devi always thought herself to be slightly different from the others. From Goldram's smile and the few words of description, she could make out that even Kaushalya was homelier and domestic than most housewives, and so—through her smile to her son—she tried to signal that she understood.

~

The whole scene was gradually becoming enriched by land, particularly as the undulating mountain range of the Arakan Yoma covered with dense jungle of teak swung into view along the western coast of Burma. The steamer slowly headed closer to the Irrawaddy basin, referred to as Irrawaddy Delta, facing the Bay of Bengal. The entire scene in its natural splendour was such that Kartarlal could not take his eyes off of it and inadvertently heaved a deep sigh. The impression of the sublimity of the view on a simple heart and the unbridgeable distance from the abstraction of such awesome beauty could not have been expressed by a novice but in such an immeasurable gesture as a deep sigh. No doubt, entwined with the emotion was a strand of gloom of having left behind the warmth of his friends and classmates in the familiar streets of Daska. The path before him was lost in the misty distance of uncertainty, of the unknown new world. The present, he perceived only as a blur in his imagination.

His parents assured themselves of returning to Daska after

the round of visits they had to make during their sojourn in Burma with better equanimity. Mathura Devi was secretly happy because she was hoping to meet her brother, Chetsingh, whose three of five children, too, were resident scholars staying with her son in Gyogon. The brother and sister had not seen each other for years now. Chetsingh was employed—courtesy of Goldram— in the railway booking office in Prome, about five hours away by train from Rangoon. She was sure glad to see him come to receive them on the jetty in Rangoon. Goldram was struck by their similar facial appearance when he saw them in an affectionate hug, except that Chetsingh had a tanned look whereas Mathura Devi was all milk and roses due to Punjab's countryside weather.

Few minutes on the deck, and Goldram's attention was diverted by the scream of a woman dashing towards the prow of the boat where the enclosures of the bathrooms were. She was throwing up all through the run for the water closet. Her husband, it seemed, had rushed to fetch the deck attendant; he brought a change of clothes for his wife and waited outside the door of the toilet. She left behind in her wake an uproar which had not subsided, for there were other such cases of people in dire need of similar help and prompt attention. Kartarlal also noticed that there was a physician in his white-long coat, trying his best to alleviate the distress, which clearly indicated the spreading epidemic of some form of cholera.

The sea breezes were laden with pungent and nauseating smells. Goldram also saw food being cooked and gormandized by some. All together vouchsafe, Goldram thought, the inevitable vast humanity peopling around wherever on the globe they may wander. The sounds of the sea and the voices and human activity of the deck subsided with the coming of night, except for the movements of the restless ones who were smitten by the ague of their illness.

By about eight o' clock in the morning—the sun having risen

from the depths of the ocean somewhere—the steamer was plying its way up the Rangoon River, a tributary of the Irrawaddy, to be docked in the jetty of the Rangoon harbour. On the ground, people, mostly of Burmese origin, could be seen in a flurry of activity, getting ready for the passengers flowing down the passage and providing them with a steaming morning cup of tea. There was a visible earthly pleasure that glowed in their eyes after having their feet on firm ground after three days and nights of rocking on the waves of the Bay of Bengal. The tea vendors, restaurateurs, porters, coolies, the bookstall owners and the staff of waiting rooms, in the best outfits and uniforms, looked forward to making a quick extra buck. Some local residents, who had come to meet their relatives or guests, waited on the other side with their private conveyances.

The agents of motor taxi cabs and hansom cabs, with a practised alert eye—like that of a preying bird—scanned and picked prospective passengers. Available among the horse-driven cabs were the higher or better versions that had a full-fledged enclosed cabin with windows. These were mounted on four wheels with a little stepping platform improvised with a steel angle and square plate provided for passengers to climb from the kerbside into the comfort of the cushioned satin or chintz-appointed cabin. These were usually taken by genteel customers among the passengers to be driven to different high-end parts of the city. There were some, like this family from west Punjab in India, who were travelling farther on to Gyogon and were to be driven to the sprawling and busy railway junction of Rangoon.

The first striking scenes that puzzled Kartarlal were of the uniformed staff and scavengers of the Municipal Committee of Rangoon (MCR), with their long hoses for squirting water on the roads, followed by a troop with long brooms to wash the roads of Rangoon clean of horse dung and its stink. This was done before the traffic of the day began with the Bentleys and Austins carrying the British VIPs to their offices. At regular distances on the road were small squarish covered inlets with 'WH' (water hydrants) embossed on them for the hoses to connect to the underground water supply pipeline. These were also meant for fire engines in case of emergencies, as they raced down from the fire station with their bells ringing when conflagrations broke out anywhere in the town.

The railway platforms for the short-distance local trains, like the one that Goldram and the family had to take, were located to the extreme west of the mainline stations. Theirs was the local that ran between Rangoon and Insein. Gyogon, their destination, was the second last station before Insein. Being a railway employee and daily passenger, Goldram felt like he was back on familiar ground. He knew the foot bridges and the platforms like the back of his hand. After they left the cab—which was quite similar to the hansoms of London roads (commonly termed as 'ghodagadis' here)—and entered the premises of the huge Rangoon station, Goldram continued like a running commentator to point out details to Kartarlal. He showed him the ticket counters, the platforms in semi-darkness full of passengers and other places of interest as they passed and trudged along to their platform for the local they had to board.

They did not have to wait long on the platform.

Goldram could make out the local coming out of the shunting area. The engines were letting off steam, getting refuelled, being filled with water, and the carriages were getting washed. A train of around ten carriages snaked out of the area and parked by the side of the platform. As it was a local, there were not many passengers and among the existing ones were some who didn't have to go beyond halfway to Kyimyindine. Nikko, years that spanned between when he saw the Japanese bombers there and the time they left Burma, still remembered the names of the three stations after Kyimyindine: Kamayut, Okkyn and Thamaing. They had to go beyond these before getting ready to step down upon Gyogon's platform.

The coolies, in their red shirts with numbers displayed on the brass badges tied round their bicep, stacked their luggage of bed rolls and suitcases under the seats that Goldram and his family occupied. These red shirt toilers crawled all over the platforms. Upon the arrival of a train, they sat in a row along the edges of the platform to claim customers emerging from the wagons that came to a stop in front of where they happened to sit. This lottery system was mutually understood and accepted, adhered to as common code of conduct. Humanity refines its laws and systems for convenience through commonly accepted and agreed-upon forms, without external authorities imposing upon them. In many cases, perhaps, this runs better than the government-imposed machinery of law and order.

~

It was a place that even today brought a lump and overwhelmed Goldram. Strange indeed it is that without even being conscious, one gets attached to little things, like the residual smell of 'ye nang' (the crude oil coating that protects the wood from incessant seasonal rains with which the exposed wooden parts of the house were coated, year after year, before the six-month-long rainy season from May to October set in) applied to wooden homes. The dimmed scene of the football ground and the surrounding vegetation, the shrill guffaws at the long slipping save of the goalie comes back to mind to cause a twinge of nostalgia.

Another event associated with the season brings Goldram back to centre stage, adding to his shored memories. The night was still darkened by the low nimbus looming to shed its weight and thunder across the Gyogon sky with bolts of fierce lightning. In the middle of the night, in close vicinity of the Goldram house, the very first house on the turning from Cohen Road was commonly seen as a house of ill repute, inhabited by only three ladies of commerce. It remained lit and livened by sounds of music until the wee hours of the morning. Soon after the lights blinked out and the last huge car departed from the front gate, from the dark backyards of the house was heard a gunshot followed by an uproar.

'Help! Help! The robbers! OH! Escaped with all our gold! Help!' the female voices cried.

They were joined by the guards and other servants of the house. The chief guard had tried to take an aim at the two running figures, their longyis tucked and tied like loin cloth. They had been wearing skeleton masks and their bodies shone with sweat and protective oil. This furore nearby woke Goldram. He reached for his longish spear and, without a word, lunged to open the door to the rear staircase. Across the lawn to the north, reaching the gravelled Cohen Road after its left turn at the end was the exit from Goldram's premises. Kaushalya, who too had woken up due to the noises, called out to her husband in a calm but authoritative voice, 'You are not going anywhere. Don't they have their guards armed with guns and all? They can take care of themselves. They always do!'

'Oh, Kaushalya, don't worry. I'll be back in a few minutes. It will be futile if I delay going.' He left his pleading wife and the sleeping little ones, and almost ran down the stairs, wielding his weapon. To overtake the two robbers, he went across the empty ground in the north, adjacent to the gravelled Cohen Road as it turned past the Gujarati mansion. But as the two noticed Goldram with his spear in the middle of the road, waiting to intercept them, they escaped into the thick woods through a little pathway.

Helped by the pitch darkness of the night and the clouds, they had a lead and escaped into the thickness of the bushes and the creepers hanging from the forest trees. Goldram, with determination, followed them for some distance, daring them with challenging calls. For a moment, he thought he was within reach when they came out of the camouflage of a brambly bush and took a sharp turn. He made a quick thrust but missed his target. He refrained from following them further deep into the wood and turned around to go back to the awed and waiting Kaushalya.

The ladies of the infamous house had been watching the whole drama from their balcony. The guards and a few other men from the neighbourhood had joined the pursuit but they had remained at safe distance. The guards too went back, after giving Goldram a salaam when they saw him returning home. It was only after the arrival of the police team that a full-scale pursuit of the robbers began. Goldram later learned that the police were successful after two hours' of tracking, and all the gold jewellery was recovered and returned to the ladies. The criminals were chucked into Insein jail for six months' rigorous imprisonment.

~

Pagoda Road was the first stop from Rangoon to Insein. It was named after the noblest of structures in the whole of Burma, as the Golden Temple of the Buddha, the Shwedagon, was within walking distance from the railway station. Close by it was a lake. It was used as a picnic spot by the people in Rangoon and its suburbs. Boats were available for pleasure trips from the boat club at the lake, enjoyed by young and old alike. You could row them yourself or hire a boatman to take you around the little islands interspersed across the rippling surface. Ducks of a variety of colours and spotted fledges floated round with their little ducklings, quacking and flipping around them. Some fish and frogs could also be seen swimming underneath the water's sunlit surface, leaping playfully. At certain points, amassed undulated flotsam brought up a tarnishing stink within the sylvan scene.

Not far away was the gurdwara, which came alive with zealous devotees and volunteers offering to make things easier for the visitors on the festive occasion of Guru Nanak's birthday. The poor and the needy waited patiently to be served langar in the open kitchen. Children, who naturally became familiar with one another easily, ran through its marble corridors, screaming for no reason. They chased each other and created a nuisance for the serious devotees sitting in the main hall, listening to the reading of the *Granth Sahib* or the collective singing of the congregation followed by the hymns, the Shabad. Even the noisy distraction was accepted as part of the celebration, except there was a hint of the inevitable but mild chastisement from the female volunteers, the better minders of these children. Families came for the occasion from places within easy reach of Rangoon, either by local trains or by ferries. It also turned into an occasion for old acquaintances and friends to get together and spend some cheerful moments of leisure.

Lanmadaw, the next station, was known for the stretching greens of the racecourse and the football grounds on the western side of the station. On the eastern side was the military hospital, which also had an annexe containing the veterinary hospital. It was mostly meant to tend to the cavalry or the horses from the racecourse club and the polo club. Beside the civilian population of the small township of Lanmadaw, closer to the hospital was the cantonment area with properly laid-out quiet lanes lined by cottages for the army personnel. Each cottage and bungalow had a small manicured, prim and green front lawn and a kitchen garden of sorts in the backyard. Behind this was a row of quarters meant for an officer's batman, employed servant, ayah or a driver.

There were two more intervening stations before the midway two-minute-long stop at Kyimyindine. This station had an imposing brick-structured station master's office and residence at the rear, where an Anglo-Indian was usually appointed. Kyimyindine was a comparatively big town, better known for hosting the All Burma Hockey Tournament. It was a suburb populated with a genteel and sophisticated community that sought seclusion from the crowds and noise of the city, with its markets well-stocked with groceries.

9

Goldram felt as though he were back in paradise as he breathed in breezes of the familiar surroundings of the Gyogon railway station—the rustling bamboo groves along the periphery and the thickly growing mango trees in the sprawling compound of the Chinese gentleman, Mr Lee Xizang's bungalow (which alone had a private tennis lawn). Mr Xizang had a huge glass-fronted shop on Frere Road in Rangoon, stocked with bolts of colourful silk or artificial silk, rolls of silk carpets, rugs and wall hangings woven by hand with pure silk thread in attractive, traditional, idyllic and very restrained Chinese designs and colours. They were all highly priced, evidently for the class of people who knew the aesthetic value of the merchandise.

In the evenings, one could often observe English and Eurasian individuals engaged in lively tennis matches on the courts. These games would persist until the need arose to illuminate the area with artificial lights, extending the duration of play. Occasionally, pedestrians passing by on the adjacent road would pause, captivated by the spectacle, before eventually continuing on their way.

Those passing usually came from the artisan and labour community who conveniently lived in eastern Gyogon across the level crossing where all the moulding and manufacturing industrial units were located. After their day's work, they came to the bazaar area in Gyogon to buy their supplies. They came almost always in twos or threes, constantly talking and sharing their experiences of the day, sightseeing or window shopping along the market roads. A general diffidence was seen in their lowered eyes and their voices were a bit subdued when they passed by other shoppers emerging or entering brightly lit and fine shops. Baby perambulators were manned by maids who deferentially waited outside the shops or followed the ladies and gentlemen a step or two behind with folded and wrapped umbrellas, ready to be of use.

~

Kaushalya was a mindful woman. A few days earlier, she had received a telegram from her husband Goldram stating the date on which the family was to arrive at the Rangoon harbour and the approximate time that would take to reach Gyogon. She got the wheelbarrow readied and told the mali, Dashrath, and the guard, Dal Bahadur, to go to the station to receive the family. They had started off early and had to wait about half an hour on the platform before the party was seen emerging from the second-class carriage of the local. The stewards rushed towards where the party had alighted from the train and stood on the platform. They met the extended family from far with smiling salutations and hastily went inside the carriage and began to lug out the baggage onto the platform.

As the train moved out of the station, they carried the holdall and the suitcases out of the station from the side entrance through the waiting room to the pushcart outside and loaded the luggage onto it. And then, without waiting for the family, they began to trundle along the newly carpeted station road. They then turned right into the red gravel Cohen Road, towards home. After saying hello to the station master and exchanging pleasantries with him, Goldram began to lead his parents and Kartarlal at a leisurely pace towards his home. All the while he described the neighbourhood they passed through, familiarizing them with the topography and making sundry remarks about the residents of the houses they went past. Mangal Sen was happy to see that those who met them on the roadside were cordial and respectful towards his son. It was around noon that Wednesday, and since it was a working day, there weren't many people on the road; all the men, women and school-going children had already left their homes.

Kartarlal arrived, transported from a district town in Sialkot on to the new soil of heavy monsoons and breezes laden with the aroma of mangoes and the rustle of bamboo groves, with the houses standing apart with enough elbow room between them, except for a small kitchen garden and a small hedged-in plot in the front. He darted his smart and observant eyes all around him to get the feel of the new place where he was going to begin a fresh phase of life under the tutelage of his very competent elder brother.

Kartarlal held his mother's hand as he walked alongside her, attentively listening to what his brother was telling them about the locality. He knew it was he, after all, who would have to find his footing in the neighbourhood and get adjusted to life there. For the time being, he had been observant enough to have registered the way leading from the railway station to what was going to be his home—at least for a few years to come. He had about six years before he finished his engineering degree—that is, if the sailing was without impediment—and then a year or two before he landed a good job, which, sure enough, would keep him away from the family in Rangoon. Such a prospect brought back the continued upheavals of periodical transfers to his mind, which his elder brother Goldram had had to go through before settling into his present job and even thinking of purchasing property and owning a small estate in Gyogon.

~

Kartarlal knew, though could not totally understand, that it was Goldram who had, a few years ago, taken their eldest brother Gurmukh Singh to Burma and spent all that was required to get him established in a comparatively smaller town, Maymyo, in the colder climates and weather conditions of the northern Shan states. Close to the main road that led to the heart of the city, Gurmukh had been able to set up a provisions shop, which had living quarters attached for the family behind it. Uncle Uggar Sen gave whatever ready money he could muster for it but Goldram, being in Burma already, took upon himself the responsibility of getting his elder brother established in the business best as he perceived under the circumstances before he left for Rangoon. He knew Gurmukh Singh was quite adept in keeping accounts and checking and preventing leakages.

But there was another aspect to this disposition, one he may not have been completely aware of. True consciousness required the focus and urgency needed to finish a job at hand, independent of external influences. Right from the beginning, even their father had noticed and failed to point out the scant signs of the attribute when Gurmukh was asked to help his uncle at the family agency office for a few years. Nothing but his lassitude was the cause of being asked to discontinue midway during senior school, which was the same case when he voluntarily gave up his studies after high school. His disinclination was, in truth, his insouciance upon it being pointed out. Never did he learn to live a life in which there was any balance between familial, social and commercial commitments or obligations and time for luxuriating.

Mangal Sen's usual healthy pink face turned crimson when he had learnt of the misdoings of his son. Gurmukh—his father was told—sometimes, though not often, used to go missing from the shop for a couple of midday lean hours. He had been seen by a neighbour hovering around a particular balcony of a house that belonged to Mr Surjit Singh Walia, the manager of the local branch of Laxmi Commercial Bank.

Walia's daughter, Sonia, was an undergraduate hosteller at Sialkot Dayal Singh College. Gurmukh had become friends with her quite some time ago when they were both students at school. It happened when students of the science section were holding a conversazione and Sonia was manning the table dealing with biology of blood flow in the veins and arteries of humans and animals. Under the microscope, she had stretched out the web of a frog to clearly see the blood flowing in its veins and arteries. Gurmukh had walked up to the table, not driven by any curiosity regarding a scientific enquiry but—as he frankly admitted to his friends—because he liked the look of the simple and amiable face of the girl behind the microscope. For some minutes, in all seriousness, he peered into the eyepiece of the microscope. Then with the wonder of a child in his eyes and a mischievous smile on his lips—and though as it turned out to be an intelligent question—he stuttered to get into a conversation with her. 'It's amazing really, but how does the body maintain a constant and steady flow of blood through the blood vessels in spite of the knots and the veins with their sharp, angled turns, which are wide and narrow at different places, with ends and twists and turns?'

Sonia, too, had been watching Gurmukh through a wide window as he meandered along with a couple of friends through the corridors when he was heading for this particular hall. She had noticed how shy and diffident a boy he was, so she presumed him to be an intelligent but quiet chap. Even then, she had decided to take the initiative and talk to him. She replied, 'It is a wonder of nature, really, but we explain the phenomenon as synchronized coordination between the heart that pumps the blood with unwavering regularity, and the natural flexibility of the vessel material.'

The crowd behind him jostled in the queue, which had gone awry, and pushed Gurmukh further on. He smiled at her with his face turned and moved on with the momentum of the shoving crowd.

The keen desire for companionship and of knowing each other better led to prolonged chance meetings in market places to finally meeting in a mutually understood and decided place—a secluded teashop, Mohan Restaurant, near the Clock Tower at Ghantaghar Chowk in the southern end of the town, away from the canal. After Sonia joined the college in Sialkot, she chose to be a hosteller and was home for any considerable length of time, but only during vacations. Their meetings became rare but more intimate. Sonia was able to arrange their meetings at her own place when she knew the coast at home would be clear, with her mother gone to participate in a kirtan and father evidently away engaging in managerial duties in his office. Emboldened by escaping notice, such meetings became more frequent.

Good fortune, as they say, visits briefly, giving you a chance to prove your mettle for better results. Word got out about the clandestine affair that had been going on for some time undetected. Mangal Sen heard it from Jagat Gupta from his neighbourhood, who happened to see Gurmukh more than once in the chowk area getting off a cycle rickshaw with a girl and walking into Mohan Restaurant. It was alarming enough for him to inform the family, which he did without delay. His gratification seemed only short of a burp and felt he had satisfactorily fulfilled his social and neighbourly obligation.

There were not only two individuals involved, but two families who had been neighbours for generations and had always cordially met as friends in all local festivals and fetes. Boys and girls from nearby streets played games together until late in the evening under street lights or sometimes in bright moonlight.

Likes, dislikes, preferences and avoidances may have sprouted secretly in some hearts among the bashful girls and boys, which were expressed or veiled by their lowered eyelids, but never had reached the pitch beyond a secret rumble. High passions and simmering emotions hardly ever blew the top; there were no emissions of smoke and lava. The behavioural proprieties among the lads and lasses seemed ingrained as a way of life that passed down from generation to generation. Of course, freak events did happen. And if the intrigue was between families of a class of equals, the matter was handled by the families deftly enough that the scandal was snuffed before it caused any flares, saving the families and the growing children from disrepute.

At other times, the *l'affaire* involved two disparate classes, like in a case where the son of an ironing man had lured and eloped with the daughter of a well-known Sikh family who owned a provision shop. The young ones had courageously shot for the stars and now their families had no choice but to wait anxiously for the return of the wayward individual. They anticipated receiving reprimands for their misdeeds, yet ultimately, they had to come to terms with the fact that their union in wedlock was inevitable.

Such incidents left the families drained in every respect, and for quite a while, they became the object of public sneering. Jagat Gupta, in his eagerness to earn praise and goodwill of the family of Mangal Sen, had hurried with his own conclusion and did something that had quite adversely affected everyone. When Jagat found himself surrounded by silence that bespoke resentment, he got up to take leave, feeling a little embarrassed.

The family understood Jagat's concern and had already taken a forgiving stance towards the matter. It is true, they knew, that young Gurmukh, after the encounter at the conversazione, had always displayed a special leaning towards Sonia; and sometimes, when Sonia thought it was proper, she had called Gurmukh home herself. This may have happened a few times. Even the Walia family did not remain ignorant of the goings-on. A friend and good colleague from the bank came to Sonia's father's office one day and in whispering tones told him what was making the rounds in the neighbourhood about his and Mangal Sen's family, and that the heat of such a mongering scandal may singe the fair names of the two.

Like Gurmukh's family, the Walia family too found that a little lecture behind the curtain was good enough to remind their youngster of the moral fabric of the society of which they were a part of and where their social canon put a limit. All through the time of her mother's stern homily, Sonia stood timorously and heard her mother out with a dry mouth and wet hands. They desisted from unnecessarily creating a scene and bringing about an atmosphere of fear in the child's mind by harsh or punitive measures. Stress, they as educated people knew, could cause so many other different psychological complexes, which in turn could cast a shadow over their whole future life. They, therefore, took steps, guided by their wisdom, to prevent that from happening. Whether or not the children were achieving the pinnacle of success in their chosen fields within the congenial atmosphere nurtured by little constraints of discipline, they still grew up as normal, physically and mentally healthy members of their social environment. They were not among those infamous blemishes of their families who occupy hospital beds, rehabilitation centres or those who add to the fouled prison cells.

The smaller towns still had the ethos of such vibrations, which breathed strength among the people, making them keep to the ways of righteous life and making sure they were not easily swayed. Of course, there are elements that always find a convenient path in the presence of temptation and opportunity of least resistance to follow and throw all dangers, punitive fears and moral drags of the conscience to the winds and take the plunge. They may quite inadvertently land in a penal enclosure or a reformatory, rather than attaining the fortune they had hoped for, by the very act of transgression.

Part Two

10

1935–1940

Goldram's homecoming and the unification of the other members of the extended family, who though hadn't met one another in person but knew each other by name and their relationship to Goldram, was a joyous event. There was Nasha and Nikkey, cousins to Goldram and daughters of his mother's brother, Chetsingh, who was a booking clerk at Rangoon Railway Station since his transfer from Prome. Their elder brother, Prakash, too, had later sought to stay at Goldram's house with the other children when he joined the medical college attached to the Government Civil Hospital in Rangoon. Prakash and his sisters came only when their examinations drew close. It was, therefore, the paucity of space in the very small apartment at the railway quarters, alongside the boundaries of the station, allotted to Chetsingh's family, and also the extremely noisy neighbourhood that made concentrating on studies almost impossible.

Prakash was a couple of years older than Kartarlal. He had already joined medical college whereas Kartarlal still had two years to go before seeking admission into the engineering college of Rangoon University. They were first cousins and yet, as it turned out later, became more rivals than friends. Maybe it was due to the uppish attitude of Prakash, whose sharp tongue was tempered with sarcasm and condescension whenever he talked to Kartarlal. After all, Prakash was a collegian at the best medical college of the city. Also, he habitually never ceased talking—bragging rather—about the late evening concerts or an occasional fete he went at college. He had whined to his mother, whose favourite he was, to get him a blue pinstripe suit made of light material paired with a matching tootal necktie, which he wore to these concerts. He groomed his hair with lime cream from 'Evening in Paris' and drenched himself in perfume. He returned late, but the first thing he'd do the next morning was boast about his dances with the most sought after and pretty girl, Jeannie—with whom he had danced twice in the course of an evening.

No one particularly enjoyed listening to him letting go of his bag of hot air, except the naughty little Biro—aged nine—who was so thrilled that she couldn't check her bubbling screams and shrieks at the description Prakash gave of the concert. She did the same when she first saw Kartarlal on his arrival and was introduced to the family group. It seemed to be her natural bugle call of welcome rising straight from the gut. This brought forth a small smile on Kartarlal's face. He quickly became friends with two of his nephews Nikko and Neshki, eight and six, who right away came to sit, snuggling by his right and left sides.

They also became Kartalal's earliest admirers when he found ready acceptance on the cricket field in Gyogon. He was specially looked up to by Nikko, who was a little more perceptive and could see that Kartarlal's muscular build powered the easy boundaries he hit. He became a fan of his uncle Kartarlal after that and secretly cherished his image as the strongest man in the world. He never failed to be there on the field whenever Kartarlal took the crease for batting!

Dashrath and Dal Bahadur had already met the family at the railway platform. Panditji, the cook, and Khwema, the ayah for the children, came to bow low in obeisance and wished them a warm welcome. Panditji, as a routine, handled all the cooking for the family. In fact, Panditji was a retired army man who had served as a maharaj, or head cook, responsible for the entire kitchen of his unit. Goldram encountered him sitting alone on a bench at the railway platform, wrapped up in his blanket with a small bag and a long bamboo staff by his side. Joining him on the bench and engaging in conversation, Goldram learnt about Panditji's credentials and story since his retirement. Discovering that he was a Brahmin and ready to take on a cooking job in a household, Goldram at once decided to take him on to join his house staff. From that point on, he was affectionately called Panditji by everyone. Due to his temperament and training, Panditji proved to be a reliable cook. He served the Goldram family until after he was hundred. By then, the family had evacuated from war-torn Burma and Panditji returned to his native village in United Provinces. His unwavering loyalty was evident through his efforts to locate the Goldram family in the divided east of Punjab and his annual visits to meet them all.

Mangal Sen was given the only easy canvas chair to relax in and Mathura Devi reclined on the cushions of the settee. After a brief welcome hug and a kiss from his wife, Goldram returned to the sitting room to sit by his father. Soon after, when some sweet drinks began to be served by Panditji, Kaushalya came bustling in and went straight to her father-in-law and mother-in-law to receive their blessings by bowing and touching their feet respectfully. She then went to her husband and whispered to him, 'Tell the elders to come inside. Let them rest in their bedroom before they are ready to eat.' Goldram told his father and mother to go inside with their daughter-in-law to the small bedroom she had appointed and prepared for them. They could have their cold drink there and rest a while before lunch was served.

Santosh and Biro were daughters of Kaushalya's elder sister, Sheila. Sheila was married to Dev, who was a doctor in the civil hospital in the city of Mandalay in central Burma. Being the eldest among her sisters, Sheila was held in great esteem and generally looked up to for her wisdom—though not all took her advice seriously. Of all the five sisters, she was the plainest looking and had a slightly darker skin. She didn't care to highlight her features with any kind of cosmetics. However, the bright moon of respect for her age had its dark side as well. Ignoring other younger children of the family romping around during the melee of the celebration of a marriage, she called her eldest son, Shakhty, to come and have an extra apple. She was the self-appointed caretaker of the pantry and had the key to the closet. As she opened the door to pass the extra apple to him, who came running with one hand trying to save his glasses from flying off, she also let out the rich mixed aroma of fruits stored inside. When her husband sat down to the community lunch in the afternoon, she took a round particularly to see if his plate had an ample helping of the green-pea dish and whether he received the most luscious leg pieces of chicken that had been cooked in butter.

But her daughter Santosh, who was staying with her aunt Kaushalya, was of quite a pleasantly contrary temperament. She was the most helpful among the lot of children staying with her. Without being told, she got up early and, before she began to get ready for school, attended to her little cousins. She gave two of her young siblings a quick bath. The tubs were filled up fresh in the morning by Dashrath from a well in the compound and, therefore, it did not require any heating up; it was already warm when drawn from the depths of the earth. Santosh helped them get into their washed and ironed school uniforms while Dal Bahadur put quick swishes of Kiwi black polish to their all-weather long-lasting naughty boys. She packed their lunch and shoved the tiffin boxes into their bags. She, too, finished her morning chores so that she could accompany her siblings to the Gyogon rail station to catch the 8.10 train to Rangoon and reach the school by 9. The schedule was strictly followed all through the five working days of the week.

The children in the family were taught and encouraged to follow the rule of self-help. They were expected to fetch their own plates filled with the breakfast they wanted. They were strictly told not to waste food or have leftovers on their plates. After finishing their breakfast, they were to leave their plates in the sink. Before heading to the local station to catch the train to Rangoon, where their respective schools were located, they had to wash their hands. The schools were run by various private religious trusts, like the Sanatan Dharm Mahasabha, Islamic Madrasas or those run by gurdwaras. In these institutions, boys and girls were separated into different classrooms and prohibited from interaction. Most other schools were coeducational.

Saturdays and Sundays were off days for them, but the two brothers, Nikko and Neshki, always had some plans ready for the two welcome weekend days with their friends. For the upcoming weekend, Nikko and Neshki had planned to go fishing at the lake. The lake was in the middle of the vast rubber plantation on the west side of the main railway line from Rangoon to Insein to Prome Road. Early in the morning, all friends got together and started to get their fishing gear ready. They collected flesh worms from beneath the stray stones or by digging into the mud around the roots of trees. These worms were then kept safe, firmly lidded in a fifties' cigarette tin they had picked up from garbage heaps or the dry gutter alongside a road. And, of course, they would not forget the old cane basket to store the bounty of their catch.

One after another joined the group of friends when a signal (a whistled tune) was sounded in front of their homes in turn. Bunny was the best at whistling, though everyone in the group knew how to whistle.

11

Besides Santosh and Biro, their younger brother Rakesh was also a resident student at Goldram's place. Because of his plump appearance, he was teased with a sing-song line, 'Fatty, fatty, bring my catty, ate up all my ghee.' He was also jokingly called 'fatso'. Rakesh had a slight squint in his right eye. Given to over indulgence, he succumbed to his greedy appetite by openly gorging upon extra helpings of butter and home-made strawberry jam, or even stooping down to sly manoeuvres every time he sat down at the table to eat. All his clothes always seemed two sizes too small for him; his flesh bulged from every side out of his clothes. His shirt buttons kept breaking loose and the space between two buttons always opened in an oval through which a roll of abdomen flesh peeped out.

Rakesh thought he was the best at tickling the funny bone in people and took it upon himself to be the joker in the pack to bring cheer and laughter in any company, like a professional clown. But while telling a joke with his squinted eye slightly closed, he would start laughing even before he had come out with the punchline and didn't care whether anyone else present laughed or not. The sound of a forced half guffaw did sometimes break the silence of discomfiture from a corner. The purpose of it all, covertly, was to distract or break the focus of people around so that he could sneak up and reach for a savoury snack. Having evoked some response to his oft-repeated wise cracks, Rakesh thought he had earned his two square meals. Later in life, growing up to seek a vocation that would suit his temperament, he languished. He became such a nuisance that his own family members wanted to shove him aside or shoo him away like a vexatious insect.

Kinta, their youngest sister, was in Mandalay at that time. She, like Rakesh, had rounded pink cheeks that gave her face a moony appearance. By temperament too, she fell into the category of her funny brother. Eating was her preferred activity. Sometimes she ate far too much for her to contain and digest, causing her to throw up almost as soon as she had finished eating. Her greed for her preferred dishes was so much that even when she grew up, she irresistibly ate more than her system could accept. Feeling too full, she would plunge her middle and ring fingers deep into her gullet to help her throw up and make her feel easy and ready to eat another meal of her choice. She had secretly devised this process to enjoy eating her favourite foodstuffs to her fill and eat more until her taste buds and guts were on the point of revolting and blowing out.

1945–1956

Kinta had married much below her status, very much against her parents' liking. The man belonged to Maharashtra and she customarily went to live with him in his home town, Aurangabad. Her system perhaps couldn't endure her weird eating habits, and gradually, her nerves took the toll. Soon, everyone in the family was shocked to learn that she met her end with a brain haemorrhage after a bout of eating and throwing up by stimulating her gullet into a spasm with her fingers. She hadn't reached the hospital alive.

Rakesh, by then, had planted himself at Biro's house. She was a stick in the mud, now wedded to Kartarlal, who was an engineer in the engineers corps and posted in Delhi. Rakesh was always seen lounging around idly, doing nothing and just putting on more flesh as he gormandized upon the freely available cheese and butter. He devoted a lot of his time to cultivate his wry quirky smile, or at best, messed around with the servants in the kitchen, the driver Baladutt, or the gardener Thambi. Kartarlal missed a beat if he happened to overhear some of the hullabaloo thus created. He didn't want to start an argument with his wife over trifles and bitterly swallowed it all and kept quiet to stifle his abhorrence. This affected his natural hypertension, which had grown and settled in his system as a symptom of high blood pressure. 'Not a very happy sign', the doctor had remarked when he first took his blood pressure after a fit of anger or suppressed anger would leave Kartarlal livid. The doctor suggested that he learn to be calm and also bring about changes in his food habits.

Not long after his marriage, Kartarlal discovered that Biro not only had a loud mouth but also had a sabre for a tongue. She also had a knack for looking the other way or coming to Rakesh's defence when she needed to. Having no other interests like reading or listening to good music in long hours of leisure, especially during the summer, she developed an expertise in picking up moments of attack, for which she kept her powder dry and artillery well-loaded. For Biro, the marriage was maybe consequent upon her curiosity and infatuation during her pubescent ages. But her mother had the shrewd mind of a planner. Her own immediate family had been centred, and she was worried only about her own progeny. She had been shattered when Kinta had died, not long after her marriage.

~

Experience did not teach Sheila much. She was a megalomaniac and always intent upon imposing her own order on life. She saw in Kartarlal a simpleton from a country background, educated to become an engineer, who would in due course—supported by his brother Goldram—be placed comfortably in a good, well-paid job. It was like getting an all paid for and ready-made groom for her daughter. The boy could as well be easy prey and accept the new blinkers and reins, ready to view the world as she, his tour guide, wanted him to see it. She knew how and when to make her move, like a spider that has a flailing fly caught in its web. For now, she was just a predator crouching on the muscle of her strategy. She took care not to breathe a word or give the slightest indication of her plans, not even to her sister Kaushalya. She knew, from experience, that all things get settled down after a little storm in a teacup caused by any untoward occurrence. She remained quite unmoved from her focal interest on which she had all sights trained, although it was still blurred by the time to come.

~

Rakesh, having gone through his matriculation, barely ever tried hard enough to get a job and settle down in life independently. A sardar in his class, when he was doing a diploma in automobile engineering in Bombay, remembered him only as someone who ate two topping plates of rice and then slept until aroused from his slumber to have his afternoon cuppa by the canteen attendant before he closed down the kitchen until dinner time.

Rakesh never questioned the origins or reasons behind receiving plates full of food that catered to his desires for breakfast and dinner. Finally, it had to be Kartarlal, the most affected, who one day forced Rakesh to sit down with him, wrote some applications and dashed them off to several different departments of the government. He instructed Rakesh to keep track of the mail henceforth and let him know the follow-up action he had taken or had to take so that he could help him out. Left to himself, Kartarlal knew Rakesh would rather just let it be. The prospect of getting bound by the ten-to-five routine was quite unthinkable for Rakesh. He was so totally given to his whimsies that to follow any schedule seemed ridiculous to him.

Rakesh, a drifter in Gyogon, seemed to have evolved into an even bigger drifter later in life. But it would not completely seem so. He was quick to learn all the devious ways of the streets and bazaars of Delhi to pocket an extra buck from under the table by ingeniously placing officials in crucial positions within systems through the common practice of greasing the wheels to speed up progress. Rakesh, with his shrewd and scheming mind, made the best of the very junior position he held in the government machinery in the Disposal Department. He seemed to have the gene branded by his mother's hand. He looked after the rejected or condemned rail and automobile iron and steel spare parts. Their storage in the open yard meant for scrap, and later, of their disposal—to his advantage. Some of these pieces, which came as condemned, were in a reasonably good condition. In fact, he established contacts with respective departments to reject and condemn useful parts, which later could be disposed of at relatively good prices. He had, at the nether end of the disposal, some small-time manufacturers and spare part sellers lined up in the market. His education was slipshod, but in the ways of the world and in practical dealings, he was among the highest degree holders.

Friends and some close relatives, who were ready to part with a good measure of a slice of pie, were beneficiaries. One such was Dewan Saheb, the husband of Soumya, the youngest sister of Kaushalya, who—to almost everyone's surprise in the family—had almost overnight become, what commonly is referred to as a 'lakhpati', or a millionaire. Their eyes bulged with amazement when they saw his pockets overflowing with banknotes as he emerged from his white Ambassador with a poker face, handing out a few of those notes to his little brats and grandchildren before entering his bedroom, where his wife waited for him. Proudly and with some bravado he emptied his pockets into her lap and bent to give her a kiss. Indeed, he was glad to notice a moist glow rising in her eyes, accompanied with her smile that required no lipstick to radiate the grace and her own brand of straightening her neck and giving him a sweet sidelong look. He felt elated. On his evening walks, he doled out money in one and two-rupee notes to poor boys and girls from the nearby slum jhuggi-jhopri dwellers.

And soon enough, within a span of four or five years, Rakesh had lined his pockets with enough pelf to purchase land, get a house built, marry and start a family. His old father, Dr Dev, whom he most resembled in his roly-poly built, lived with him until his last breath. His mother had succumbed to an agonizing, but not long-lasting, illness at the All India Institute of Medical Sciences in Delhi. It was her throat that was held in the terminal talon of cancer, doctors had later revealed.

Part Three

12

1935–1940

All the places in the drawing room were occupied and each person was generally keen on being the first to be heard. Almost all of them began talking together in chorus. In the process of getting introduced, especially to Kartarlal among others of his age, they produced close to a noisy din. It created an aura of warmth, which wrapped especially Mangal Sen and Mathura Devi in its welcoming arms. They were overwhelmed by the respect Kaushalya had shown in her very traditional welcome by bowing low to touch their feet and receive their blessings. Kaushalya, too, was truly happy with the huge hug that her mother-in-law gave her. Holding her hand, she addressed her father-in-law, saying, 'Please come along with us to your room,' and led them into the small bedroom that she had gotten ready for them so that they could rest a while before going for a bath and eating their lunch.

Having to share common space in the house, meeting at almost every meal and the clash of school timings with activities like sports and music classes did not always make such a get-together possible. Yet, as time passed, equations had formed and small groups of the like-minded had come together. Some came by compulsion, like Biro for instance. She was very bad at numbers and because of her wandering mind, she could hardly ever, for any length of time, concentrate on her sums and wasted a lot of her time creating mischief and teasing others who were poring over their homework and getting ready for the next day.

Goldram was aware of Biro's plight; he had seen her periodic school report cards and had signed them as her guardian. He, therefore, thought it would be a good arrangement to entrust Kartarlal with the responsibility, and asked him to devote about half an hour daily to help Biro out with arithmetic. This surely didn't go down well with Kartarlal because he didn't want to cut down on his cricket-playing time and the time he spent meeting the new friends he had made on the field. But Kartalal was also quite aware that his elder brother's suggestion was no less than a mandate. He acquiesced. But Kartarlal got to decide the time slot.

He was firm when he said to Biro, 'I shall take you up with your lessons from four to half past four in the afternoon. I hope it will be all right with you. If there has to be any alteration for any reason, we'll sort it out.' Biro didn't know why, but she giggled a little, and with that mischievous smile still on her lips she rolled out, 'Oh yes, yes, I understand. I'll be all right and be ready with my books and all.'

By dictating the timings for the tuition, Kartarlal had managed not to disturb the schedule of his evening sport that he loved so much. It also gave him a little time to socialize with his new friends. Two boys who became his new favourites were: a Tamil boy, Narayan, who happened to be his schoolmate and was also good at studies, especially mathematics; and a Sikh boy, PP, short for Pritpal Singh. Kartarlal quickly became familiar with PP because they both spoke the Punjabi language and could converse in their native tongue. They were soon on visiting terms and Kartarlal was welcome into their household, especially when they learnt that he was Goldram's brother. The family was located in the western part of Gyogon, not far from the cricket field. And because Nikko and Neshki inseparably trailed along wherever

Kartarlal went—Nikko being more forward—they became friends with both Narayan and PP as well. Neshki seemed to lag behind, but he was never far when he saw he was missing something interesting like a treat of sweets or an extra bit of pocket money Nikko was getting from their father. Goldram was a man who went by the principles of strict moral discipline in every aspect of life, and yet could not sometimes help the indulgence of his generosity.

~

It may be recalled that a few years earlier, after the storm that Gurmukh's affair had created in Daska's teacup, on the urgent suggestion of his father, Goldram was asked to think of ways in which Gurmukh could be truly employed so as to not leave his mind in wild and empty dreams. Goldram gave himself a few days to ponder and understand what exactly his father wanted him to do, and then he had brought up the matter with Kaushalya.

'I know, Kaushalya, that it would be adding a burden of responsibilities on ourselves. Yet, as the wise say, the self must suffer in sacrifice to be able to help others. Gurmukh, you know, is a drop-out and he is not inclined by long way in academics and would, therefore, need to be self-employed, if not fixed in some petty clerical job. This would be time consuming indeed to find.'

Kaushalya, at once, fell in line. She thought and came up with a modest alternative, 'In that case, what should be done without losing face in the family, is to create an outlet, a shop in a town, perhaps, in a newly upmarket area, where the prices would not be very high. I know it would mean sending him to some remote region. Maymyo, I read in the papers a few days back, is popular with new settlers from Assam and Nepal.'

'Right,' said Goldram. 'It would be sensible to have a small shop for daily provisions—small stocks of all daily needs and some choice toiletry. The location shall have to be well-chosen.

I shall have to apply for a loan for around two thousand rupees to set up the establishment and set the ball rolling. You can understand the loan shall be deducted from my salary in small instalments every month.' Goldram felt the weight come off his chest after his little talk with Kaushalya.

He had travelled back home to Daska to do what his father had desired of him. But before he left for Punjab, he had taken a brief reconnaissance tour of the town of Maymyo. With the help of a local property dealer, he was able to pinpoint a place for the prospective business for Gurmukh. In fact, he did all the spade work and got the place readied. The rest was done as routine.

Gurmukh settled into his new life in Burma, and for him, life began moving smoothly since the day he reached Maymyo. Weather-wise, as the place was up north in the mountains, it had a cold and bracing climate throughout the year. It got a bit chilly during the months of January and February. His family was prepared to face some rigours of the seasons, new environs, language and ways of life—some of which, of course, Goldram had already explained. In time, the new Punjabi family fell in step and were acclimatized.

~

After a brief stay of about ten days, Goldram's parents decided to leave for Maymyo, where Gurmukh lived. Mathura Devi told Goldram to make all the necessary arrangements for the journey. He sent a telegram to Gurmukh: *Parents reaching Maymyo coming Sunday, 30th of May. Receive at the railway station. The time of arrival of the train is 8.30 a.m.*

The send-off was rather emotional. Kartarlal shed tears clinging to his mother, while his father tried to placate him. 'There now, you are a brave boy. And we are not going far away after all. You come to Maymyo to visit us all during the coming holidays, okay? Your little nephews must now have grown big. Your mother tells me that your aunt Kaushalya takes good care of you. So be happy young man. Don't forget you're here for a purpose. Be the good boy that you are.'

The scene amused Biro to no end. She giggled and gave Kartarlal sidelong secret glances. The brief pacification of her teacher from his father tickled her into side-splitting laughter. Although the amusement was at Kartarlal's cost, he didn't quite mind Biro's giggles. He secretly liked her plump cheeks and regular small shiny row of teeth, especially now that there was a pink glow on her rounded cheeks following her effort at suppressing her shrieky guffaws of laughter.

Teaching class four arithmetic to Biro was child's play for Kartarlal, although initially, some time had indeed been wasted due to Biro's tendency of indulging in her mischievous pranks. She was inventive in her choice of pranks to tease Kartarlal. Yet, as time passed, the tuition developed into some sort of satisfactory and even-keeled routine, and in the allocated half hour, a reasonable amount of work began to be covered. On All Fools' Day, she offered Kartarlal a plate full of diamond-shaped milk sweets, all beautifully covered with a lace handkerchief. But an alarm bell rang inside Kartarlal when he saw this total transformation in her behaviour; he noticed a twist in the corners of her mouth. Nonetheless, he picked up a piece of silverfoil-covered barfi and took a wee bite and was appalled when he found that his mouth filled with a foul, acidic taste.

It was just a second too late when Biro cried out, 'April Fool! I cut a cake of washing soap into this shape. Sorry! I'm so sorry. I'll get some water for you to rinse your mouth.' She ran to the kitchen and fetched a glass of water for Kartarlal, who was grinning all the time Biro was gone until she came back with the glass of water. He took it and went to the washbasin, rinsing and gurgling to clear his mouth of the filthy taste. Biro dug her hand into her skirt pocket and offered an éclair to Kartarlal, smiling broadly and, for once, candidly declaring that the sweet was genuine. 'Come on, take this. This is quite okay. It will freshen up your taste and breath.' She unwrapped another éclair, put it in her palm and popped it into her mouth, leaving no doubt in her teacher's mind. Suddenly, she laughed out loud and Kartarlal joined in the laughter. For the first time, Kartarlal noticed that the glint of naughtiness had disappeared from her eyes.

That day's teaching session was spent on Biro's practical joke. She continued to be apologetic about the whole episode until Kartarlal, now in a reconciliatory mood, declared, 'Let's call it a day for today's session. You try to do your homework by yourself. I'll go over it later sometime. We have this match today between our team and the team from eastern Gyogon.'

'Good luck. Bye,' she said and impulsively waved to him as he walked towards the exit. She heard his cheery, quick steps on the wooden stairs as he climbed down. There was a new spring in his step and it looked like he was almost dancing down the stairs. It was a strange joy that filled his whole being. Perhaps that's why he had a good time batting at the crease in the match against the eastern Gyogon team. He walked like Caesar re-entering Rome in a triumphal march after his victorious campaigns to extend the Roman Empire to the western coast of the Albion. Poor country boy, he didn't know what he was walking into.

Prakash began to feel sidelined as the understanding and intimacy between Kartarlal and Biro increased. The first seed of jealousy between them had been planted. Prakash was a happy-go-lucky bloke, so he took it all in his stride and moved on. Indeed, time treads over and decimates the last vestiges of the greatest and most gloriously etched empires of human history. He was aware of his own popularity among the crowd in college. For sometime now though, he had been hovering around Jeannie. She, too, was readily coming forth. The intimacy grew between the two and therefore, Prakash, without any qualms, gyrated away from Biro. The vacant space was already filled with the new arrival of her preferred maths teacher, Kartarlal. Prakash internalized his cauldron of anger and vengeance because his sense of rivalry was picked up by the nosy Rakesh who had spread a rumour that Prakash had written 'I will kill Kartarlal' in his diary.

Such is the attribute of shifting adolescent attachments. Lamenting his unrequited first love, even Shakespeare's celebrated Romeo, who, in deep melancholy, lost awareness of the the time of day, might have lingered in the sombre shadows if hadn't, uninvited—though persuaded by Mercutio—gone to the revelries of the Capulets and met Juliet. Almost unaware, he cast off the heavy burden of memories in the lightness of their dance and the world around him seemed to brighten.

Kartarlal, like other children, fell into the groove of his own studies, his cricket, and now the welcome break of having to spend half an hour with Biro. The growing intimacy between the two did not go unnoticed. Kaushalya, with her keen sensibility, was the first to get a whiff of the peculiar development. At the first opportunity, she broached the subject with her husband. Goldram listened attentively to Kaushalya's observations and nodded thoughtfully. After a brief pause, he said, 'Yes, now that you mention it, I have noticed a change in Biro's demeanour as well. It's as if Kartarlal has developed a special connection with her. But what could be the reason behind this sudden shift?'

Kaushalya pondered for a moment before responding. 'I wonder if it has something to do with the time they spend together. Kartarlal has been helping Biro with her studies, and I've seen them engage in deep conversations. Perhaps they have developed a unique bond during these interactions.'

'Oh yes, there is indeed a noticeable increase in the friendliness between the two of them. Kartarlal seems to be spending more time than usual with her, in spite of the heavy schedule he's cut out for himself. I've seen him linger around her even after the lessons are over. It would be better, Kaushalya, if you took up the matter mildly and diplomatically. My disapproval, as you know, may blow up something so trivial. What you can do is approach the affair via her elder sister, Santosh. She is cool-headed and would know how to deal with her boisterous sister. And keep everything under covers', Goldram observed. 'You're right there. I shall go about it just as you have suggested,' Kaushalya responded.

The practical person that she was, Santosh swung into action at once. She wrote to their mother in Mandalay. She also asked her mother to write back soon so that she could show the letter to Biro and then give her a small lecture on the side. Santosh was satisfied with the contents of the replied letter containing an admonishment intended for Biro. Santosh showed it to Biro to pull her reins and keep her course. But she did not show Biro the other part of the letter—which she, too, couldn't quite make sense of—in which their mother had instructed Santosh to not be too harsh on her little sister so that the applecart of her schemes don't get jolted. This was only suggestive in the letter and not clearly stated.

13

Kaushalya was glad that her sister had wasted little time in coming down to brass tacks. Sheila, going by her discretion, did not think the time was right for Kaushalya to know of her objectives, though she also knew that without Kaushalya's intervention, she could not possibly accomplish all she had planned. But then, she was intelligent enough to have patience, telling herself: 'All in good time. I know how to tackle Kaushalya. She's always been such a simpleton and gullible who could be fooled even by a smart modern-day child. Our own father had been such a believing fool at heart that the servants and attendant staff at home and in his photography establishment smiled into their sleeves at Mr Mackerah's bumbling foibles.'

On the contrary, Mr Mackerah was by far the most English gentleman in the whole family because of his regular dealings with British officers. He used to dress up in his three-piece suit and never went out without a bowler. Such men, though, are easy victims of jealous, petty and ambitious people. Mr Mackerah, especially, was a target of religious bigots because he was known as an eminent member of the Burma Arya Samaj and a crusader for conversion in the country. Yet, he lived his life as an upright religious man and never crossed the line between the willing aspirants and those who generally were subject to coercion or lured by the glitter of gold. As an unprejudiced individual, he even chose the treatment of a Muslim hakeem (a physician), Abdul Afreed, for his kidney problems.

The laboratory tests revealed high levels of uric acid in Mackerah's blood. His complications only increased after the hakeem started his treatment. The frequency of his intestinal disturbance also increased. He began to feel weak by the week. It was rather late in the day when the doctors at the military hospital—where he was being examined courtesy of his friend Colonel Macduff—discovered that he had been poisoned with mild dosages of arsenic by the hakeem. Over the course of a year or more, his metabolism had been affected by the ingestion of arsenic. The nails of his fingers and toes began to change colour and texture, showing signs of the drug. His urinary tract was obstructed, his kidneys and the prostate gland were affected and he fast deteriorated towards dysfunction.

His eldest son Chaitanya Dev, who was studying at Banaras Hindu University in the United Provinces of India, was summoned. He abandoned his master's degree course in European history and rushed back to be at his father's side during his final time. Mr Mackerah's younger son Sudarshan, born to his first wife, came rushing from Meiktila. Such a fast deterioration of health was quite unthinkable and it took everyone by shock.

Mr Mackerah had always enjoyed the very pink of health. When his five daughters—whom he never failed to mention with a sense of pride—were growing up, he made sure that everyday after breakfast they all went for a long walk. There was a winding path into the hills starting about a hundred yards from behind their house. Taunggyi, being in the mountainous region of the northern Shan states, enjoyed pleasant weather all year round, much like the weather in Maymyo. The hillsides were covered with pine trees and the place was considered suitable for sanatoriums. There was one run by Dr Stephen Brown. It was named after the erstwhile Viceroy of India, Lord Hardinge. Hardinge Sanatorium was always fully occupied. It was located on the other spur of the range, running westward. The climbs were gradual and never very steep. Mr Mackerah told his daughters to carry umbrellas if the weather seemed bad and to not miss their walk even if there was a thin shower. In these expeditions, they were almost invariably joined by the two sisters from the Bose family in the neighbourhood. Indeed, there existed a warm and intimate friendship between the families. The little arrow-like scar mark on the ridge of Nikko's nose came from the stitches he had to be given when he hurt himself while prancing and spinning in the Bose's drawing room.

Besides being blessed with the salubrious climate and the sweeping vistas of beautiful landscapes, Taunggyi was a well-laid out township and also Kaushalya's home town. It was therefore the natural choice of vacation of the Goldram family during Nikko and Neshki's summer holidays; they spent at least two weeks or more there. During the strawberry season, Mrs Bose sent a basket of fresh and luscious fruit from her abundant garden's yield, and the children in Goldram's house in Gyogon had lots of strawberry jam on their toast or parathas that Kaushalya made under her mother's guidance during her stay there. More easy-going, her other sisters did not have such laborious enterprises. But they always got a taste of it for there would always be some in one of the three ceramic jars she brought with her.

Sheila also came to Taunggyi during this time from Mandalay. However, they saw to it that their visits didn't coincide for more than a few days to avoid burdening the household. Of late, Chaitanya Dev had come to join his ailing father and had continued to stay on. Like a true Gandhian, he wore only khaddar products. He wore white khaddar suits and his solar hats and shoe tops, too, were covered with khaddar material. Sudarshan, younger than him, was a qualified dentist and he had come to practise his dentistry in one corner of the ground floor. He had all the latest equipment available there.

Even though there were other servants and attendants, poor Ujagar Singh, part cook and part odd-job boy, didn't have a moment's rest during the extended family's visits. He had a sparse curly beard on the fair skin of his face and wore a patka. The children had great fun by distorting his name from Ujagar Singh to Gajar Singh. They shouted his name aloud and let off a chorus of shrill laughter, for they all knew 'gajar' was the vernacular for carrot. Ujagar also joined the kids in their hilarity, although the joke was on him. There was an atmosphere of joviality created all around. The families thoroughly enjoyed the children's innocent jokes and cherished being in one another's company away from their daily onerous homework.

Every year, they found each other to have grown bigger, and their relationships too turned more complex. Secrets began to be kept from one another. Yet, they all looked forward to the summer holidays to go to Taunggyi. Life in that house was staid and sophisticated, with living rooms on the first floor separated from the ground floor by a flight of stairs with a single landing at the turn; the photographic studio and the dental surgeon's chair also occupied the ground floor. So the family used different stairs to come and go from the living quarters and made sure to not intrude upon the business areas downstairs.

~

Goldram had always had the option to take his immediate family to wherever his younger brother, Dayal Singh, was posted as a station master in Burma. The family were thus able to travel the length and breadth of the Burmese mainland. It had taken quite a few years for Dayal Singh to be promoted. He had been posted in those early years to smaller inland stations where the important express trains did not have any stops; the trains just ran through the land. Dayal Singh used to stand on the platform of the station to pass the two-feet-large iron ring with 'Line Clear' written on it, witnessed by the engine driver as the train went past the station. The driver hung out with his arm hooked, ready to take the ring into the moving engine, which was then handed over to the station master at the next stop After the 'Line Clear' operation, Dayal Singh went straight to his Morse instrument and rattled off the message of 'clear passage' of the train telegraphically to the station master of the next stop.

Long before he took Gurmukh back with him to Burma and got him settled in Maymyo, Goldram had come over to Daska to fetch Dayal Singh, the next brother in line. It was godsend that Goldram was in a well-established job in the railways, and because of the proficiency in his work, he was in the good books of his senior officers, especially the chief engineer. He was able to put in a word for his brother to facilitate his admission into the Railway Technical Institute located in Pegu, not far from Mandalay, for a course in communications, culminating in a diploma.

By dint of his proficiency and good practical work early during the session, Dayal Singh was recommended for a stipend during his training period, with which he maintained himself during his stay at Pegu. His first posting after the completion of his training was at a small station in central Burma called Shanywa, which was connected by a branch line to Thazi, slightly north of the huge junction. Shanywa was Goldram's family's first holiday destination after Dayal Singh's posting there. The small village was about half a mile away from the station and Dayal Singh's railway quarters.

One afternoon, everybody was alerted by the raucous furore that emanated from the middle of the village. Considering the station master to be of some importance, a man came running from the village to the station to seek help. He started to speak, still out of breath, 'Sir, a young man has committed suicide for a girl he loved...she didn't love him back so he has drunk some poison.'

Dayal Singh was a cool-headed man. He went into his room for his first-aid box and selected a small bottle. He gave the man a powder—nothing more than bicarbonate of sodium, but a larger than normal dose—and said to him, 'Let the young fellow swallow this powder and drink three glasses of water.'

The man rushed back to the village and found the boy writhing in pain, foaming at the mouth, lying on his cot. Putting a hand under his back, he got him into a sitting position and made him swallow the powder and drink glass after glass of water until he held his stomach and began to throw up. They brought an old basin out for him. The greyish content of his vomit was streaked with dark brownish viscous matter. Perhaps he had bled inside the stomach and the blood had clotted. After the spasms of hiccups, he calmed down and the family heaved a sigh of relief.

They gave him some fresh lime in a cup of water mixed with a little salt and sugar. Soon afterwards, the boy turned on his side and was fast asleep. The news of his recovery was given to the station master, who was with his brother and his family at the time. Feeling relieved at the fortunate outcome of the ordeal, they had a good laugh over the boy's impetuous behaviour.

One evening, not long after the suicide incident, another such event stirred the quiet atmosphere of the little village of Shanywa. A man with a very bedraggled appearance arrived. He had moist bleary eyes, a salt-and-pepper beard that was unkempt, a small piece of cloth around his head, and wore a longyi of nondescript colour and a broad black-and-white chequered shirt. He came with dust all over him, as if from a sandpit, and walked into the station master's office. He hunkered down on the floor a little away from the table at which Dayal Singh sat. Out of the blue, he began, as though picking up a narrative from where it had been dropped the day before.

'It was your younger brother—I was told later—who shot a couple of pheasants this morning in the woods beyond the paddy fields. I have a handkerchief here that can protect anything wrapped in it from a gunshot. And this is my claim! You bring your gun and come out. I have a pheasant, and we shall place it on a branch of a tree on the platform and tie it up in this handkerchief. You can then shoot it from any distance and see that it won't be affected at all. If you want, I'll sit there myself.'

Considering the matter as a big joke, Dayal Singh, who was temperamentally jovially inclined, laughed. He tried to dissuade the stranger from indulging in such dangerous experiments and told him to accept two rupees in alms and go away. 'Now take this and go and have some grub. You look famished,' he said. Dayal Singh didn't want to waste his cartridge as he had to travel long distance to buy his ammunitions.

Dayal Singh thought he was done with him. But the man continued to stand his ground. 'You may call it an experiment, Sir. Let it be an experiment. I won't climb the branch. We'll just let this poor creature be sacrificed. But, Sir, I believe the mantra given to me by the wise old man from the mountains will surely hold. He demonstrated its efficacy to several of us.'

'Well, if that is your wish and you insist, let's try it out.' Dayal Singh left him crouched in his room and went back to his quarters and returned with his gun. Also trailing behind him, chaperoned by Kartarlal, were all the holidaying nephews and nieces, screaming and shouting, clearly thrilled to see their uncle carrying his gun.

On seeing the station master return, the stranger began to walk up to the end of the platform, and there he climbed a tree. Everyone else kept following him. He had brought the bird with him, which was later tied to a branch with his colourful kerchief; it was apparently covered with a magic mantra. His face remained quite grim; only his mouth made subtle movements, as though reciting some verses to himself. Dayal Singh was smiling and laughing a little with the children all the while. The man came up to Dayal Singh and said, 'Sir, now you can go ahead and have a shot at the bird. Watch the magical imperviousness of the mantra-blessed kerchief.'

Dayal told the children to go and stand at a little distance from him, and they did. He then chose a spot with his gun and took aim from where there was no obstruction of leaf or branch. He could clearly see the small bundle sticking out from the highest branch. He didn't take long as the distance was quite short. He pulled the trigger and hit bullseye on the first shot. There was nothing much of the bird or the kerchief left when the stranger brought the blown bundle down the tree. The bird was dead and bleeding and the cloth was all in shreds, turned into a haphazard sieve by the shot from the cartridge. The stranger was shocked and stunned. He hung his head, made one or two furtive glances at the smiling gunman standing astride, surrounded by the children all in a daze. He just walked away, maybe with a lesson or two from the experiment that had jolted him into better sense than believing any Tom, Dick or Harry claiming to have mastered the occult supernatural powers.

14

Goldram didn't remain off duty for more than two days. He left the family to enjoy the holidays and left for Gyogon by himself. In Taunggyi, of course, out of family obligations and as Kaushalya was visiting her parents, he extended the stay by another couple of days, but never more than that. It wasn't decent, he believed, to stay at the in-laws' for more than a few days.

Some rather bad news awaited him when he got back home. It was a postcard, scrawled over in Gurmukhi, from his brother Gurmukh in Maymyo. The few lines conveyed that a disaster had overtaken the business. It must have been a gradual process, Goldram thought. Over a period, Gurmukh must have borrowed money to replenish the stocks in the shop and had not made enough profits, nor had he checked or controlled the expenditure within the family. Even their father, who was living with Gurmukh, was kept in the dark about the erosion that was happening at the business end. The postcard did not bode well for Goldram as he had to bear the brunt of losses incurred by the negligence and total apathy. He would have to pull the reins on the finances, especially the wasteful expenditure, at the first indications when borrowing became imperative.

Goldram felt a twinge of pain and guilt when he explained the situation at Maymyo to Kaushalya. He had hardly finished paying back the loans he had taken from his provident fund since he got Gurmukh established in the business. Kaushalya was the one who had managed the house so deftly that they had been able to sail across the rapids without braving any major upheaval or social discomfiture. He was quite aware of what Kaushalya herself had to endure, but she did indeed prove her familial mettle and went through it all with a hard nose. She had seen dark and low nimbus clouds turning days into gloomy nights, and also the orange-tinged golden clouds spreading along the horizon, auguring of bright days to follow—all of them passing, one giving place to the other. Goldram sometimes wondered what he would have done to face up to the vicissitudes without Kaushalya's support. He felt warmly in his heart about how he had learnt some tough life lessons so casually from Kaushalya at home.

'You know Kaushalya, you don't have to worry about finances; we have some reserves by the grace of God. And besides, having paid off all borrowings, I can still get some loans from my accounts at the office. Above all, I want you to be reassured that I am well aware that I have to draw a line on this sort of overreach. It shouldn't be taken casually. Nothing can go on and on infinitely. Gurmukh has been irresponsible from the beginning but he cannot expect even his well-wishing brother to shoulder the troubles or adversities of his reckless handling of his affairs forever.

'And now he is the father of four boys and a sickly girl, who I'm told, can't survive the double pneumonia that has jammed her lungs. Yet, this is no time to take reckoning of these things. I just have to get him out of the woods and leave him with one last word of worldly wisdom. Both my parents are there too.'

And so, Goldram spent the next week in Maymyo, paying his brother's outstanding debts and talking to the wholesalers who had supplied stocks to his brother's shop. Gurmukh, with a bowed head and extreme discomfiture in his eyes, walked along with his brother. All the while, images of his life in Maymyo criss-crossed his mind and made him feel guilty, making him bend his head lower. Instead of arraigning himself for sloth and lassitude while managing the affairs of the shop, he at times, found himself blaming the circumstances and the whole nature of things around him for his failures. And yet, he could not muster enough courage to lift his head, look directly into the eyes of his brother and speak to him, for he knew that all explanations would sound rather flimsy. There is indeed no alternative for hard work. The *Bhagavad Gita* states, 'Let a man be lifted up by his own self; let him not lower himself; for he himself is his friend, and he himself is his enemy.' External help and denunciation are but passing shadows of clouds sailing across the infinite sky.

Goldram stayed a day or two longer to be with his parents, who, in their innocent fondness for their dear Goldram, would have him extend his stay further still. According to his planned schedule, in keeping with leave of absence from office, he could stay only until the weekend. Then he left for Rangoon. His parents, especially his father—an intelligent businessman—knew what had brought Goldram to Maymyo and what he, in his khaki trousers, was doing from morning till late in the evening. Mangal Sen silently blessed his son. Mathura Devi, too, had some inkling of what was going on but she never said a word or interfered in the affairs of men as an understanding good housewife. She had faith in her son's competence to take responsibility for whatever he took upon his shoulders. He had, after all, come all the way from Rangoon and it must have been for good reason. So his mother was certain that whatever the matter was, it was in his safe and competent hands and that he would see it through. She also forgave Gurmukh for his follies of indolent negligence that had led the family to disaster.

Once in a while Mathura Devi had to remind Gurmukh that

his working hours were supposed to be spent not in his living quarters at home chit-chatting, but on his official gaddi at the till in front of the open entrance of the shop. His mother did not approve of the twist of unwilling resentment on his lips, like he used to do while going to school during childhood. She could see the same idler in him today and she showed him his place sternly enough. He thus walked up to his gaddi like a whipped puppy. Although younger in years, Goldram, too, briefly but tersely, said to him, 'Be your age, attend to the shop a bit more seriously. You have a large family to take care of. I am answerable to my senior officers. I can't get a leave of absence so often. I'm sure you will understand. I must leave on Sunday and report for duty on Monday morning. Take care. Give it all you have; more devotion, more attention. I'm sure all will turn out well. Our parents expect a great deal more from you!'

With Kaushalya's robust and ready support, life in Goldram's house in Gyogon did not take long to regain its balance and they forged forward at an even-keel. Yet, there were moments when Kaushalya thought she could hardly contain the anxiety churning inside her as they skimped on kitchen expenditure and the budget for other household items. She had regulated the expenditures and had left no corners to be cut. Every need of every individual had been taken care of—from the weekly payment to the washerman, to monthly bills of the merchandise from Ghulamali (the proprietor of the flourishing local provision shop) and the periodic visit to the central market of Rangoon for special purchases. Clubbed with such shopping trips was a visit to either a close family friend, like Parmanand Kaushal, or more often to Tarachand, the Superintendent of Police, first cousin of Kaushalya's mother.

~

The weekend after Goldram's return from Maymyo, Kaushalya had turned in late. She had waited for all the children to return from Friday's late-evening engagements safely. She found Goldram awake, a very unusual phenomenon. He was known to fall asleep as soon as he hit the bed anytime between half past nine and ten. Within two minutes, he had thrice shifted on his sides. His restless twisting and turning continued even after Kaushalya came to bed beside him.

'Something seems to be terribly upsetting you,' said Kaushalya softly, not wanting to disturb her husband further. Just in case he cared, she was there to help him get the load off his chest. So he did, as though he had been waiting for an opening. He had been pent up with emotional turmoil because though he was in wringing agony, he didn't wish to disturb Kaushalya's much looked forward restful sleep. She had to get up early in the morning and be ready to brave the next day's routine chores. He had, therefore, dithered to broach the matter uppermost in his mind.

'You know, Kaushalya, I don't get easily perturbed. My salary statement is not much of a great concern; the piled loans will surely be paid off in the course of a few years. But of late, I've noticed the very sensitive barometer of the gracious features of your face troubled under subtle shadows, and truly, I've wanted to talk to you about it...and about related matters.'

Kaushalya smiled in the semi-darkness of the room, lit by the street lights a little away from their windows. She was truly happy for the kind of understanding Goldram had always shown towards her and his respectful eminence of her place in the family. She, therefore, walked in the halo of unspoken grace and authority. 'Oh, I know how the silent waters run deep in you and how sensitive you have been to understand and fulfil all needs at home. I'm amazed at times that before a word is out of my mouth, you tell me what my requirement is. But as far as the expressions of my face are concerned, I know, I just can't help it.

'You are quite right. Everyone in the house looks up to me for anything they want, especially the growing ones. There is no end to their demands to increase their pocket money. The markets are crop-full of glittery goodies for the growing kids—branded shirts, trousers, suits and dresses, styled and branded footwear, dress materials, lingerie, cosmetics and the rest. Their friends show off and their desire is fired. Our times of sobriety of fashion is past, it seems. Flaunting money and bodies is the order of the day.'

'It's true, as you say,' Goldram said. 'But for certain things, you better put your foot down. Who's going to question you? Fashions are passing things, a nine days' wonder, and luxuries are meant for the stinking rich. Besides, during the phase of life when we receive education and prepare to face life squarely, as the wise always say, we must live austere lives. They must concentrate only on their studies and keep themselves in check from being distracted by fanciful thoughts. It has always been a difficult proposition. Friday evening parties, dances, concerts and lakeside picnics must not distract the impressionable minds of the young. There will always be time for such indulgences. There is no harm in being a little harsh while imposing the kind of disciplined schedule you consider right for them. Let them crib if they want. Can't I see that you have cut down on your personal needs? They must not feel the crunch of want and must not squirm under the stress of the grind. But luxury, no! Education is attained only the hard way, the life of austerity.'

'Oh,' Kaushalya said, 'this has taken a weight off my head. Perhaps there's is more on your mind. Get it off your chest once and for all. I can't bear to see you afflicted by the gloom of oppression.'

'There's not just one but two things that I have been fretting about. There's this vexing shade of repetition considering the episode at Gurmukh's end, and I don't like that at all. He is my brother and my moral responsibility, but all told, I don't like it a bit. Besides, as a grown man, he has to understand and take on his share of responsibility of the mess he creates. Being older, he must keep in mind that I am running a large household here. Indeed, I have a mind to let him know somehow that as an able-bodied head of his family, he must bend it to his best and pull up his socks before resorting to dashing off an SOS. Being of the same blood, I'm sure he wouldn't like to create any more embarrassing situations for himself and the family.'

Acutely conscious of the constraints of time and place, Goldram still allowed the gushing lava to flow. 'And then I wonder,' he said, 'whether you have gathered from the *Gazette* how the conditions of war in Europe are affecting the east, especially Indochina, the region we are a part of. Japan has been cheesed off and is deeply embittered by the sanctions imposed in a secret meeting by the US, UK and Netherlands in the form of oil embargo. Japan, the eastern end of the Axis, has, therefore, systematically begun to harass the British, French and Dutch colonies in this region—by sea, land and air attacks—in an attempt to destabilize their colonial governments. Countries like Vietnam, Malay and Siam have already been attacked by the Japanese and here, in Burma, we could face the same fate any time. I hope our mali has the trenches in the patio ready to use in the time of emergency.

'I have seen the imminence of grave calamity in the dark clouds of Sir Rolland's eyes. Last week, he and Governor James Baldwyn began to talk about the general safety and security measures being put in place for the city of Rangoon. Also, I got a hint of the large-scale preparations for the evacuation of the civilian population. I can foresee a gigantic task for myself of getting the family safely back home to India. But for the present, it is long past midnight and soon enough, you'll have to be on your feet again to oversee the daily grind.'

Sure enough, soon Kaushalya—whose worries exacerbated with her husband's apprehensive cogitations and hadn't yet gone into a slumber—heard the regular breathing and soft snoring of her husband. She could tell herself that all was well and she, too, could now claim some rest and doze off. Still not quite at peace, both of them lapsed into the penumbra regions of the subconscious. From outside of her billowing mosquito netting, Kaushalya could imagine the house in peaceful sleep. Dal Bahadur, not able to endure the first onslaught of sleep during the first quarter of night, had his chin down the third button of his uniform. The cows in their sheds were heavy-lidded, half covering their innocent eyes after slowing down the mastication of cud and cuddling close to their calves who were already asleep; the stale and pungent smell of cow dung still hung in the stillness of their shed. The winter sky was clear and the stars bright in their celestial glory. The mali had safely covered the well for the night.

The peaceful stillness pervaded the front lawn, leading up to the entrance gate into the house, and the lamp post across the lane was still dimly lit. Little moths and flying insects rose from the overgrown grass and whirred round it, sometimes knocking against the glass of the bulb and the enamelled shade to make wee ticking sounds. With the habitual mental survey of her household in God's protection, Kaushalya woke up at the first break of daylight around six in the morning.

She found, as usual, Goldram had already left his bed and, as was his habit, had gone down where the mali had already arrived for duty. He went round the cattle sheds, caressing the cows and the galumphing little calves; his heart was warmed by their soft grunts and tentative moos. He then went to the flowers and vegetable beds, caressing them all as though wishing 'good morning' to each little sprout. He plucked out the browned leaves here and there as he went from one row to the next. The mali gathered some fresh vegetables for the day and went up to deliver them to Panditji in the kitchen. Panditji, looking at the quantity of the vegetables, would often enjoy a mild joke, when the mali said, giving him the armful of morning gleanings, 'I've brought a gift for you, Baba; sorry but nothing better than some extra work to do,' and they both laughed.

Both of them had been with Goldram for several years. The mali, an Odiya man, was quite a stripling when he took employment with Goldram. He had married a Burmese woman and now had two children whom he had named Lav and Kush, after Lord Ram's sons in the epic *Ramayana*.

15

The world war that began on 1 September 1939, with Hitler's Germany sweeping the comparatively unprepared target, Poland, was now at its height. The rumbling of tanks, the rapid machine-gun fire and the boom of exploding artillery fire from the dive bombers continued, bringing more and more death with every new sortie. The raining death did not make much difference between the soldiers of the Axis countries or Allied forces. They all lay bloodied, spread-eagle on level land on both side of some imaginary line called the front, or in trenches, with one common expression of shocked surprise mixed with pain or fear but ubiquitous innocence written large upon their faces.

Children at school were let off early. Nikko, as he emerged from the gates of his school building wondering about it, was struck by what he saw. The cover page of the previous day's *Rangoon Gazette* was lying on the pavement with a huge illustration, showing an eagle with widespread wings swooping down on a small cringing rat. 'Germany' was scrawled across the eagle and 'Poland' was on the rat's image, painted with a huge splash of red. Nikko was so awed by the sight that he remembers it even today.

~

By the time Kartarlal finished school and joined the university in the department of Civil Engineering, Biro's mischievous attentions for him had turned into fondness. She found herself thinking of him in her idle hours and making imaginary conversation with him—sometimes even laughing to herself at her own naughtiness. But when Kartarlal came face to face with her, she found her mind going blank. For all kind of reasons, it was not very often that he could give her the usual lessons in maths. A lot more time was required to focus on his advanced studies. Also, he didn't want to get out of touch with his batting as he was now playing for his college.

He had also become quite familiar with his bearings in Gyogon as his older sister-in-law used to send him to the Insein market for her personal shopping. Biro and Kartarlal's growing fondness for each other had traversed beyond the passing of notes and perfumed letters. Now they touched and squeezed each other's hands. Forgetting everything related to propriety, Biro would sometimes openly call out to Kartarlal, when he went out in the evening, to bring paan for her and did not forget to write in her next note to him how she found the paan having the sweetness of his love.

Just then, schools and colleges closed down for summer vacation. Kartarlal, whose college results had been out since April, seemed to be just relaxing and hibernating. Within himself, he was eagerly waiting, looking forward to step into the world of the grown-ups and becoming an independent, earning member of society. Kartarlal had, with the encouragement and help from his brother, applied for the post of Associate Estimator Engineer in the district of Pegu in central Burma when the vacancy had been advertised. And Goldram, without losing any time over it, had told Kartarlal to write an application and mail it forthwith.

An answer from the concerned department was expected any day now. Even before receiving the positive response from the department, Goldram had already had a word in private with Kartarlal.

'You know Kartarlal, until now you have—whether in Daska, or later here at Gyogon—been living a safe and sheltered life; sailing, as they say, over charted waters of the deep. The congenial atmosphere at home is built with values that all observe, not as an imposition. The world outside is a harsh world. There's no end to man's greed; resorting to violence or violation of norms needs no provocation. It's a way of life for some. Away from home, you are going to be exposed to this new kind of merciless world for the first time. We have lived, grown up and have had our habits formed in an atmosphere permeated by universally accepted moral values. That imbibed is indeed the conditioner of our inherent character. And yes, it is a tough shield against the assailing contrarieties. Yet, what I want you to be careful of is that a smooth tongue can easily deceive you into doing something that you would, in the cool of your mind, disapprove of. So it's always better to brush it aside and lay off those who are overly humble, who come as your well-wishers and inveigle you into devious ways with their suggestions of how to get around the law with impunity.'

Thus Goldram casually put across the wisdom of his years while launching his ingenuous Kartarlal into a new order outside the home and the cricket ground. He left the rest upon Kartarlal's own devices on the spot, face to face with a live situation. The last thing he told him was that he must never forget that his conduct in the discharge of his duties was going to reflect on the family's reputation.

~

They were sitting in the second-class waiting room of Rangoon's railway station, where Goldram had come to see off Kartarlal as he left for his new job. Meals would be served at Kartalal's berth in the cabin. However, as the train came to a stop by the platform for the passengers to board, Goldram bought a surahi for water and a packet of fruits for Kartarlal and led him to his berth in the cabin. He found a convenient space to tuck Kartarlal's luggage and spread a sheet over the cushioned berth. Goldram sat with Kartalal on his reserved berth for a while and then went on to reassure him that Mr Sammad Husain would receive him at the junction of Pegu station, and that he had been instructed to take care of everything about his boarding and lodging for his comfortable stay there. Sammad Babu was an old colleague and friend of Dayal Singh's as they had happened to be appointed at the same station after the completion of their training.

Upon Kartarlal's arrival in Pegu, Sammad was promptly at the station to receive him. Sammad gave Kartalal his first meal at his place before taking him to the lodge. He truly took care of his welfare just like any member of his own family would. Kartalal's digs had been properly cleaned and tidied before he was moved in.

During his stay of around seventeen weeks at Pegu, Kartarlal's encounter with a gentleman called Hansraj Bharadwaj was enough to vouchsafe the veracity of what Goldram—he thought wryly—had been sermonizing to him. He had respectfully kept quiet and heard his brother out with a sense of misgiving and considered it all a great deal of magnification of some stray streak of malevolence in society. All kinds of people employ all kinds of means to earn a living, Kartarlal had thought. But he was yet to learn that sunlight has seven colours of the rainbow and how imperceptibly microscopic *bacilli* could infect man with fatal illnesses. It is from personal experience that lessons are learnt, which then turn into unforgettable pieces of wisdom—something that Kartarlal got to encounter.

Young and in sanguine health as Kartarlal was, he was sweating profusely even under the fan in his office. It was a warm day of June. Kartarlal could feel drops of sweat trickling down his spine, from the middle of his shoulders to his lower back. He had to wipe his upper lip every few minutes as beads of sweat appeared. Rahim, the peon, announced that a Mr Bharadwaj, who sought to speak with the engineer sahib, was waiting outside. Immersed as he was in the perusal of other office files, Kartarlal thought of the visitor as a vexing intrusion, an outright distraction for him. He grew more irritated when he saw the peon pressing him to give the visitor a hearing, an unusually obsequious smile creasing his dyed, bearded and skinny face. Not allowing his temper to get better of him, Kartarlal told Rahim to send the gentleman in with a word of caution to be brief in whatever he had to say and not take up a lot of official time.

Mr Bharadwaj was in his late forties, plump, suntanned, with dark circles under his big, rolling eyes. His cheeks were pink in spite of his dark skin. However, this pinkness was the effect of last evening's session of booze with his wayward friends, with whom he drank not by peg but by bottle. He walked in carrying two small boxes—apparently packed with sweets—and a small bag—quite possibly full of bank notes. After all, he had come to introduce himself to the engineer, with whom he visualized a long relationship of exchanging favours. He came in gingerly and took a seat facing Kartarlal. Mr Bharadwaj noticed that though Kartarlal's complexion was fair and pink, he was clearly an Asian. He felt emboldened. After the formal exchange of salutations, he began to loosen the strings of the small bag he had placed in front of him on the table and opened it partly to expose the wads of bank notes inside. With a broad grin, he squarely looked at the engineer. Against all his expectations, what he met in response from Kartarlal was a poker face; his breath was more akin to the whistling sound of an aroused cobra.

'Sir, I am the oldest contractor for the railroad laying

company, Phayaji Enterprise,' he began to speak, 'and as your records will show, I have done a lot of honest business with this department and I hope to continue it with your sympathies in my favour. As a gesture of goodwill and friendliness, I've brought a gift for you. I look forward to a long and cordial relationship with you and your office. I thank you for your kindness to have given me your time and this present hearing.'

Not having received any rebuff ever before—nor fearing any now—Mr Bharadwaj got up in some added assurance when he suddenly heard Kartarlal's terse voice of controlled anger. 'Mr Bharadwaj! You may be done with your part of the meeting, but I am not. So please sit down and hear me out carefully. I don't know who gave you the liberty to come and behave as you have done. So long as I am in office and in charge here, never dare to offer any kind of gifts. Different officers have their different ways of dealing with matters. And so far as the work contracts under me are concerned, the transactions are done through the invitation of quotations. So, at the time the advertisement is put out, send in your competitive quotation and wait for the due date on which your quotation will be viewed alongside those of others and the date when the decision is taken will be declared. Now without any further argument, please pick up the stuff you brought with you. And whenever next you wish to talk to me, make sure to get a prior appointment. Have a good day.' With that, Kartarlal concluded the meeting and rang the bell on his table for Rahim.

Bharadwaj opened his mouth a little to say something but noticing the stony look on the engineer's face, he stopped short. He went on to sheepishly collect his paraphernalia and—red in the face—turned around and went out, almost crashing into Rahim who came rushing in answer to the call of the harsh office bell.

Seasoned and hard-shelled as Bharadwaj was, he could not

check himself from giving himself another fling at his luck. Just before stepping out of the office door, he turned around to face the engineer. In a very subdued, yet patronizing, voice, he began, 'I'm afraid you may consider me impudent, but I say this just out of being much older and experienced in the ways of the world. You are quite right, Sir, to go by the rule book in your day-to-day dealings with people.'

The look of disapproval in Kartarlal's eyes and the couple of harsh words that escaped his mouth (he was trying his best not to embitter the relationships at the very inception) did not deter Bharadwaj from continuing. 'The problem arises when you deal with people who, quite unlike you, are unscrupulous about any moral considerations. In fact—and I say this not to change your mind—during my professional career, my observation has been that even the staunchest sticklers of upright conduct are tempered with time. They erode to fall in line with the devious, maybe through the pervert persuasion of the staff at lower levels. The sooner you see the point, Sir, the easier will be your transition. You will kindly forgive me, Sir, for my impudence, but I would call my prolonged meeting with you an imposition.' Then he quickly turned into the corridor and down the staircase leading to the ground floor.

Kartarlal heaved a deep sigh of relief and wiped the sweat from his forehead. He was glad to have kept his cool during his first encounter with a crooked contractor. He was also happy that, if nothing more, he had given him a warning to not just walk into his office whenever he felt like it but to make an effort to seek prior permission or an appointment.

Kartarlal had always looked up to his elder brother as a supremely intelligent and knowledgeable person. He had tried to imbibe the entire spirit of what his brother wanted to instil in his mind. And now after his experience with Bharadwaj, he reminded himself how important it was to always be mentally prepared to face an exigency like this. In about five to six months, after careening across the uncharted terrain and dealing with little jerks and jolts, Kartarlal had managed to make a tangibly respected place for himself—not only among his colleagues, juniors and seniors, but also in the neighbourhood of Pegu. Missing out on the luxury of his favourite sport, he spent some evenings playing chinlone, a game of bouncing a cane ball, with a few students of the local technical college who enjoyed talking to an engineer.

Kartarlal's life had soon begun to acquire a smooth sailing stability. He had started to live a reasonably contented life with dreams of a future in which Biro always claimed a place as his partner. Family bonds were strong in him. Once in a relationship, he remained committed; he was not a playboy but one who belonged. He regularly kept in touch with the family at Gyogon, Rangoon and Maymyo, and he hoped to visit and share with them all his experiences sooner or later. He wanted to share joy and laughter over quaint little stories about Sammad Babu and Bharadwaj the contractor. He would especially describe to his brother how he had dodged and shooed away Bharadwaj's baited visit—a moment when his breast swelled with pride. He would talk about his visit to Maymyo to meet Gurmukh, his family, and his dear mother and father over a long weekend by taking an off on Friday.

And this was exactly the way things transpired. During the five days he got off around Diwali, Kartarlal—for the first time—bought gifts and toys for the kids at Gyogon, fondly spending his hard-earned money as he had done when he had went to meet the family at Maymyo. It was truly a very happy festival for the family at Gyogon with Kartarlal arriving back home with arms full of gifts for almost every one in the house, especially for the Gurkha guard, Dal Bahadur. Kartarlal had met Dal Bahadur's distant relative Pashupat, along with his family in Maymyo, where a cluster of a few Nepalese families—running away from drought and famine conditions in Nepal—had come to settle down, close to Gurmukh's residence.

~

Two or three days into his furlough, Kartarlal had begun to feel relaxed in the warm conviviality of home when suddenly he was left shocked and stunned by a telegram from Maymyo. The head of their family, Mangal Sen, their father, had been found dead in the toilet due to—what doctors found later—a brain haemorrhage. His stocky and well-built body was found slumped over the washbasin, his head having collided with the faucet, with blood from his head flowing into the basin.

Gurmukh and his son, Bhagat, Singh had carried Mangal Sen's body to first give it a thorough wash. They had then laid the body on a stretched out white sheet on the floor of his bedroom. Gurmukh had lit an earthen lamp and placed it near the head as a ritual. Swaran Singh, Gurmukh's other son, had hurried to the local post and telegraph office in the main bazaar to send necessary telegrams to the family wherever they were in Burma and Daska.

Kartarlal, the youngest and having lived with his parents until they left for Burma together, was the most affected by their father's death. He was in Gyogon on a visit and Goldram wasn't back from office yet. Having read the telegram, he broke the news to Kaushalya, almost sobbing. He quietly left her in the kitchen and slunk into his bedroom. Kaushalya came running after him, caressing his convulsive shoulders and head while he lay on his face and sobbed into his pillow. She sent away the curious children hanging around dazed by the sight of their young uncle crying like a baby. Indeed, there was a faint, tentative sob or two from the little twins. But stunned by the whole scene, they quietly walked out to where they had left their tin rails and train with other toys.

In the evening, when Goldram returned and Kartarlal had slept and rested in the afternoon postprandial siesta, he once again broke down on the shoulders of his brother. Even Goldram, a man of rare emotional exhibition, wiped his flowing eyes with the extra hanging length of his turban. With a consoling embrace and soothing and encouraging words, Kartarlal began to slowly breathe normally. He wiped his eyes and nose on his handkerchief and accepted the glass of water Kaushalya had brought for each of the brothers.

Part Four

16

1941–1945

It was December 1941 and the American fleet in the Pacific at Pearl Harbor, Hawaii Territory, had been struck by the Japanese bombers on the 7th of that month. It had been a surprise attack launched from two aircraft carriers. The Imperial Japanese Navy conducted these sorties with the primary intention of deterring the US naval base, aiming to halt American interference in Japanese plans to attack US, British and French territories in the Philippines, Malaya and Indochina. Some of these colonies had already been victim to the ruthless Japanese forages followed by the occupation forces. It was all because of the European sanctions—especially the oil embargo—decided upon in Amsterdam, that Japan was targeting Burma to replenish its stocks of oil, rubber and tin.

The next phase of the Japanese advance into western Indochina was inevitably expected to be the British-Indian colonial extension in the east, or the province of Burma. Goldram, by his sensitive perceptions and sensible inferences drawn from deeper and intelligent reading of the action happening in the war arena of Europe and its consequent fall out, had begun to feel apprehensive. This was reflected in the attitude of the piqued but powerful nation of the Axis in the east, Japan.

~

Goldram dwelt upon the causes of anxiety that had been, of late, fretting away his otherwise very stable mind processes. He had been speculating upon this, at that moment, in the context of his and his family's life. He did not miss bullseye by a mile when he openly said to his wife on a sleepless night that he feared it was not going to be long before the Japanese war machine would come rolling down the streets of Rangoon.

'You must start collecting, in fact, separating things—the most precious things and the things that you'd not like to take in an emergency. They may be left behind with the uncertainty of ever returning. Oh, the agony and the very thought of abandoning the warmth and comfort of this precious home you've built with your love and devotion from the laying of the first brick in the foundation! It must be only the things most valuable to you, of manageable weight, and those that can be contained in the smallest space to make it convenient to carry. I know, you may think my apprehensions are, perhaps, overblown premonitions. But I have been watching closely how the Japanese armies, since their successful attack on Pearl Harbour, have been speedily trampling over the Indochinese areas like Vietnam and Malaya and have already advanced in our neighbourhood up to Siam. To my mind, it won't be too long before Burma will be within range of air strikes, tanks and rolling cannons from their advanced military bases. I know of some preparations afoot in official circles for the evacuation of the government staff. Ominous as it may sound, we may soon be on our way to India. In their effort to save as many English lives as possible, they have stipulated flights from Rangoon to Calcutta; besides, there are special steamers to ferry the officers and their families.

'Also, as a gesture of goodwill towards the honest and faithful servants of the British government and the Crown, the offer has been extended to some chosen officers of Indian origin. And what

I've heard is that my name has been included in the list of the privileged to be airlifted.'

Kaushalya, who habitually kept herself abreast of worldly news, had never dwelt at any length on the developing situation or drawn far-reaching political conclusions. She was used to forming intelligent ideas on the basis of observations of reported events she thought were cogently connected. She hardly had time to linger or ponder any further. She knew though that her husband would not panic over a fancy, and so, she took seriously what he had said that night and mentally began to prepare to leave everything behind. It required a lot of courage, but she started to put away stuff, like bank notes and gold, and packed them in a sort of belt that could be bound around the girth in an emergency situation when they would have to just walk out. She was not quite sure, but tentatively, she packed a suitcase with a change or two for every one in the family to lug along if conditions allowed it. In appearance though, life went on as usual, except for a quiet gloom that permeated the whole house, for the sword of Damocles menacingly dangled over their heads every hour they spent in Burma.

~

It was Christmas Eve. It had been a fortnight since the Japanese had attacked the US naval base at Pearl Harbour. The day in Rangoon was gay and bright. The Christians in the city and in the suburbia of Rangoon, joined by several others of other communities, had festooned their house-fronts with bright coloured lights and streamers, and the large symbolic star which would be lit up in the evening. Most Christians in Gyogon were up and about since morning after a quick early breakfast, crowding the market places accompanied by their children in their best festive outfits, some even looking like Santa Claus. A galore and variety of Christmas trees and sweets and other little toys were on display to be bought dangling from the branches of the little pines or cypresses. The people were without a worry during their Christmas vacations. But all that changed in an instant. The passing shades of apprehension on the faces of some knowledgeable gentlemen seemed to have suddenly materialized. There was panic and chaos all around as the trenchant sound of the siren began to pierce and echo across the quiet blue Gyogon sky. The merry preparations were all awry.

~

In the northern end of the market, Nikko, just across the hedges and the barbed wire boundary of his house, had been climbing guava trees since morning. He had his sights set upon the upper tufts through which the sun came streaming into his eyes. As a natural reflex, he narrowed his lids; the strain of the whole effort broke small beads of sweat on his face. His young skin appeared to be pink and sometimes golden whenever he basked in sunlight. He tried to spot the nests nestled in the crisscross of twigs when he thought he had heard the noisy clamour of fledglings and the whirring wings of the sparrows coming to roost by sunset—especially the yellow sparrows and not the common brown and black ones. His curiosity took him to explore the higher reaches of the trees to spot the nests of these sparrows so he could discover the younglings or the pale sparrow eggs in them. Nikko had come upon a nest on the first tree he had climbed and felt lucky. So he went on to the next one in the row and was climbing up to the nest he had spotted when he heard the piercing siren. Through the leafage, Nikko saw aircraft formations advancing southeast towards the airbase at Mingaladone—about five kilometres away from his house.

The aircrafts arrived making small waves in the sky. Within

minutes, the fearsome boom was heard from the direction of the airbase. Having heard so much about the activity of war, Nikko could make out that he was indeed witnessing action of the great war. He even heard the rumblings of shaking furniture and trembling picture frames against the walls from his house. He noticed, too, some aircrafts flying in the other direction; perhaps, they'd finished their bombing sorties. Then suddenly, he saw an unusual sight in the sky followed by a flash and a loud bang: one of the aircrafts was struck by the anti-aircraft guns fired from the ground. There were flames and thick, wavy, black, coiling trails of smoke as the aircraft came down with a tailspin. From the burning aircraft, he saw an object shoot out; it turned out to be the pilot whose parachute had opened up like a huge white umbrella against the clear deep blue sky. It came whistling down, shifting along the direction of the north-westerly wind. Several other planes met with the same fate.

It was a sight that struck fright in the innocent heart of the schoolboy, his head full only with stories from comics. For a while he watched the gigantic cosmic sized fireworks; aircrafts screaming across the blue sky with trails of smoke and fire, and the dive bombers as they came down, their machine guns indiscriminately firing rat-a-tat-tat-tat on the civilians.

Quite stunned, dazed and tremulous all over, Nikko jumped off the lower branch, landing straight down on his bottom on the grassy ground, and hurriedly squeezed his feet into his Bata Naughty Boys. Breathless, he ran towards the nearest rear staircase, up into the safety of his home. He found his Ameji (he had been taught by the Burmese ayah to call his mother Ameji) fully prepared to go down into the trench in the patio which—thanks to Dashrath the mali—was now well equipped and ready for use. Immediately after the siren pierced the skies with warnings of air raids, Kaushalya called out to all children, including those of the ayah, to hurry up and get inside the safety of the trench.

~

It was on this dreaded day that the bloodied shadow of the terror of the war hit Rangoon. The schedule of long distance and the local trains had all gone haywire. Goldram got back home only as dusk had started to darken the mauled sky. Panditji, with dinner ready in his kitchen, waited for the family to come out of the trench. Goldram arrived with an aura of good cheer. Nikko had felt a lump of emotion choking him while he waited for his father to return, and had burst out in sobs as soon as he saw his sky-blue suited form descending the stairs with a reassuring smile, crowned with his signature white turban. His presence brought more light and cheer than the kerosene lantern could have ever done. The moonless night was further darkened by the city that was plunged in the mandated general blackout as the precautionary warning had announced two weeks ago.

As usual, Panditji had set the low round table in the middle of the large living room with cane seats around it for the family, with only a small dim lantern placed on a low stool in the corner. They all came up by the steep and straight rear stairs from the trench, and after quickly washing their hands and feet, they were seated around the table. It was now fully laid with hot and tempting food. The children grew busy with loading up their plates with their favourite dishes and homemade cow's butter. Goldram, on the side, wanted to have a quick important word with Kaushalya and they carried their plates to the drawing room. Together, they had to take care of the welfare of the family during the forthcoming hazardous trek back to India, across the border of the Arakan mountain range.

'What you must understand is that the time to leave has

come. Even official notifications have been issued for a general evacuation of the civil population, government employees and their relatives. Special ferries are being arranged to accommodate as many people as possible for travel from Rangoon jetty to Calcutta harbour,' Goldram hurriedly let her know. 'For the families of graded officers like me of the Burma Railways, airlifts had been booked.' But Goldram went on to explain to her, as he thought was necessary. 'But, though at the cost of self-sacrifice, keeping in mind what strikes me as quite reasonable—a suggestion put forth by my mother—I had to forfeit this privilege. She would not care, she had said, to go safely back to India leaving the other three sons and their families in lurch in a strange land. Besides, lest we forget, there's your elder sister in Mandalay.

'The family in Taunggyi, I've been informed by Sudarshan, have been fortunate to get assistance from the army base of getting a transportation lift as soon as possible in supply transport trucks that ply between Manipur, through Pallel, to the last checkpoint, Moreh, in the Indian Territory. You know, the commandant of the base camp of the army in Taunggyi had always been a patron of your father who was the proprietor of the best photography establishment there. The family will be carrying an authority letter from the commandant of the base at Taunggyi to make things convenient for them. Therefore, we can stop worrying about them; they would reach India much before we are likely to make it there. I'm sure they will be in much better shape, too, as they'd be travelling faster and without any dearth of foodstuff. But us being with a larger group of family members, we shall have to go through a lot more difficulties and problems. According to the reports coming from the wayside camps, paths are mostly bumpy and slushy and wind through the thickly forested Arakan ranges into Imphal, the first big Indian town and capital of Manipur.

'There's much more to tell and talk about, but life is to be lived here and now. Start taking care of the preparations; put the last knot on the packed baggage. Since we are not sure about the means of transportation, it would be better to be more mindful of what all has to be left behind. I shall take care of the rest. And so, good night and good luck.'

~

The second bombardment on Rangoon on Christmas, as expected, was more widespread and intense. Consequent upon this, the fate of Goldram's family's countdown for the departure from their home was sealed. The British government in Burma had made hectic preparations for evacuation—besides having put an air raid precaution system in place, a bill of dos-and-don'ts was issued officially as an advisory to regulate life in the city during this emergency period. But when it came to transportation, priority was given to the British, both on flights and bookings on the steamers leaving from Rangoon and Akyab on the west coast. The English were seen carting away not just their prized period furniture pieces, but also their fine bone china dinner sets. The sick, old and needy were left to fend for themselves as they were denied passage and even inhumanly chased away from the ports and airports where they had crowded.

~

The next morning, Goldram had started to tick tasks off his priority list. The first thing he did was use the public call office booth just outside his workplace to get in touch with his brothers far from Rangoon—Gurmukh in Maymyo and Dayal Singh at Shanywa. He was able to get through to Kaushalya's elder brother-in-law too—Dr Dev in Mandalay. He gave them all strict instructions to treat the developments taking place around the whole country seriously and to prepare for a long journey back to the safety of India. With the widespread bombings in Burmese towns, the time it would take for Japan to penetrate Indian Territory was anybody's guess.

Something terrible did happen. The night before the large family group travelling under Goldram's wings reached Imphal, the place was heavily bombed. Since the evacuees in thousands were trudging through the slushy mountainside, several dead bodies were lying alongside the tired, wobbling and sore. Despite the heartache, the courageous cavalcade continued to climb their way to India. All through the journey, these gritty survivors passed a word of encouragement or a smile of cheer to one another by looking back at their companions over their shoulder or across the bunch in front. They were hit by the strong stench of rotting human flesh and faeces when they closed in on the precincts of Imphal. Indeed, it was close to the stench of an infernal pit.

Goldram told his family to not waste any time thinking about the situation and to pack the bare minimum to meet their needs on the long journey. They had to reach Shanywa as soon as possible. What Goldram had planned was that the whole family should first get to one rendezvous, and then from there, they would chalk out their plans to move forward. In many different ways, Shanywa, where Dayal Singh was now posted, was quite centrally located and within easy reach from Rangoon in the south and Maymyo in the east, with Mandalay being its nearest neighbour, slightly to the southeast. Its exact location was somewhere midway between the two bigger rail junctions of Thazi and Pyawbwe. To replenish his monthly provisions, Dayal Singh used to travel to the crowded noisy bazaar of Pyawbwe in the first week of the month. It was both a place for the people of the neighbourhood to get together and also to purchase weekly provisions. Dayal Singh, too, for his domestic supplies and, especially for the purchase of batteries for his newly bought Philips radio, would go there. With the war having reached the doorsteps of Burma and with the delivery of newspapers becoming erratic, listening to the hourly news from BBC about the current situation had become a necessity.

The grown-ups among the boys—Kartarlal, Prakash and Sukhdev—and also Sammad Babu, crowded around the radio. At times, these gatherings lasted beyond midnight. Dayal Singh, of course, would join them only when he had ten to fifteen minutes to spare from his busy schedule of looking after trains running through his small station. And, indeed, there were some local trains which made a brief stop there, and still took a good fifteen to twenty minutes before their departure from the platform.

The gatherings around the radio during the late evenings and nights of the blackout were great fun, despite the shadow of apprehension of the Japanese bombers bearing down upon them. Japan's gloomy shadow was fast spreading from Rangoon to other bigger cities, like Moulmein in the south to Toungoo in central Burma. The bus depots and railway stations were getting more crowded every day with people seeking to get to the north of the border between Burma and India; many hoped they could cross over into the safety of their homeland, the Indian subcontinent.

~

Over the second week of January, the numbers in Shanywa began to grow. The women and children arrived before the elders, having wound up things and packed and locked their homes to join the family in Shanywa. The extended family were mostly growing children in their early teens and some were even younger. For them, being together was a good enough reason to get into the mood of holidays and extended picnics. In a place without other civic provisions such as amusement parks and similar outlets, they drifted in small groups of their liking through the bare bazaar to while away some time and devised other activities to entertain themselves. They went for idle sightseeing walks through the busy local market and shopping lanes. Sometimes, they invited others and a few acquaintances from the neighbourhood if they had decided upon outdoor games such as oundoo—which they had learned from the local children—and played during the evenings across the railway lines from the platform. They enjoyed these moments the most because all were involved and it required a lot of running to safeguard their territory. The whole crowd was divided into two; these groups were the masters of their demarcated jurisdictions and had to save them from marauders and invaders. During most of the evenings, the whole of the empty lot resounded with shouts, shrieks and screams of laughter. Even the passers-by were attracted and stopped a while to vicariously enjoy the game. Among other outdoor activities was the flying of kites, climbing of trees, hide-and-seek, cops and robbers, hopscotch for smaller girls and top-spinning or gilly-danda for boys. The girls also played korda chapaki—a traditional game from Punjab—and the grown-ups whiled their time, if and when they had any, by playing cards or a game of dice.

17

The nights were still long during the middle of February but the days tended to be warm. Dawn broke early for them if Harbhajan, Dayal Singh's sister-in-law, brought the morning tea early. One bright morning, the two large rooms allocated to the women of the family (they called it the 'ladies' pavilion') were bustling very early with a cacophony of trenchant voices. It seemed as though two or three of the women were in a hurry to say their bit.

It was surely some fierce argument but it was not clear what it was about. Basho, Chetsingh's daughter, standing by Kaushalya's side, was trying to say something in support of her very affectionate sister-in-law, 'I swear, I'm telling you I saw with my own eyes.' Basho's hair was tangled and dishevelled and her eyes were wide with a bulging look. She had been sleeping close to the newly galvanized iron-sheet trunk, and it must have been a very slight creak caused by the little drag of the trunk that had awakened her. She had not quite gotten up, but shrewdly, with half-opened eyes, had tried to gather the goings-on.

She saw, in spite of semi-darkness (at about two in the night), the form of a woman in a sari digging into the half-opened trunk, which she knew belonged to Kaushalya. The woman was quickly rummaging and, finally within minutes, her hand brought out a small flat box. She had tucked it into her petticoat and covered it with her sari and had slunk back into her bed in the space portioned out of the main bedroom by a curtain. It was only when she was passing a bit close to the night lamp that Basho was able to place the silhouette as that of Gurbans—wife of her cousin, Dayal Singh. She had fallen asleep in the quiet that fell after her little cameo in the semi darkness of the ladies pavilion.

Early in the morning, Kaushalya was going for a bath and had found her trunk all upset and in shambles when she had opened it to get a change of clothes for the day. In her casual check, she found that her jewellery box was missing. She at once rushed out to the men's quarters, shouting that thieves had come at night. 'My jewels have been stolen. The jewellery box is gone! Please come and see! They've robbed me.'

Goldram, followed by Kartarlal and Dayal Singh trooped into the room where the trunk had been lying. Giving the room a searching look, Goldram's first observation was, 'No door facing outside has been forced open. Nobody from outside could have gained entry into this room except from the passageway between the two ladies' rooms. Almost the whole empty space in the rooms is occupied by the beds of the sleepers. There's hardly any sign of an intruder from any other door or window in the adjacent rooms.' To this, Dayal Singh added, 'And after cleaning the kitchen and all the rooms, the two servants go away to their hut not far from the station.'

Basho, who had been awake in the middle of the night because of the stealthy sounds and movements, went and stood by Goldram. She pulled at his arm for him to bend and hear her whisper. 'Cousin Goldram, I was sleeping close to the trunk and I was awakened by the little creak the iron trunk made when it was shifted slightly. I was stunned by what I saw but I remained still in my bed. I clearly saw the form of a woman in a sari lifting the lid of the trunk and plunging her arm into it. Within a minute, she brought out her hand holding a flat box. She hid the box underneath her sari and tiptoed back into her room, there, behind that curtain. As she was crossing the passage where the night lamp burnt in its dim hazy light, I could make out that it was sister Gurbans who was easily moving about from one room to the other.'

Gurbans and her younger sister, with a few curious children—who too had risen by the noise and had stood in the doorway to watch the bizarre event—rushed into the room. Gurbans couldn't wait for Basho to end her ear-kissing tale to Goldram. Her guilty conscience, dark and heavy with all kinds of apprehensions, could no longer bear his ears being thoroughly poisoned against her. And for no apparent reason that Goldram could see, she pounced on the young Basho as she was trying to tell Goldram what she had witnessed last night.

'How dare you, you little devil! What cock and bull stories you are telling brother Goldram? I saw you pointing towards me. And Kaushalya, how can you believe the little scheming liar and start asking me questions? I'm already under the blight of a curse, and now you wildly start pointing fingers at me!' a guilty Gurbans blurted out.

'There's no need to shout and create any unnecessary fuss. You do go to the loo and wake up a few times at night. And befuddled in her deep sleep, Basho, a child after all, perhaps was left in confusion. Listening to her and asking a few questions would only clarify the situation,' Kaushalya steadily said.

Having observed the whole situation, Dayal Singh considered it proper to intervene. 'Gurbans, you better go back into your room and get busy. Get the breakfast ready. We are a family and we'll sort these things out. And please talk respectfully to your elders. Sister Kaushalya is like a mother to us all.' The angry note with which Dayal Singh ended his speech took the wind out of Gurbans's sails. Indeed, Dayal Singh had his own private reason for getting a bit vexed with Gurbans, and he alone knew of it.

One reason that all knew of was that even after about five

years of Gurbans and Dayal Singh's marriage, there had been no signs of her fecundity. After a thorough check-up at the hospital, the medical officer there had declared her completely infertile and incapable of bearing any children. Invasive surgical assistance was not yet available and test tube babies were a distant reality. The psychiatrist had told the family to be careful and deferential towards a growing streak of belligerence and spitefulness in Gurbans's temperament—her character as a whole. She may develop a streak of peevishness in her conduct. This was truly evident, even to her mother who was still alive at eighty-seven in northern Burma and had had eight children in all. Dayal Singh knew much more, above and beyond, these traits of Gurbans. Therefore, he knew he should privately deal with her quirky conduct. So he had sent her back to her room with a single rebuke and glare of his choleric eyes. On the side, he was also able to convey to Goldram, 'I'm sure you'd believe me when I say that I will settle the matter to the satisfaction of all without causing loss of face to anyone, except for a bitter pill the guilty must swallow.' Goldram always had faith in Dayal Singh's worldly wisdom and his ability as a hard taskmaster and shrewd arbiter. The day that had augured an unpleasant atmosphere found the clouds dissipating as soon they had formidably appeared.

The jewellery box was later located by Chhotey, the odd-job boy, before dusk. He found it beneath the haystack, where he had been putting fodder together for the buffalo. Dayal Singh was in the habit of having a buffalo or two wherever he was posted to have a ready supply of milk and butter. Apparently, Gurbans had told Chhotey to take the box to Kaushalya with a story to tell. All improvisation was the brain child of one who absolved the guilty in public eye. But the dark of the alleys grew thicker still, deep as they already were.

~

The evenings were livened up especially by Sammad Babu, who was full of jokes and told them with such élan. One that had made him the king of jokes went something like this: A naughty teenager rounded three goats from the meadow behind his house. He numbered the goats in dark red ink—1, 2 and 4—and let them go free into his school compound, asking the guard to be his accomplice. The droppings and the stench alerted the staff the next morning. After sniffing around, they knew it was goats. The frantic principal and the staff searched and located three goats with numbers 1, 2 and 4. Even after desperately searching the whole building for almost an hour, they could not find the goat they presumed was bearing the number 3. The totally harrowed principal had to suspend classes for the day and call for police help. 'Hurrah!' the students shouted and enjoyed a holiday. And 'Hurrah!' cried Sammad's audience in the dim light of the lantern in the corner of the room, already dark with its brown walls and yellow ochre roof.

The times and conditions were of apprehension and anxiety, especially the demon fear arising from the declared intentions of Japan after the daring dive bombing over the American fleet moored in Pearl Harbor. But together in each other's company and with free time on their hands, they agreed to while away their time between breakfast and lunch playing cards, of which two extra decks had been bought from Pyawbwe. Dayal Singh also bought a chessboard and set of chessmen. Another game that was an option to keep them engaged during rainy days was the ancient game of dice. Sometimes, when they were together, Goldram enjoyed playing with his brother, though he knew Dayal Singh excelled at it and would always beat him. So Goldram never played for stakes as he always lost at these gambling games. Yet, he did have fun playing and being a part of the jovial company.

The other families, together or in groups of twos and threes, began arriving at Dayal Singh's centre in Shanywa. Goldram had to be parted from his family for a while as there were more arrangements yet to be made. In Gyogon, he had left two cows with the mali. He could use them for milk for the family and could also sell them for extra earnings to spend on the maintenance of the family. He had left the mali with a room on the ground floor to be better placed as the guard and caretaker of the property. Always a positive thinker, Goldram did not intend to sell the house. He covered the furniture, and had all the wardrobes and sideboards covered, sewn up and locked properly. He gave special instructions for the sewing machine to be properly covered with a sheet and kept safe because he had noticed how Kaushalya had sorely loathed leaving her machine behind. He had packed the orderly file he'd maintained of the papers pertaining to the landed property and the precious sword with mother-of-pearls on the gilded hilt. The sword was sealed and locked in the drawer of the cabinet in their bedroom.

In the office in Rangoon, too, he had plenty unfinished work upon his huge desk. His personal attention was needed to wind up matters in his own punctilious manner before he could leave. At the sight of Goldram in the office fussing around his work table, Sir Rolland, who had just entered the room, said to him, 'Good morning, Goldram. Now, no member of staff is obliged to be present in the office. All official work has been suspended. Indeed, I don't see anyone else here on this floor; maybe there are a few on the lower floors, but I see you in full concentration fussing over a heap of files and papers on your table.'

'Oh, good morning, Sir! I'm sure you know that I had to decline the government's very gracious offer—which was surely by your recommendation—of the comfort of air flight to a safe distance from the advancing shadow of the Japanese war machine. But my mother didn't have the heart to leave my other siblings here exposed to danger and wouldn't take the easy way out. So you can understand that we were left with the only choice of trekking across the back-breaking terrain of the Arakan Yomas. I've sent my immediate family already to what you can call a base camp of the whole extended family who were spread out in different parts of Burma. My younger brother Dayal Singh, as you know, is the station master at Shanywa, where the rest of us shall come together before setting out for the "long march" home from the border town of Tamu. As for me, I'm here to wind up the matters myself and arrange things in order just in case conditions alter and I happen to return to the same seat.'

Sir Rolland said, 'God bless, Goldram. I'm certain that reinforced British troops will be back before long to retake the lost territory in the state. And come peace, things should be back to normal.' He added with a wry smile, 'Hopefully, I may return to my same chair. And to you, I'd say, you keep in readiness. You will get a call from me, and Godspeed indeed, for a promotion to becoming Associate Chief Engineer of the Toungoo district.'

Both of them guffawed in good cheer, yet a streak of dubious apprehension smeared it as the laughter trailed to silence.

18

1945–1951

Sir Rolland was true to his word. Goldram did get a letter from him, inviting him to take the position he had promised. That was soon after the curtain went down on the war at the onset of autumn in early September of 1945. By then, Goldram had—with his retirement benefits and ambitious plans—already launched a moulding and machine workshop in the industrial area of Badami Bagh in Lahore (now in Pakistan). Though in a couple of years he was uprooted from Lahore as 'refugees' and had to face a sea of vicissitudes with his wife, five children and his old mother of seventy, getting knocked about from Haridwar to Delhi, to finally settling down in the industrial town of Ludhiana in east Punjab.

Upon their arrival in Ludhiana, Goldram and his family found themselves amidst a tumultuous scene. The town was inundated with an influx of refugee families, all seeking shelter and stability after the partition. The streets echoed with cries of anguish as families mourned the loss of their homes, belongings and cherished memories left behind in Lahore.

In the midst of this chaos, the refugees struggled to rebuild their lives from scratch. Goldram faced the heartbreaking reality of losing his ancestral inheritance and the flourishing business he had established in Lahore. The once-thriving machine workshop in Badami Bagh now existed only in the fragments of his memories. The burden of responsibility weighed heavily on his shoulders as he navigated the maze of challenges that came with starting anew. Despite the hardships, a sense of resilience permeated the air as the refugees banded together, supporting one another in their shared journey towards recovery. Ludhiana became a melting pot of diverse cultures, languages and traditions as families from different parts of India found solace in their collective struggle.

Slowly but surely, Ludhiana transformed into a beacon of hope, with makeshift settlements turning into bustling neighbourhoods and small businesses sprouting up to provide essential goods and services. Goldram, fuelled by determination and an indomitable spirit, tapped into his entrepreneurial skills once again, starting a modest venture that would slowly help him rebuild his life and provide for his family. As the years passed, Ludhiana became a testament to the resilience and strength of the human spirit in the face of adversity. While the scars of partition remained, etched deeply into the hearts of the refugees, they also carried with them a renewed sense of hope, unity and a shared determination to rebuild their lives in this new land they now called home.

Gurdial Singh, a friend from Gyogon in Burma whom Goldram had happened to run into in Ludhiana, suggested that he settle down in Ludhiana and offered a room in his house as makeshift homestead. But not very long afterwards, he began to show signs of impatience at the presence of Goldram's family; probably behind the curtain were the instigations of his termagant wife. She didn't know that Gurdial used to be a frequent—though uninvited—informal guest at Goldram's table in Gyogon.

Sir Rolland's offer letter reached two years late to Goldram. He couldn't even reconsider, and had to decline the offer Sir Rolland had made. There was no scope to get in touch with him. Sir Rolland had since retired and gone back to settle down permanently in Perth, Australia, his home town.

~

Goldram then found himself in the middle of a deep mire in a new and strange scenario, especially because of the manner in which work in local offices was done. With hordes that were still arriving from across Wagah, the Pakistan border, the foyers of every office of the rehabilitation ministry were crammed with twisted long queues, and the hot and humid waiting halls were filled with the miasma of human body odour and bad breath. Besides, the whole work culture displayed no evidence of self or mandatory imposed discipline, and that made Goldram feel as if he were in a different country. Yet, he was back in India, in Punjab, a place where he had belonged and loved. After each gruelling day, he was fighting hard to find his footing in this baffling new environment. It seemed to him that everyone's prime concern was their own personal interest and not the destitute refugees who, bereft of their homes and chattel in this almost hostile environment, were putting together the necessary items to create a semblance of homes to nestle into.

Since Goldram was handling so many different aspects of the work single-handedly, setting up a new factory day after day proved to be extra strenuous, especially where temperatures ranged between 45°C in the summer and plummeted down to 4°C in the winters. He had to travel the distance between the other government offices, walking from his rented apartment, or at best, hiring an affordable cycle rickshaw manned by a fellow whom he pitied. Added to other difficulties was his primary concern of providing for the expenditure of the family. All his savings and the last collections for the supplies made in the name of his allied factories were touching the bottom. The ball was just getting ready to roll on the latest venture of his that he had launched on similar lines to the one in Lahore.

It was during this period of utter straits for Goldram's family when Goldram came to know of Kartarlal's location from another common acquaintance from Gyogon. He dashed off a postcard to Kartarlal, who in the corps of engineers of the Indian Army, had been posted in the Roorkee Cantonment in the United Provinces. He hadn't seen his brother, who was more like a son to him, for a long time. For it was early during the family's sojourn at Gujranwala in the heart of Punjab that Kartarlal had applied and gotten selected in the service of the armed forces. Since he was a qualified engineer, he was assigned to the corps of engineers at Roorkee.

Kartarlal didn't take long to respond. After two days, he was at Gurdial's address. It was indeed like Bharat having come to meet Ram during his period of exile. Their embrace overwhelmed them both; Kaushalya, too, wiped her eyes and began to get Kartarlal's favourite dishes ready. The children were happy to see their dear uncle there with them, especially Nikko, whose iconic hero Kartarlal always had been.

The brothers then walked up the corner of the lane where a branch of the Central Bank of India was located. Kartarlal withdrew three thousand rupees from his account and handed the money to his fatherly figure, his elder brother. Goldram's throat was choked with a mix of emotions. He wished that he had more savings so that he could immediately shift the family to a place independent of any obligations.

This was the only part of the family that Kartarlal could identify with since he had left Daska. Their mother, since the passing away of her husband, had shifted from Maymyo to live with Goldram's family. The emotion they shared was mutual and could not be put into words, nor could it be understood by any outsider, not even by his wife, Biro, who had spent her growing years with the family. Secretly, perhaps, she knew that all siblings stayed at Goldram's because it was merely a matter of convenience. Her own conclusion from her probing with her naughty but sharp mind was that some members had been exploiting Goldram's generosity. Goldram's magnanimous gesture was beyond the reach of her experience or understanding to take in back then.

But now, with such a gesture from Kartarlal, Goldram's eyes too had moistened.

~

After a long wait in the queue when it was Goldram' turn to face the magistrate—the custodian of the evacuee property for the district of Ludhiana—Goldram thought he saw a somewhat familiar face. As he presented his official application for the allotment of land for his prospective workshop and a place of residence, he moved a step forward and had to crane his neck to address the gentleman in the chair of authority, and rather hesitatingly asked, 'Am I addressing Mr Lallchand from Daska, Sialkot?' The magistrate looked up, startled, and within a split moment, he stood up. 'Oh, for God's sake, Goldram! My dear friend! Come around into the enclosure.'

So Goldram did. He went round through a passage into the enclosure of the barred balustrade. The people waiting in the queue watched in wide-eyed wonder as the two friends embraced with dewy eyes. Lallchand offered his friend a chair by his side and sent his peon to fetch water for Goldram to drink, along with a glass of Goldram's favourite shikanjvi.

'Just relax and feel at home. Lunch break is in about fifteen minutes; then we'll talk.' He gave a quick surreptitious look at his wristwatch and turned around to deal with the next person in the line. Looking at the queue, he took a deep breath and knew that in spite of all his efficient dealing with the ongoing paperwork of the applications, it was going to be a long and arduous day as usual.

He spent just about half an hour with his old classmate. It was enough to get mutually updated. Quickly they trotted through happy memory lanes and the rest was left to be picked up on a later day. Goldram—when his meeting with Lallchand ended and reached home to his family—discovered that his friend had allotted him the choicest piece of land for his factory on Grand Trunk Road, and also a lovely two-storey house in a Christian neighbourhood close to the Sacred Heart Church on Ms Brown Hospital Road. All this was in lieu of the claim he had put in with the rehabilitation department of the ministry for the property he had left behind in Pakistan. Goldram, like others in the queue, had come to put in his application for such allotment being made against the approved and registered claims cleared by the rehabilitation office in Ludhiana.

If there were any hopes and dreams of returning to the paradise in Gyogon, Goldram abandoned them and replaced them with his desire to some day go and find out details about his property there. At the time of his evacuation from Burma and after crossing the border at Tamu, the Government of Burma had issued him and his family a folder, somewhat like a passport. It contained all the relevant particulars regarding their Burmese connection and their Gyogon postal address. But the struggle against the almost insurmountable vicissitudes of getting settled in life again after Lahore seemed to have drained him of the last ounces of energy. All things Burmese were relegated to the farthest corner of his mind. He hardly ever thought of it; and if at all he did, it was only in his dreams or during the rare commodity of leisure when he would recall memories of Gyogon with Kaushalya.

All this was not very long after he had crossed the peak of

fifty. Lately, at the end of his strenuous day of knocking about from one government office to another, he included in this schedule a few hours to go to the neighbouring city of Jullundur. When he got back home, he felt exhausted and depleted from the physical stress and anxieties of every possible kind that came crowding when he was by himself. Kaushalya sometimes found him fast asleep and snoring softly before she had even been able to lay his table. She loathed shaking him by the shoulder to wake him for his wash and dinner. Always a great sharer of the day's happenings with his wife, those days there was something he carried in his heart as a secret and didn't feel so good about it. Once or twice, he had felt as though his heart had tremulously missed a beat now and again for about fifteen minutes. He didn't want to alarm Kaushalya, but he was just giving the symptom a little time to become clear before talking about it and going to a doctor. Nonetheless, he began to take precautions then and there and ate a frugal dinner instead of his usual bellyful (for he always tended to eat a little more than his appetite allowed because the taste of Kaushalya's cooking went down his gullet like butter).

~

His children were growing. Nikko was now going to college, the twins would be finishing school in a couple of years, and the spoilt youngest boy had drifted into the debasing influence of loutish street boys. He had recently been caught smoking and was spanked for it. Goldram was informed that the little chap had been initiated into having a drag on the fumes of brown sugar. Without the benign and sturdy support of the quietly moving Kaushalya in a transformed ambience, Goldram thought that he would've been totally lost at sea. His heart ached to see Kaushalya growing grey, and over the years, she grew imperceptibly but surely emaciated as she went about managing the house without much domestic help. Yet, she always came up with monetary assistance to Goldram with what she sagely put aside from her kitchen budget for what they call a rainy day.

Goldram found himself sadly presaged with various conditions, when suddenly good news poured in godsend. During his last outing away from home to Patiala, Goldram had run into a member of the royal family of the Patiala state. After meeting his customers, he entered the Ritz for lunch—a good and tried restaurant—and before he knew it, found himself sharing the table with a plump Sikh gentleman. A little later, as he got into casual conversation with the man opposite him, they grew familiar with each other's credentials. The man turned out to be Raghavendra Singh, a brother-in-law of the present ruler, Yadavendra Singh of the Patiala state, after whom the sports stadium was named—Yadavendra Stadium—the best stadium in the whole province of Punjab.

Goldram was amazed by the unexpected changes life brought in its perpetual flux. There was a time in Gyogon when he used to have long spells of leisure; he had time to take the family out for picnics and he never missed his Sunday morning long walks which ended with a swim in the small waterbody ensconced in the midst of the orchard of rubber trees, a part of the stretching wooded area on the western side of Rangoon-Insein Road. Sometimes, if he so desired, he would play a card game with some of his neighbours. Now, from the moment he went out with his almost weather-beaten briefcase till he returned dog-tired and hit the bed, the ceaseless activity—like a Persian well with its tinkling lever and creaking bar—engrossed him so completely that he didn't realize he had lived through only ten hours of the day. Time seemed to have been squeezed into one quick moment and it vanished in the blink of an eye, leaving behind a tired and depleted Goldram.

The sad part of it all was that little work was done by the

end of the day. The shine from his shoes was gone, his Madras cotton suits had wilted into khadi shirts with hardly straightened collars and the khaki trousers were bulging at the knees with no signs of an ironed crease. He walked the dusty potholed roads—with its post-rain slush pervaded with horse and cow dung stench—of Ludhiana with unyielding courage. The smoke from a thousand braziers that lit the homes and the streets filled the dusky evenings. He was welcomed with the screams and shouts of children playing or flying kites as he entered Kucha Harnam Das, the lane in which he and his family lived. They knew that Mr Goldram, as usual, had his pockets full of toffees to be given away to the eager expectant little ones, children of Goldram's neighbours, and they let off shouts of joy.

Goldram saw glimpses of a silver lining in the clouds when, one morning, Raghavendra Singh unexpectedly made an appearance. It turned out that he had come to propose a partnership deal in Goldram's 'The East Punjab Agricultural Engineering Works', with fifty thousand rupees as a direct investment. From his first meeting with Goldram in Patiala, Raghavendra had gathered enough information about the concern and had pondered long enough to join hands with Goldram in his venture. He had learnt that Goldram was financially in a hand-to-mouth condition at present, but due to his engineering qualifications, he secured the much sought-after monthly quota of three-ton pig iron and three carriages of hard coke supplied by Tata Steel Company from the office of the agriculture engineer in Punjab. The material was meant for the manufacturing of agricultural implements like chaff cutters and cane crushers along with small items like picks, axes, shovels and rakes for farmers' use. The royal was also impressed by the fact that Goldram was the elected president of the Quota Holders Association, Ludhiana.

The procedure for finalizing the terms and conditions of the partnership was completed at the local district courts. The timely influx of money eased the situation and the works were soon underway in earnest. Raghavendra, too, was happy with the deal as the proceeds were good. It allowed him more leisure and more luxury, and he spent most of the time in his erstwhile Patiala haunts. All this left Goldram a bit cheated, for he alone had to manage things in the market and deal with the correspondence too. Soon he hired a clerk to do the office job of bookkeeping and correspondence and work next to the peon, who was the all-round odd-job man.

~

The smoothly rolling diurnal cycle didn't last very long. The disruption was caused due to a natural configuration. It was 1951, midsummer, when the monsoons brought good news for the farmers and peasants; the weatherman forecasted a good and normal rainfall. But as the ill-fated Ludhiana district had it, there was more than ten days of incessant thunder and showers. Days and nights seemed to merge into each other in the prolonged semi-darkness. Muddied water inundated the roads and railroads, turning them into swirling streams and rivulets—all that, of course, was the concern of the local municipal corporation office. About half of the area in which Goldram's factory was laid out was covered with loads of hard coke, the weight of which seemed to have made even the surrounding area into a veritable broad crater. Consistent rain over the last ten days had filled it with water that rose to almost half the height of the stack. The moulding shop lay in sandy carbon ruins, and no work could be done for months, thought Goldram, terribly downcast. The machine shop was not affected much, although the roof had sprung some big leaks. The support of stilts and legs on which the roof rested over the lathes and other presses were sturdy enough to withstand the inclement conditions.

Gradually, most of the staff and workers had to be dispensed with. With work almost stopped and income from the workshop coming to a standstill, it was difficult to maintain the staff. Except for the expert head-mechanic, most of the others had to be laid off. Even if the rain stopped, it would take a long while for the work in the foundry and workshop to begin and get back on track again.

Even as a man with grit and positive outlook, Goldram was shaken for some time. His anxiety was augmented by the letter he got from Raghavendra stating that he would like to come and have a talk with him. His premonitions came true—the royalty of Patiala revealed his true colours. His pocket money, for which Goldram had sweated, was now just a trickle, not enough to pay for his indulgences. He resorted to what minds like his could think of as the ultimate answer. Yet, putting on a smiling and affable front, Goldram did not feel any discomfiture in broaching his design.

Raghavendra Singh said, 'I can understand that you have been hit by a natural disaster worse than any. This water I see has half submerged the whole of our reserve fuel for the smelting cupola. My problems are different. I need ready money. The stipend from the royal treasury does not suffice to meet all my expenses. So under the circumstances, the proceeds from my investment—you so generously shared—have been put in abeyance; for how long it is anybody's guess. Under this painful pressure, I'd prefer to have our partnership revoked. I am prepared to go through the paperwork at the courts at any time you suggest. But my only request is that you try and understand my predicament and within two or three months' time make it convenient to return my investment amount.'

Goldram replied, 'Well, Raghavendra Singh, whatever may be the obligations that are confronting you, your very politely stated request has pushed me into a corner. I'm already facing tight pecuniary difficulties due to what you rightly stated was a natural disaster. Major work has come to a standstill. We are in the market because we still rake in pennies from accessories and repairs for our subsistence. You are asking for a huge chunk. Well, I have greater liabilities than you can imagine; give me time, more than what you mentioned. Let the limit be six months, and if god be willing, I should be able to send you back not disappointed when you call next time. Now, before you're back on the road to Patiala in your Chevy, I invite you to your favourite Ritz in Chaura Bazaar to sit at your preferred table and eat lunch with me. The blight of calamitous circumstances has struck and annulled our business cooperation, but let it not mar our amiable relationship.' Such was Goldram's geniality that it neutralized the bitter and hard feelings of the wayward prince, though he had come to have it out with Goldram.

'Oh sure, come, let's go get some beer and be in good cheer,' he said. With good humour returning and with no hard feelings, they rode the Chevy on the road to the clock tower, turned right into Chaura Bazaar and stopped in front of the Ritz. Raghavendra handed over the car keys to the valet and climbed the few steps into the cosy air-conditioned restaurant along with Goldram, smiling a bit quizzically.

~

It came as quite a surprise when Kartarlal visited Goldram in Ludhiana. As he faced his elder brother, Kartarlal—who had gone straight to Goldram's office from the railway station—was in a confused state of helplessness and anxiety. He wore the blanched look of a first-time tight-rope walker. His face was dark and drawn with simmering tensions. Biro's parents had prolonged their stay with him as their son in Jhansi had sent them packing to Biro's (apparently because good bread was not available there, and because it's so damn expensive, he'd said). Sheila's machinations, germinating from her idle dark mind, found it convenient to reach out to her daughter, Biro. In spite of the latest experience with Raghavendra Singh, Goldram met his brother as genially as ever. After pleasantries and welfare enquiries, Goldram said, 'I hope all is well, Kartarlal. You'd said in your last letter that you would be soon leaving for NEFA under some border roads project. Instead, you are here.'

Kartarlal's discomfiture broke his heart before he could blurt out, 'Brother Dayal Singh after his retirement and with his paltry pension has to be sent monetary help every month. I've been doing the best I can for the sake of the family but now I find myself in a tight spot too. Maybe against the small amount I was able to offer you before, please lend me some money. I'm stuck badly!' He had shot off—his mouth groggy with indoctrination—all before he thought he'd falter. Kartarlal could kick himself in chagrin for having mentioned the last bit. He couldn't regret it enough and knew not how he would atone for the bleeding affront he had caused his dear and beloved brother. And in the ensuing stunned silence, Kartarlal sat there in front of the fatherly figure of his brother, his head bowed and eyes focused on his shoes.

'Go home and rest. Don't be morose. I'll see what we can do about the matter,' Goldram said. Goldram had been able to sense the pecking of a hen, perhaps more than one hen, and patted his brother's shoulder. They both stood up. Kartarlal bowed and touched his elder brother's feet. He said, 'I shall not be able to go home and nor will it be possible for me to stay the night over. I have to be ready for my departure to the border duty tomorrow. What time will the next train to Delhi be?'

There were tears in Kartalal's eyes. He very much wanted to take Kaushalya's blessings as she had given him a mother's love during his student years in Gyogon. He also wanted to hug the children, who were grown up now, but he hadn't seen them for quite a while. Goldram sent his odd-job man to the neighbouring Mohan Restaurant—whose quality Goldram patronized—to fetch some snacks, a repast of stuffed parathas and lassi, because he knew there would be time enough for Kartarlal to eat something to last him the five-hour journey by train, for which there was still an hour and half to go. Again and again, Kartarlal's eyes rose and rested on his brother's face, now sadly weathered, creased, tanned and rugged.

Kartarlal's heart was heavy with emotion, but he couldn't say everything he had come to say. It was only after Kartarlal had washed, eaten and wiped his pink and full lips with fancy tissues did he speak. Goldram waited, the innocent childhood image of Kartarlal coming back to his mind, and then he emerged from his office with his arm round Kartarlal's shoulder. He felt the soft tremor of his body from a smothered sob. They stood on the kerb of the Grand Trunk Road until a manually-pedalled rickshaw came along and was hailed to stop. Kartarlal stepped up to the high seat of the rickshaw while Goldram waved him to be careful and give his love to his children. Later, he mentioned the brief stopover and their meeting to Kaushalya, but he did not as yet share the details of the matter concerning which Kartarlal had come.

Early next morning, Goldram woke up and sat at his work table by five and with a clear head—no anger or bitterness tarnishing his mind—wrote out a brief letter and a long bill of his expenditures, amounting to around thirty thousand rupees. These were the expenses he had borne since he had fetched Kartarlal from Daska and provided for him until Kartarlal had drawn his first salary in the job Goldram had gotten for him. He mailed the missive for Kartarlal's benefit, especially for the hangers-on in his family. With this, in small print at the bottom, he wrote, 'Make sure your respected mother-in-law goes over it. Clear the payment of the accompanying bill before I can reciprocate.'

He sent the letter by registered post to be sure and carefully preserved the acknowledgement slip. As he knew and expected, Goldram never again heard Kartarlal mentioning the money which he had been given to understand by the doctrinaire that Goldram had generously doled out in the time of need. In his heart of hearts though, Goldram never thought of it more than giving a hand to the fallen to rise.

19

Despite facing difficulties while building his life in Gyogon, there was hardly any moment where Goldram had felt financially depleted. But now in Punjab, Raghavendra Singh's demand for revoking the partnership and the thought of Kartarlal trapped in a state of anxiety and distress plagued Goldram's mind incessantly.

However, the harsh reality was that Goldram's resources were limited and sending some money to Kartarlal would have made his situation even worse. The mounting debts, particularly the one he owed to Raghavendra Singh, became an increasingly pressing concern. Goldram had always thought that he would be returning to Gyogon someday and that is why he had not sold his property there. But in order to untangle himself from the present financial burden, Goldram had to make a tough decision: selling his beloved home in Gyogon.

Giving up on his dream to return to Burma was excruciating. It meant that he would be not just selling his home but losing the Burmese part of himself that he had worked so hard upon. Severing ties with the community he had been a part of was impossible to imagine for him, but he had no choice.

With a heavy heart, Goldram set a plan in motion to settle his debts and manage his expenses. Uncertainty of the future was a constant companion, but the unwavering resolve to straighten his life provided the necessary strength to let go.

1942–1945

After Goldram felt that he had gotten over the last stitch on the sheets that covered the furniture, bundles of the bedding and curtains and had safely put away the kitchenware, he was ready to join the family that was gradually getting together at Dayal Singh's centre at Shanywa. It was the first week of February 1942. Goldram left Gyogon with a heavy heart, seen off only by Dashrath who went to the railway station with his good master with whom, over the years, he had developed great love and had shown unimpeachable loyalty. He went up to Rangoon with him. Across the over-bridge, they walked to the platform where the train that Goldram had to take for Thazi and on to Pyawbwe junction was ready. Dasharath carried the few pieces of luggage that Goldram had packed for himself to see him through up to Shanywa.

The mali's eyes were wet with tears of separation as he bent down to touch Goldram's feet, but Goldram held him in his arms and gave him a consoling pat on his back. He felt the mali's body shaking with the spasm of a suppressed sob and they bid each other farewell. Dasharath then rode back on a local to Gyogon with a heavy heart. Panditji and Dal Bahadur, too, in time, left for their native homes with cherished memories wrapped in sadness. They had become a major part of the Gyogon household and were now going away, not knowing if they would ever see each other again.

~

Goldram was happy to be back among the family. But the vague uncertainty of a long odyssey from Moreh across Tamu's border inside Burma, up to Imphal deep in Manipur in India, filled even his brave heart with apprehensions. He was fully aware of the situation from which, he knew, there was no easy way out. The Japanese had jumped into the world war in full awareness of what they were fighting against. And since the Japanese attacks on Burma were going to continue relentlessly until they were in full control of the state, the attempt and effort of those affected to get to the safety of their native land had to be tenaciously undertaken and followed. Though how long the peace and safety there would last was anybody's guess.

Finally, the entire family was now gathered in Shanywa. They understood the cause of getting together and also knew that as soon as Goldram arrived, the days of treating their stay at Dayal Singh's as a protracted holiday were about to end. They were soon going to be on their way into unknown regions, through the mountain ranges of the Arakan. The adults, including some women, too, began to have meetings until late into the night to discuss and decide upon the route best suited to them. The route taken had to cause the least trouble to the children and ladies of the rather unwieldy family of forty people—mostly consisting of three to twelve-year-old children.

The routes, considering distances from Shanywa onwards up to Kale, along the banks of the Chindwin River, were chiefly decided by Dayal Singh and Goldram with a great deal of input from Sammad Babu who was more familiar with northern Burma. Sammad Babu had sent the details of the family travelling together up to Kalewa Railway Station in advance. He gave instructions to some he knew could facilitate their stay and their passage at station restaurants all through the rail journey. Kalewa was a small town in the northern region of Burma. But even here, Sammad Babu's influence was telling.

All this brought a wry smile to Goldram's face as he went around the table every time they sat down to eat. He moved from table to table to see if there was a burp, the indicator of gratification for the young and the old, as they gobbled down their morsels. It also amused him to notice that the crockery in the remote and not-very-neat surroundings too bore the trademark of the best caterer in contemporary Burma—a man who dominated the rail or restaurant cars and restaurants at the important stations or junctions—M/s G.F. Kellner Caterers. But what took the cake was a counterfeit appearance—something that Goldram, with the keen observation of an engineer's eye, saw through at once. The crest on the plates and bowls were mere prints, and even the prints were poor and shoddy that gave away the fakery because of the amateurish print in place of the embossments of the original. Yet it seemed like the owners of these restaurants smugly basked in making the impression of being part of the first-rate elite catering organization.

Goldram enjoyed the few moments of amusement in solitude. Only later, when he had some moments to spare with Dayal Singh, did he ask his brother if he had noticed the Kellner's crest on the plates in the restaurant of Kalewa Railway Station. He hadn't. Then Goldram went ahead and told him about it and expressed his wonder, 'How do the business people, plying their crooked trade away from alert and equipped police of big cities, get away with counterfeiting and then gloat upon their success!' He laughed a little and said, 'For them, the smugness of a poker face is part of their shrewdness; having befooled the customer, patrons and innocent people is akin to a great triumph.'

Goldram could share these jokes with Dayal Singh because, in addition to the material reality of the content, their responses were made about the subtleties at the core of the matter. They commented upon the condition of life, and were spontaneously in unison and could turn the hilarity of the laughter to one of a bonding timbre. Gurmukh, having stayed the longest in Daska and having hobnobbed with the commonalty while he minded the brokerage in the grain market, had never cared to look beyond his matriculation. He was a willing dropout, disdained disciplined education and had no sophistication of attitude whatsoever. Kartarlal, on the other hand, was young enough to be a son to them, and he didn't dare intrude.

~

Sundar Dev, a military hospital veteran who had served across Burma, was also part of the travelling party. Recognizing the need for an emergency first aid kit, he meticulously prepared a compact yet comprehensive solution. The kit resembled a mini hospital enclosed within a sturdy German silver box. Painted on the lid was a white circle with a deep red cross, accompanied by the words 'First Aid'. Within the kit, Sundar Dev had thoughtfully organized various essentials—medicines, bandages, gauzes, volatiles and smelling salts—ready for any emergency situation. The supply included an ample quantity of aspirin and quinine tablets, as well as anti-allergic medications to address vomiting and severe diarrhoea caused by waterborne diseases like cholera.

The news from the border and across was alarming. The sickness had acquired the proportions of an epidemic and seemed to have been rampant in the camps around Manipur River and terminated in not a few deaths. The numbers that succumbed to the disease could only be imagined from the dead bodies abandoned, without much ceremony or care, on the wayside or being carried or dragged and left in the bushes around the path. The infection might have extended even deep into Indian Territory. The cavalcade of evacuees in hundreds of thousands was almost unending, and the remaining camps were crawling and cramped, like ant hills wrapped in the stench of human faeces. In fact, this miasmic admixture, along with the general odour of the green leafage and forest undergrowth, created a peculiar otherworldly subterranean aura to breathe in or choke. These little bits of news that travelled back and forth from the terminus Tamu to Mandalay gave Goldram enough ideas to share when he sat down with Dayal Singh to chalk out a rough estimate of sorts for the stuff they would require during their arduous long trek.

~

In their purview, the greatest difficulty for them to confront would be the paucity of available means of transport beyond Kalewa. While there was a train connection up to Kalewa, not all trains leaving from Thazi to Shwebo made a stop at Shanywa. Only the slower local trains, meant for all and sundry—'bazaar trains' as these were popularly known—with only inter-class and third-class compartments, stopped there. But the advantage to the family was that both Goldram and Dayal Singh were railway employees of worthy rank, especially with Goldram's connections over the length and breadth of Burma and Dayal Singh's public relations from central to northern Burma. They would be able to get a whole carriage booked for the family of an important railway employee and the whole journey of around three hundred and eighty kilometres up to Kalewa would be nothing but a comfortable ride.

Since they would be in the train overnight, they would all have enough room for every one to lie down and sleep through the night. But the children had their own secret plans to keep them busy in what was of interest to them—quizzes and puzzles, rhymes and songs in the game antakshari. They even devised a game of hide-and-seek and found a good place to hide behind the bulk of their father, their mother or their aunt. Crouching under the seats, too, was a fine ploy, but they emerged from under it with smudges on their clothing and black patches on their faces. Of course, they were spanked for naughty ventures such as locking themselves in the toilets.

And indeed, once on their way to Kalewa, this prank landed them into deep trouble with Kaushalya's younger sister, who was compelled to resort to some drastic measures. In a game of cops and robbers, Nikko and Neshki hid in the toilet and Nikko, being the elder of the two, took the initiative to lock the door. In the excitement and noise of the seekers outside, they were quiet and did not let anyone know where they were. But after a while, when the knocking on the toilet doors began again and grew louder, the two of them decided to let the others know of their hiding place They didn't seem to have a clue about how they could open the door. In the great hullabaloo, they got confused and had forgotten where the small key lever was. Totally frustrated by their frantic search, they felt completely helpless. They stood in front of the door bamboozled, yelling their heads off calling for their mother. 'Oh the door is not opening, Mummy! Oh, Mummy!' Their cries mingled with their sobs, and they went on going over and over their call, more plaintly. Guddi, Kaushalya's sister, came close to the toilet door and shouted out the instructions to get the door open. She tried to explain to the children the location of the key lever and how to turn it clockwise to release the lock. But possessed by their panic, they got more confused and ignored her and their crying grew louder and turned into screams.

After about fifteen minutes of screaming, the train came to a brief halt at a small wayside station. Guddi rushed out of the train onto the platform, climbed the stepping board along the carriage, and confounded by the emergency and aware of the brevity of the stoppage, she didn't even think of a stone and banged hard with her fist a couple times on to the ground glass window pane of the toilet from the outside. After looking at her familiar face through the opening, the children stopped yelling. With great patience, she peeped into the toilet and told them what to do and made them open the door. Guddi returned and found her hand badly injured, slashed by the broken glass of the pane.

Guddi's hand bled profusely and left her sari with spreading stains. But Nikko and Neshki joined everyone in laughter with their tear-stained faces—somewhat bashful though at their own folly. Kaushalya gave Guddi a big hug. Goldram informed the guard of the train of the broken glass pane and it was immediately replaced. Yet, the exigency of the stop got it fifteen minutes late in leaving the station, which, of course, came to an advantage to the vendors on the platform who were moving along the delayed train. Their calls became louder with added cheer. Last minute calls from the passengers out the windows were frantic with demands of what they required until the husky shriek of a whistle was let off by the engine and the train began moving forward.

As the days grew longer and the shadows shorter, February approached its end. The entire family, gathering from near and far, gradually arrived to form a cohesive travel group. The increased numbers provided mutual mental support and strength to one another. Among the adults present were Kartarlal and Prakash, adding to the family's security during the upcoming journey across rivers and mountains, and ultimately across the Indo-Burma border.

After the heavy monsoons, which lasted from May to October, the foothills of the Arakan mountain range, halfway between Pyawbwe and Kalewa onwards, were thickly forested. The verdant foliage and the wild grass underneath the trees now showed signs of mellowing browns and reds. The sight through the train windows was alive with breathtaking glimpses of stray deer, bucks and monkeys. It was the chaste beauty of nature in its very virgin form, untrodden by human presence. Added to this sight was what human hands had created: at a distance of five or six kilometres from this area was the Sagaing Bridge in its sublime glory. The whole area through which the train was now running was called the Sagaing district. The train would pass over the bridge in about five hours and would resonate with the chug-chug sounds with black smoke spouting from the top chimney of the engine and the carriages across it. But the children screamed as they looked down into the gorge between the two peaks across which the bridge had been built. The awe sent cold shivers down their spines as the train went over it—it made for a hair-raising experience.

Shanywa to Kalewa by train was an overnight journey of almost eleven hours, which as mentioned, was a long holiday and picnic for the children. As the train moved forward, the ever-changing scenery outside the windows showed a spectacular sight. The Sagaing district presented a lush and green landscape, adorned with rice fields and occasional mango trees. Interestingly, Burma boasts nearly five times the number of mango varieties compared to its neighbouring country, India.

Along the way, there were stretches of fertile land, patiently waiting to be cultivated. Some appeared bare, while others featured slopes and depressions that resembled expansive ponds filled with rainwater. These watery surfaces reflected the vibrant hues of the surrounding vegetation and the shifting shapes of passing clouds in the sky.

This picturesque backdrop served as a source of joy for the children onboard. As the journey continued, the miles rolled by, leaving the children behind in silence, gazing at the receding landscape through the swiftly spinning wheels, heading towards Kalewa. At the brief stops at small stations, they began shouting for all kinds of vendors—clay toys or colourful sweets made from sugar and desiccated coconut—going up and down on the station platform. It seemed that the independently-reserved carriage had infused a sense of bravado among them. The naughty pranks were but a part of their enjoyment and there was a spirit of general good cheer in their company.

~

The family had to be separated into two different compartments, one hitched behind the other. Gurbans was happy that she was not cooped in the same carriage with Kaushalya. The matter related to Kaushalya's jewellery box had been amicably resolved in which Dayal Singh had played the role of the chief arbiter as he knew Gurbans better than anyone and she had not dared to contradict whatever her husband had asked her to do. And since then, though Kaushalya had never again referred to the subject, Gurbans always had her head bowed and her eyes down in her presence.

Dr Dev and his family were in the same compartment with Dayal Singh's family. Chetsingh's family hit it off well with Kaushalya's part of the family. In fact, Kaushalya's temperament was such that every member of the whole clan got along with her very well. They all had had some time or occasion to enjoy the warmth of her benevolent hospitality in Gyogon. During almost all the stops of the train, short or long, there were regular goings and comings into her compartment. Even here she shared with one and all whatever goodies (like chocolate éclairs, cashews, pistachios and some homemade sweets) she had stashed away for her children. Gurbans's two younger sisters were as welcome as any body else.

~

The true Sagaing topography was on full display—rocky mountains, around which ran many a twisting mule tracks and mountainsides with thickly forested teak, their roots sometimes streaking down the sheer rock side. Darkness fell upon the tracks fast, and adolescents like Kartarlal, Prakash, Sukhdev and Prakash's younger brother Baldev Raj Gulati opted to make a foursome and play cards. Naturally—in Kaushalya's compartment—the children were wrapped in their sheets or blankets and were soon asleep in any convenient spot they found. The night brought heavy rain. A few smaller stations, like Ye U and further north Kaduma, passed by while most of the family was asleep. Some were momentarily aroused by the tea and coffee vendors' calls—loud as ever in the middle of the night—even though the duration of the stop was short there. By the time they reached Thickegyn, the first glow of light of the breaking dawn peeked above the eastern horizon.

Shwebo was the last stop before Kalewa and everyone had their last meal of the day there. All kinds of fare and dishes were available at the station's restaurant. The vendors with their hand-driven carts brought some spicy fish snacks or khowsue, the commonly loved snack of noodles and pork swirling in chilly soup. Goldram's family went in for the traditional fare: rice, dal or lentil soup, spinach cooked with potatoes and some curd. But Goldram made it a point to go round all the tables and both the compartments to make sure everyone had their choice eats to their fill. Of course, later on at smaller stations, boiled eggs and tea or coffee were always available on the platform's counters, but that did not make for a bellyful dinner for the Indian palate.

Cramped in one of the small upper berths, with a sheet to cover him and his turban bundled under his head for a pillow, Goldram woke up at the break of dawn. All his life he'd been an early riser; the habit had formed since school days. He was also aware that in a couple of hours, when their train would roll into Kalewa, he would have to hurry up to the Maung Shwe Transporters and Carriers to see to the arrangement of a convenient small semi-covered truck with two bench-like seats running along the side walls with empty space in the middle for baggage. He would have to find a poor ramshackle imitation of what the army goes roughly by term 'three tonner'. According to his estimate, the family would need two such trucks.

~

It was a bright sunny morning when they reached their terminus, Kalewa. Instructed by Goldram, the young men (Prakash and company) took the family into the railway waiting rooms that were equipped with washroom facilities, while the coolies brought their baggage in wheelbarrows or manually carried it on their backs and heads. After the use of the facility, some of the family members went straight to the railway restaurant while others ordered for their breakfast to be served in the waiting room. Goldram—perhaps the only one with a cheery smile—went around, dropping hints to eat well as availability of good food would be uncertain thereafter. He knew that traditional street food, or even what is provided by the wayside eateries such as rice and fish in watery curry with a few leaves of spinach or khowsue may not suit every palate, especially not Punjabi tastebuds conditioned by dal, roti, fresh vegetables cooked in ghee or mustard oil and curd, plain or spiced.

20

Nikko felt he still had some energy left after all the travelling and was eager to take some time off to walk down the bright, sunlit platform with his uncle Kartarlal and take a distant look at the town of Kalewa. He then persuaded Kartarlal to swerve towards a lane leading into the town just for a look around. It was a bright sunny day, sometime between half past ten and eleven in the morning. Nikko had gone through his breakfast in a hurry, his mind keen on visiting the market of the small town of Kalewa. Kartarlal was so attached to his young nephew that he took him out willingly and they walked through the broad market street lined with shops selling bright colourful stuff to attract one and all, like balloons and stuffed toys in gaudy clothes. There were bolts of silk cloth both for men and women, along with Shan bags, typical of Burmese people, cane baskets, chairs, stools and broad-brimmed headgear for rain and sun on display. There were colourfully painted dolls made from wood and bamboo dressed in folk dresses of dancers and cute actresses in a Pwe scenario. Nikko was amused to no end as he enjoyed the sights. He was especially thrilled by the music played on the xylophone, flute and the improvised violin, and he swayed with the rise and fall of symphonic notes as he listened for a while, completely spellbound.

Kartarlal bought him an ice lolly and told him that they should get back to the waiting room quickly. They were to proceed on their journey to reach Kale from Kalewa before evening and had to take the first steamer in the morning for Tamu. His father, Goldram, was not going to like it if he found some members missing at the crucial time of loading and boarding the vehicles that were going to drive them through to Kale.

Indeed, after a quick breakfast, Goldram was constantly on his feet. He attended to the members of the family, personally going to each one to see that all were well provided for; more importantly, he did so because he had to aver to each one about the urgency of not lingering over the meal.

~

The engaged trucks had been properly loaded and packed with their belongings and were waiting for them to board. The distance to Kale from Kalewa was just about eighty kilometres and the time taken to reach was not more than two hours. Nevertheless, because it was just a raw cart road, there were only two broad parallel grooves on the trail made by frequenting motor vehicles going to and fro over the rather uneven surface. During the dry season, it was dusty and the vehicles left a trail of dust behind them. During the rains, it turned into slush bordered by bamboo clumps and other wild evergreen bush and woodland along its sides.

There were some swampy patches here and there as the twisting and turning road neared the banks of the Chindwin. But the district headquarters at Kale showed some signs of life, like wayside shops selling tea, soggy biscuits and rusks, and small clusters of huts. In the distance were a few imposing buildings which housed government offices. Even the road became livelier with the sight of adventurous youngsters on their scooters or motorbikes. By and large, the journey was rough and their entrails were thoroughly shaken by the jerks and jolts of the ramshackle trucks. The delicate ones like Biro, Basho and Kinta began to throw up. The sheds and shelters along the banks of the Chindwin, where a few boats and small steamers were moored in the lagoon by the jetty, were crawling full with evacuees. The kiosks were vending food for all tastes and doing brisk business.

The pilot bus, in which Goldram rode sitting beside the driver, came to a stop by the side of the police post; the other vehicles behind them stopped as well, awaiting further instructions. Goldram went straight to the policeman on duty at the port and got all the information required—not only about tickets but also about facilities not available on the jetty or the steamer they were to take up to Tamu. It was about ten hours of sailing, with a few wayside stoppages for relaxation and replenishment of available stocks that the passengers might need.

~

The Chindwin was a beautiful sight with its bends and forested banks. It was dotted with a few small islands where fishermen—in broad-brimmed bamboo hats over their dark, sweat-stained suntanned bodies and tied longyis—could be sighted engaged in casting and drawing their nets weighty with their catch. In the distance, they appeared like toys wound up to actuate a performance. Like in the make-believe world of movies, cinematography has a subtle art to highlight the beautiful, to enhance the graces of a scene and to intensify the evocation of emotions by allowing the camera to meaningfully linger a subtle extra split moment on particular spots and situations. In doing so, it does slide over what, in contrast, would stand out to be a slur causing revulsion, as distortion or ugliness of a kind would. Yes, the natural beauty of the Chindwin takes your breath away. But when it is seen from closer quarters as its waters flow along and away from the sterns of the boat, it tells a sad tale of what havoc the river could inflict upon the mounting presence of destitute multitudes.

Along the banks of the river—wherever the topography permitted—clusters of habitation had come up. The wrath of the choleric epidemic and typhoid cases caused road blocks to the family's journey of escape and they stayed wherever they found a place of respite to nurse the sick and dispose of the dead. At times, the flotsam passing by the boat not only contained the unseemly sight of human excreta with other garbage indiscriminately thrown into the water, but also corpses of the dead whose last rites could not be performed by sick relatives. The people on the deck of the boat could not escape the whiffs of the miasma. The sickness left them pallid and limp.

Men and women bathing and washing their clothing could be seen on the sloping banks. Considering the flowing waters to be clean, they even used it to wash their mouths. The children had fun swimming and playing games they had devised in the sandy and shallow parts of the bank. They screamed and waved vigorously at the passengers on the deck of the steamer. Sooner or later, they would run into one another, jostling away from the danger that loomed from the skies. The majority of people were propelled by an inherent herd mentality, paying little attention to the dangers of their arduous journey across the unimproved kuchcha road. This road, apart from serving as a mule track, now served army three-tonners transporting rations from Imphal to Moreh, the last Indian Army post in Indian Territory. And lately, since the cavalcades of evacuees from Burma had continued and were growing by the day, some transport contractors in Imphal had started a rather erratic service on the same route. The rattling small trucks going up and down the route seemed convenient and safe (protected by a local guard with a shotgun) but were expensive compared to the bullock carts and coolies who were engaged to carry extra baggage for those who travelled in their carts.

The situation was no different on the boat's deck. Most passengers, not bothered about desired comfort, occupied the convenient places they could find for the brief period of half a day and one night. Though, all told, the total time to be spent on board would be less than twelve hours, but it was afternoon before the passengers were all in place and the boat could leave the shore. The families huddled close; two newly-weds discretely looked for a place a little away from the edge of the rest in the hall and found the covered area on the roof deck. Somewhere, a little away from Goldram's family, was a small Gurkha family. A boy, about four or five, remained busy driving a small aeroplane producing a zooming sound with his shrill voice all afternoon. The whole childish operation struck a separate trenchant note and was in contrast to the general din of the crowds in the process of settling down on the deck. His little sister, too, perhaps running a temperature, had been restless since morning. Hearing the ceaseless whimpering of the child, Dr Dev gave her a potion to bring down her fever. The effect seemed to be contrary to his expectation. She cried louder and threw up whatever medicine had been administered, along with the undigested food in the stomach. The writhing and crying child lay in her mother's lap, flailing her little arms and legs, while the father sat with a wild, agitated expression in his red eyes.

To the surprise of the all the onlookers, her father opened an umbrella and began to move it up and down to fan some air for the restless child while shouting irate profanities and obscenities in his language at the same time. He seemed to be possessed by some evil spirit or struck by a fit of whirlwind insanity. The heat of the day and the persistent crying of his child, in spite of all his efforts, had triggered him into an explosion. He pulled out his kukri (a Gurkha dagger) and began some kind of diabolical hop and infernal dance around his wife and child, accompanied by

'Aahs!' and 'Oohs!' from the onlookers. The wife, who knew her man well, was unmoved, and with a suppressed smile looking at her husband fanning the girl with his open umbrella, she gestured to the people around her to not bother too much about whatever was going on.

Indiscriminate eating from the kiosks and drinking untreated water from taps on shore seemed to cause some events of sickness among those with weaker immunities, especially among the physiologically tender and delicate children and the female passengers, leading to more cases of getting knocked down by symptoms of cholera. Dr Dev was active more than usual, seen scurrying around the passenger lounge, giving out medicine and instructions about a diet to those who were stricken. He went into the kitchen to get a capacious can of water boiled and got some salt and sugar dissolved in it. He cooled the boiled solution by letting it float in the cold water of the river. This was kept ready to be given to those who were throwing up and had diarrhoea. 'To prevent severe dehydration,' he explained, 'which can lead to death too.'

Amidst such agonizing going-ons, there were a few groups who brought out a harmonium, a percussion and other paraphernalia, and started to sing and distract attention from the common despair. They started with bhajans, devotional songs sung in chorus, that developed into a sangkeertan, in which most present joined in, keeping rhythm with clapping and standing up to tap out a dance. Once the tempo was set and going, they turned to popular Bollywood songs, which brought new life into the prevalent verve. Among Goldram's family, only the lively Prakash and his youngest sister, the most playful, Nikkey, went and joined the merriment. Indeed, it took the edge off the gloom of what had brought them together. It went on, until with the advancing night, the spirit began to lose its impassioned tempo and the gathering around the musicians dispersed. In ones and twos, they went back to their own family huddles in different directions of the deck.

~

Except for the few who were in acute agony and whose subdued groans were heard almost throughout the night, by and large, most of those sprawled across the deck fell asleep and for a little spell, all was quiet and peaceful. It was well past midnight when the steamer sounded its hoarse whistle, warning that it was arriving at Khampat, a stop for the steamer as it reached the village. Khampat spread out for about a mile along the Chindwin and had all sorts of harbours for passenger and cargo boats and small steamers plying up and down the watercourse. The harbour was lit and the hutments were visible at some distance from the shore. But the darkest part of night found most passengers asleep or half asleep due to exhaustion and there was hardly any activity on the deck except the stirring of those who needed to replenish for their children a supply of biscuits, sweet buns, drinking water or powdered milk. The doctor, of course, needed a supply of packets of glucose for emergency. Never quite known for magnanimity, this common calamity, where he found a mass of humanity, had brought out the best in him. He dug into his own pockets for medicines, bandages and rolls of cotton wool required for first aid.

There were still four to five hours to go before daybreak and another hour's upstream journey before they would reach the precincts of their last destination in Burmese Territory, Tamu. It spread out on both sides of the river, but the markets and bazaars and the larger part of habitation was on the eastern side of the Burmese inland. The government offices, police stations, post offices, schools and hospitals were all on the east side of the Chindwin, so all human activity of the small town was seen here. There was even a small cinema hall that played Burmese and Indian language movies alternately for a week each and people enjoyed watching both kinds equally. They had something novel for entertainment besides the traditional period melodrama 'Pwe', which told stories of ancient kings, queens and princesses in the background of verdant greens and pagodas on the slopes of hillsides.

The western banks were largely occupied by the evacuees, who were grouped either with family or with people whom they had met on the same path leading away from regions of danger and into zones of comparative safety. Like in Kale, here too they had erected a running shed upon bamboo poles, built with palm leaves, thatch and thin corrugated asbestos and cement sheets for a roof. There were small kiosks for police assistance, local volunteers and a small office devoted to the registration of all evacuee family members, manned by a district magistrate (DM).

On the completion of recording items of relevant information in successive columns, a yellowish beige-coloured 'Registration Card' was signed by the DM above the seal of the Burma Government and was issued to the head of the family. It contained the names and bio-data of each member.

Being an unpleasant topic for him, Goldram went about the adjuration with what could have been a forced smile on his face. He got the family together safely in one place under the shed and said, especially addressing the ladies, 'From here onwards you must be extra careful to keep count of the family members and luggage.' They all smiled briefly as he continued, 'We are going to get separated, so to say, because we would be accommodated on five different bullock carts. And though we are all going in a row, one after the other, you shall individually have to take full responsibility as long as you are in a different carriage. This is only a reminder to be extra watchful in every aspect for all that is going to be inside your carriage.' The smile on their faces were replaced by bland apprehension as Goldram left in definite haste.

Soon after, one of the volunteers wearing a badge was going up and down along with a policeman or two, patrolling the shed end-to-end when Goldram enquired about the location of the magistrate's office and made a beeline towards it along with Dayal Singh, Dr Dev and two others. He lined up in front of the office. Goldram and company entered the magistrate's room when it was their turn. Goldram noticed the raised eyebrows and skeptical expression in the magistrate's eyes and before he could object to their herding in, Goldram explained, 'Excuse us, Sir, we are five families in the group travelling together. All those who've entered your office with me are either brothers or brothers-in-law. The exigency of travelling together requires that we get the registration cards made at the same time too. I hope you'd understand and be as kind as to get our papers done all at the same time.'

The magistrate made a gesture with his hand and called his clerk. Addressing Goldram, he said, 'Just go along with the clerk to his table; he will complete the paper work for you.' Turning to the clerk, the magistrate said, 'Saung Kha, they are five families travelling together. *Hanji-panjimalouba ne!* Get the job done straight so that they can conveniently be on their way.'

'Thank you, indeed, for being so considerate and for the timely help, Sir. God bless you!' Goldram said and moved on along with the clerk to his table. He instructed Dayal Singh to give the clerk all the details of the families for their registration cards to be made while Goldram left to arrange transport for the family.

~

Across a narrow part of the river, a wooden footbridge had been built with the help of the jawans of the Indian Army for the convenience of the people, especially the baggage-carrying day labourers. Goldram had to walk for at least half an hour before he reached the outskirts of the town of Moreh. He talked to a local peasant to find out where he could find someone with spare bullock carts to be rented out. He was led to the doorstep of a well-built and colourfully-painted house of a well-to-do farmer. The stretching field in the backyard of his house was half covered with paddy and half with wheat crops.

Moreh wasn't small either. With open fields flowing with rice crops, it was interspersed by a wooded area and bamboo groves with smaller hamlets spread out at least five kilometres across. There were several peasants, too, proud of their bovine wealth, who were already helping the evacuees by providing them with transport. Some of them, like true followers of Buddha, did their job with compassion for the hapless and suffering refugees, even if it was for some extra earnings on the side. Some even voluntarily transported serious emergency cases of sick folk or for those who expected childbirth, to the nearest Red Cross Centre and makeshift hospital about twenty-seven kilometres away at a place called Pallel. Four or five years ago, a Gujarati merchant from Imphal had liked the small village and built a rather imposing pucca house for his family's holidays there. He had let out a large part of the house in charge of guards, for a brief halt and lay-by of the trudging refugees because it had a generous supply of drinking water. A striking feature of the house was that there was a life-sized coloured picture of Lord Krishna on the living-room wall.

A swarthy and well-built man, clad only in his longyi and loosely-tied scarf in checks of white and black, came out of the door that was painted green and yellow. He had a broad grin on his face when he greeted Goldram with folded hands. He motioned to the bamboo stool and they both sat down in the running veranda along the front of the house.

'*Kya sewa?*' he said in staccato Hindustani. His servant, in the meantime, brought two tumblers of water, and Goldram was glad to drink his glass almost greedily after his walk in the sun. Without wasting a lot of daylight and talking about facing the thickly dark forested mountain path in a mutually understood mixture of Burmese and Hindustani, Goldram concluded the negotiation for five bullock carts in quick time. Young drivers, one for each cart, who could also take good care of the animals on the way, were to accompany the carts. Two types of carts were available—one drawn by one ox and the other drawn by two oxen. The cane and bamboo covering hood and the ground space were not much different, so Goldram chose the one drawn by a single ox.

~

The total distance to be covered was around two hundred kilometres, and according to Goldram's estimate, they should be able to cover it in less than ten days. He had mentally planned to take the journey without any panic. Taking into account the comfort of the women and children, especially when the infectious sickness was rampant and several deaths had been reported, he had made up his mind to take enough time to take care of their well-being. It was indeed a horrifying sight to find mutilated and dead bodies not very far into the wooded verge of their path, with flies, dogs and wild animals hovering around. He decided to go slow and take just a spell of extra time at each camp before taking to the road again.

The road from Moreh across the western bank of the Chindwin to Imphal in Manipur in Indian Territory was hardly better than when it was used as a mule track by the army for the conveyance of rations for Indian troops to replenish their munitions at the Moreh base camp.

Goldram led the carts to the exit head of the footbridge and waited for the members of the family who had gormandized upon enough food to last them until nightfall. He sat on one of the shafts of the cart (to which the ox would later be yoked) and let his melancholic eyes rove over the banks of the Chindwin. The vast conglomerate of fleeing humanity was in view. The people were engaged in the almost meaningless routine activity of living with anxiety. They were angry and in despair, their unwashed bodies itched all over and heavenward apprehensive eyes were raised with a private prayer. For a moment, in his imagination, he was stuck on the word 'fleeing'; weren't he and his kin—whom he was leading with the spear in his hand—part of those fleeing? His mind went back to the first page of the *Rangoon Gazette*: a huge picture of an eagle with a swastika stamped on its wingspread, swooping down on the bleeding rat depicting Poland. He knew broadly that the existing and gradually mounting tensions among nations were all rooted in trade relations. Exploitation was based on how pressure could be built by making necessary supplies scarce and expensive and how a revenge-driven people can, in turn, come to be callous and perpetrate actions that result in the bloodshed of innocent multitudes, driving them away from the comfort of their homes to wander on strange beaches in search of new safety.

21

Kaushalya had kept a small packet of some chapati rolls packed for her husband, who had not even had a proper morning meal. Among several other families seeking safety, the five carts of Goldram's group were moving around to find a proper place to be parked under the shady trees along the shore. Goldram allocated a cart to each family of his group and told them to arrange their baggage themselves in whatever level space there was in the cart. He made sure to speak to the drivers of the carts and left them with instructions to assist the ladies in stacking the baggage and to only then yoke the animals for the trek onwards. Goldram sat on a wayside boulder and proceeded to heartily savour the meal his wife had packed and kept for him. He was glad to see extra butter that was rolled up in the chapatis. With five or six healthy cows in the shed and an abundant supply of milk and milk products in his kitchen, an extra blob of butter in his meal had been enough to bring the colour of contentment to his face. But now for long, butter was going to be a rarity. The Indian Government's supplies for the thousands of refugees during stopovers at established camps (almost every sixteen kilometres) up to Imphal and further to Dimapur was just a mere handful of rice, chickpea halves, dal, salt and some chilli for each member, which they would eat off broad plate-sized teak leaves, washed clean with rainwater.

Goldram was glad to notice the children and other members of his family among the crowd across the footbridge, about to reach the end. Each one carried a piece of big or small baggage, shielding their eyes from the high noon sun with squinted expressions. Not everyone had remembered to carry or wear their solar hats. There was sweat, yes, but because of frequent showers, the air was clean and dust-free. With few petrol or diesel-fuelled vehicles—apart from the ones that belonged to the Indian Army or the few transporters, and a few ramshackle trucks from Imphal to Moreh—the atmosphere was pollution-free.

And indeed, some of the refugees who could afford the highly-priced seats in the vehicles rode in comfort. The cleaners or helpers of the drivers could be seen with their heads jutting out of the windows, shouting for passengers and calling out loud, '*Hawaleiye, Hawaleiye!*', which the trudging refugees had come to understand as a call to get the passengers to keep boarding the rickety bus to overflowing capacity despite the slushy and slippery narrow roads that sometimes ran alongside fearful gorges. The vehicles did sometimes face small or big mishaps, which caused damage to the vehicle and injuries to the passengers; it was a disaster. All depended upon the inclemency of weather and also the adroit or not-so adroit steering.

But largely, the mass of people preferred to travel in bullock carts—slow, but stable on the road. The journey, at the speed that it was being traversed—with squeaky wheels, the rope on the bamboo shafts and wooden framework of the cart, and the tinkling of the bells round the necks of the oxen—was going to be slow, arduous and long. There was actually little distance in terms of mileage, but it came with adversity, strain and ensuing wayside vicissitudes caused by natural conditions and the want of certain essential provisions. To count among other troubles was the occasional attack of malaria and some mild intestinal problems causing both pain and fever. These were though treated promptly by our roly-poly Dr Dev, yet it was a cause enough for added delay. Like Goldram—who with a spear in hand walked for as long as possible alongside his family cart—other able-bodied men also walked guard by their own family carts, especially during the nights, with a bamboo staff to scare away stray wild jaguars or even a leopard (both of which had sometimes been sighted).

~

The camp at Kakching was found to be overcrowded. The sheds for the travellers' brief stoppages were erected on a cleared piece of land, approximately forty feet by sixty feet, spread over with cane-woven chetayis or tarpaulin sheets—if available from government stores or courtesy the Indian Army supply units—on which people could sit or lie down to rest their limbs that were aching from the jolting cart ride. It was under these sheds that the refugees sat and fed themselves on the supply of rations and lounged or caught a nap if they could, before climbing back into their carts and be off on their seemingly endless trek back home. To answer the calls of nature, some shaded and sheltered enclosures were made about thirty-five metres away from the camping sheds in a clearance in the woods. These enclosures had cesspits that were kept covered, which were cleared every day or on alternate days by hired scavengers from the nearby village.

From here onwards, the mountain terrain and cart road gradually gained gradient and started becoming stiffer to climb. Yet, up to the next big campsite in Wangjing, it did not affect the speed of animals that drew the carts much. Brief stops to tend to the needs of the oxen, to rub them down and water them, seemed to happen more frequently. The woods around the path were thick and dark, even during sunlit hours, except for what seemed to be an opening where signs of a trodden forest path led into the depths of the jungle and perhaps, to some small village in the clearing.

The blue sky was wrapped around the creeping gnarled boles

of thick swaying trees and intertwining foliage on the hill slopes through which the road passed. And at times, the sky opened up bright and blue, and the space overhead was streaked with darting and sailing flights of eagles and the oxen perked up on the downward sloping road, indicated by the louder ringing of the bells round their necks. Of course, the riders inside got sharper jolts, which the children enjoyed. They giggled out loud when they were tickled by the swaying carts, their strange sounds jabbing and splitting the prevailing silence of the woods around them. Only during the mornings and evenings did the atmosphere turn alive with bird calls and the collective flapping of their wings when they came back homing.

What alarmed the birds out of their peaceful cosy nests sometimes, even while they were cuddling their little ones under their wings, were the zooming sounds of aircraft, the Japanese bombers, which were in formation day and night, ready to dive in and bomb their targets. The birds panicked and shot out of their nests with a noisy flapping of wings that echoed for a while in the serenity of the night sky and soon died down when they returned to their nests. Sometimes, the zooming of the aircraft was followed by heavy booms of fired incendiary and destructive ammunition, whereas at other times, the forays were reconnaissance flights planning to properly bomb the Air Force stations in the darkness of night and cause worse destruction and confusion.

The quietude was filled with the constant dull sound of rain falling on the verdurous hillsides and the general haze dimmed visibility at all times, which brought all stirring to a dead stop. People or wildlife slunk into the closest shelter available. But such spells of rain, whether short or long, were frequent and left the whole landscape dank and dripping, especially the roads on which hundreds of bullock carts were slowly dragging their weight up or rolling down. They turned muddy and very slippery and extra effort was needed by the oxen to pull because of the climb. The drivers used their fine bamboo sticks on the behinds of the oxens, along with choice spicy curses meant to encourage them to go on. The rain did bring some respite to the beasts from the heat as they stood breathing foggily, widening their moist nostrils for the spell of rain to continue. The whole mountainside emerged polished, bright and shining when the last of the drizzles stopped and the sun shimmered from behind the spent clouds. The movement of life resumed with a rejuvenated smile. During the nights, of course, the chill of the wind and the rain had gripped the harrowed travellers. They could only huddle closer together as they faced a shortage of heavy clothing or coverings. They used all available resources and braved the pall of nature with the same instinctive determination as animals or insects would to fortify their resilience.

~

Goldram's family had had a quite horrifying experience earlier. There had been a short shower of rain during the forenoon after they had left Wangjing and were heading towards a much bigger camp in the village of Thoubal. It was located at a higher elevation of the mountain ridge that they were climbing. The carts were moving at a comparatively slower speed due to the slush and the steeper climb on that patch of road—it was a rather long climb of nine or ten kilometres. The afternoon sun was hidden by the tree-topped undulating ridge on the western side. So, it seemed as though afternoon had merged into the darkening of the evening. Goldram's instructions were promptly sent to the drivers and the lanterns that hung from the side of the carts were lit early. In the lamplight, the eyes of the oxens facing the dangling lit lanterns ahead of them reflected the sparkle and shone like kids' marbles. Goldram's youngest, Kuku, was thrilled by the sight and gave out an excited shout of joy when he saw the ox following their cart using its long twisting tongue to polish off the remains of the last mouthful of regurgitated cud from its mouth. Soon after this childish belligerence, Kuku began to sulk and mewl, wanting to see the ox's tongue again. But the ox seemed to have clammed shut its mouth and despite Goldram's attempts to lure the ox to open its mouth by waving a green frond of leaves close to its mouth, the ox just gave them an empty stoic stare in response.

The progress of the carts towards Thoubal was slow and steady and it would take around three more hours before they reached the camp, which was slightly to the other side of Thoubal. As the darkness of the evening swiftly enveloped them, the road narrowed. Not long after Kuku had cried himself to sleep, the driver suddenly realized that the cart was drifting towards the extreme left of the road. Before he could give a big jerk to the reins and bring the cart back to the middle, the right wheel seemed to have hit and bounced over a huge stone buried in the deep mire. The cart came down on the road with a huge bump and got toppled to the left. Despite the ox's weight and the efforts to hold the ground, the whole cart, along with the ox, went slipping to the bottom of the shallow ditch along the road. Goldram, walking by its side, was left aghast for a moment. Then realizing what had happened, Goldram sprung into action by sticking his spear in the ground and jumping into the ditch. It was largely overgrown with tall grass and was now also filled with the cries and wails of the children and Kaushalya, who frantically lifted her children, who were tangled atop one another, and sat them upon some pieces of luggage.

The other carts of the family stopped as well and Goldram's brothers all came running; with the helping hand of the driver, they were able to put back the cart, the ox, the children and other family members back on the road. Goldram's presence had made all the difference. Kaushalya and the children were back inside the stacked cart and they slowly recovered from the horrifying jolt of the experience.

'It is indeed by God's grace that we've all escaped unscathed. Are the girls all right?' Goldram asked Kaushalya. 'Yes, yes, thank God. Except for a few scratches here and there, they are all fine. We can get going now,' said Kaushalya, her confidence bolstered.

Goldram went up and down the family carts and saw to it that all were back in place and shared a word of good cheer with everyone, 'Come on now, such little odds of a mishap are not going to knock our spirits down, are they? Most of you are able-bodied young chaps. I'm sure you're walking some part of the journey just for the sake of giving yourself some exercise!' He walked past the carts as they began to pick up pace and went on to tell the drivers to get started and be very careful—that last bit, both parties understood. All were back on the trail. The vagaries of nature and the apprehension of the frequent roaring of the Japanese war planes were still a hazard they had to face.

This is exactly what happened with Goldram's family's oxen carts approaching the precincts of Imphal. After a midday meal, they were closing in on the capital of Manipur and were just about eight-odd kilometres away. It was about eight in the evening, when the Japanese bombers came with screaming jets and the fireworks across the city skies began. The news next morning was that they had inflicted heavy casualties and destruction upon the central city.

Goldram and his family were still in their bamboo camp shelter till the next morning. In fact, there was terror in the air because of the stench of putrefying human flesh from earlier attacks and the sight of some corpses lying on top of the other in shallow wayside rainwater drains. These old and new corpses had been droned over by king-sized flies of a metallic purple tint. The family had left the village called Wing Jing, but were now stranded a few kilometres this side of Imphal. Around the shelter were several clay pots, perhaps taken by the sojourners from nearby pottery works or a kiln, which were in a semi-completed state. The sheer baked red clay pots were to be used as commodes inside makeshift toilets for the campers, but they had to be thrown away into the hillside thick bush. Such was the scene in the hazy light of breaking dawn brought into view against the general bice of dripping foliage, wrapped in spent clouds along the mountain slopes that received the travellers to the camp a few miles between Imphal and Wing Jing. They had left it fairly far behind and grittily forged ahead towards their destination which was now not very far.

The gentle generosity of the Indian jawans came alive and was manifest when at some distance an Indian military supply truck, returning from Moreh base camp, stopped by the side of a trudging Goldram, who carried, besides his spear, small lumps of caked mud round his heavy-duty ankle shoes. With a raised hand, the driver signalled for him to stop the cart at the side of the road and climbed down from his seat to meet Goldram. The army man seemed to be a subaltern, or perhaps he was—what in Hindustani would be—a subedar. He was a man of polite manner and etiquette. The driver spoke to the jawans inside who then brought out packets of food supplies like tea, powdered milk, wheat flour, butter, some packets of biscuits and other eatable oddments. The jawans brought out a camp stove and got it going for the convenience of the famished refugee travellers. All the family members came out of their carts and partook in the luxury of sweetened tea and bread and butter; they ate to their fill whatever they found to their taste. Goldram went around and saw to it that they all had enough of the provisions offered by the compassionate jawans of the Indian Army in transit. Kaushalya and Sheila got busy and made some parathas to go with the tea. Goldram, as ever, was ready to share some laughter and enliven the gloom of their general condition. He smiled as he went around and particularly addressed himself to the doctor, to whom he was closest in age, and said, 'Feels like a feast at the king's table,' and laughed. Everyone else joined in. This feast was neither here nor there, but only in imagination or fairy tales. Such moments felt like the patches of bright sunshine falling on their faces after spent rain clouds began drifting away. With their batteries recharged, the family went back to their lairs in the carts and joined the general caravan snaking up to Imphal.

~

The travelling crowd proceeded further to make it up to town after they had reached the camp on the outskirts of the capital. Goldram had suggested that it would be better to travel in the dark of the gathering night. He could visualize that if at all there were other bombing sorties at night, it would in all probability be on the city proper as it had all important targets like the army and air force bases there. Wisdom lay in letting the night pass, and yet nothing was quite predictable in case of these air attacks; they could come from anywhere and at any time.

The influence of the capital's proximity showed. There was a vast, properly covered eating court with benches and running tables. It was not liveried, but there were boys and young girls waiting on people who came for meals or snacks. The menu was not very ambitious but met the common needs and demands of the travellers, who were quite aware of the constraints and circumstances in which they all were. But to be served with hot and freshly cooked food at the table was indeed something to be elated about—it seemed other-worldly. No more yearning for home-cooked mother's kitchen fare. Rooms, too, were available for the very old or the sick, but generally people preferred to be close to their possessions through the night and retired into the comparative safety of their respective bullock carts.

Also, without wasting any time by languishing in one place more than necessary, they had to continue to be on the move. Though geographically they were well within Indian Territory, they still had to cover about 150-odd kilometres before they reached the railway station of Dimapur across the Naga Hills. The Naga Hills were less forested than the Arakan range. The mountain path wound through steeply rising, undulating hills from the foothills in hairpin sharp turns. The roads were better though—smoother with fewer potholes, though not carpeted, frequently used by army trucks or other sundry motor vehicles.

There was no definite bus service in place, but some drivers from private transport companies, working in tandem with tourist establishments, plied their jalopies to facilitate some part of the journey of the refugees on the march. But only few could afford such long rides. There were some rather steep patches where Goldram thought for certain that the ladies of the family—such as Mathura Devi, frail with age and spells of ailing, Sheila and Kaushalya, who had taken ill with malaria fever according to Dr Dev and were struggling to traverse the distance between camps—had to be seen to and special arrangements had to be made.

It must have been the most primitive kind of a hammock and distant from the idea of a palanquin. Goldram got a few strong sheets tied at both ends, which he slung through long and strong bamboo staffs; these could be carried by two sturdy Nagas—one at the front and one at the rear. This made for a comfortable carrier for both who shouldered the weight and who were carried. They climbed the rocky path and sang in tune, playing fragments of their local folk songs, which brought about a rhythmic rocking to the suspended weight. This was so soothing to the old and the ailing that they soon dozed off, and later, when they woke up from the nap, felt better in fine fettle, breathing fresh mountain air.

~

The Naga people's agriculture was spread far out on the slopes of the hills and valleys in a terrace formation and appeared to be a picture-perfect hillside scene with the village huts in a cluster away from the fields. Large banana leafage with dewdrops shimmering in the morning sun waved in the wind and tiny human figures in their bright reds and greens, and some merely in a longyi with bare upper bodies, were getting tanned in the sun. They could be spotted even from distant twisting roads over ridges, teeming with the moving multitude.

The climbs were rather steep at several points and the speed of the carts slowed down to almost a man's walking pace. Goldram found Nikko getting restless on the floor of the cart. He was running a high fever despite the aspirin and quinine given by Dr Dev, who was exceptionally fond of Nikko. He had red eyes and a burning body and could not stand the jerkings within the cart. Goldram engaged a Naga coolie to carry Nikko on piggyback and go slowly, swaying on the climb under the open sky and sharp breeze. Later, Nikko, years after their migration from Burma to Punjab, would nostalgically recall and graphically describe the experience to his dad's friend Habibullah when he had been summoned by Goldram to Lahore to get his factory going. Nikko, at that time, in eighth or ninth class at a Lahore government school, was learning to ride a horse and a bike with Habibulla's help during his free time.

Nikko would vividly recall the feel of the clammy, sweaty skin and the pungent smell of the sweat of his carrier, and laugh with the lean and rather emaciated Habibullah, who would shake Nikko's hands with his rough and cracked ones. With the same deft hands, he showed Nikko how a coin would magically appear and disappear by a sleight of hand (apparently by just shutting and opening his fist and pointing at it with a screw driver) to the great merriment of the little ones around him. They all giggled and urged him to show more such magic tricks. And indeed, Habibullah would entertain the kids until they would spot Goldram with his white turban entering the factory yard from a distance. At times, even Goldram would join in the fun and laughter. This was an indication that his deliveries and collections were going smoothly. He would liven up the mood and bring broad grins to every face by ordering some pakoras and tea from a tea stall in the neighbourhood. Nikko, within himself, felt proud of his dad, who freely gave so much happiness to everyone around.

But back on the journey, among the five family carts, the one occupied by Chetsingh's family was the most cheerful. Goldram's aunt, that is Chetsingh's wife, was fond of popular film songs but when she tried to sing she could never catch the right tune; her voice ended up in a ragged falsetto and made a laughing stock of herself in the company. Her eldest daughter, Bimal, didn't have much sense of tune or rhythm as well. But her two younger daughters sang very well and took turns to sing for their mother. If they were at a stoppage at a camp, they decided to have a bit of entertainment, and young ones like Biro and Rakesh from the other family carts, with Prakash and Kartarlal, joined in the fun. The morose elders, too, brought up a faint smile in response to the frolic and made a chink in their armour to let in some fun. They were determined to forge over their condition and the time spent in transit.

~

The long march replete with upheavals created indelible lifetime memories for the family. Their mixed bag of experiences during the whole odyssey were like the stories of the *Mahabharata*—a storehouse to be narrated to the raised eyebrows of friends and relatives and sometimes neighbours as they would make 'aahs', 'oohs' and 'wows' in response to the most bizarre events that happened across the difficult terrain of the Arakan and the thickly forested Naga Hills. In any case, with the continued moving cavalcade of humans, the ferocious wildlife had receded deeper into the thickest parts of the jungle and rarely was a leopard or a jaguar sighted.

At about midway, perhaps a bit ahead of Nagaland, was the town of Kohima. It was another comparatively bigger town, larger than the tiny villages dotting the vast expanse of vales and mountainsides. While these small hamlets didn't appear clustered with many houses, even from the distance of the cart road, there were straggling terraces of agricultural sustenance and support. The bigger township was called Senapati, and indeed, it must have been named after a renowned general of the ruler's army, who, through his valiant deeds in past glorious battles, had given the town its name. A flag in colours of blue, green and red with a coat of arms printed across it still flies on an iron rod planted into a concrete base in the centre of the township and celebrates a famous victory under the said general or the senapati. The tale that hangs by it is told in several versions like legendary anecdotes that surround a hero, who, like Robin Hood and his merry men, may have been just a brigand of sorts. The stoppage at Senapati was significant as medical facilities of a hospital were available and the old and the ailing could be taken care of by doctors and trained nursing sisters. Dr Dev, too, quickly went into the town and replenished the more frequently used medicines. With proper medical care and a better diet, the weak and sick got back on their feet and were ready to take on the road.

22

With regular stops at camps, the large family of forty led by Goldram wobbled along with their share of gripes or at times throwing up the bland food doled out at the camps farther away from towns and supply depots, until they hit Kohima.

At Kohima, they would have to abandon the bullock carts they had hired at Moreh. Some of the refugee travellers had already changed carts at Senapati. This wasn't mandatory, nor were there any check posts. The entire arrangement and process was at a social level, which was considered for the benefit of all the stakeholders involved in the maintenance and rentals of the ox carts. However, this was all a part of governance and the state remained uninvolved. The process of changing and transitioning was consistently hassle-free and seamless. The gears of this system turned smoothly because of the lubrication of human understanding, even though such mechanisms might only be achievable to a certain extent. The conflicts and disputes arising from bribery were absent here, representing the inherent tension between the state's directives and a law-abiding public. This system naturally evolved among people who were left to their own devices.

It took three days to travel between Senapati and Kohima with an overnight stop at Karong. The road on the way became somewhat more lively with appearance of other means of conveyance like bicycle riders with heavy bags or sheaves of tall mountain grass, fodder for cattle and pedestrians chatting and smoking their country made si-lei, a granular tobacco rolled in tobacco leaf—a crude version of a cigar—clearly indicating a leisurely manner of going about, sometimes even across villages for domestic and social errands. Amidst all this was the cavalcade of pedestrian 'pitthoos', piggyback carriers of the sick and disabled, the palanquin bearers and, of course, the rocking bullock carts. The scene would not be complete without mentioning the occasional 'Hawaleiye' ramshackle buses speeding up and down the road to Kohima, and the roaring sky lions—the Japanese bombers raining death as they dive-bombed their targets which included railway bridges, major connector roads used for the movement of the troops and heavy artillery to the front area, hangars of airfields and formidable army cantonments equipped with radars and powerful anti-aircraft guns and gunners that shot down some of the menacing bombers.

~

The stoic Goldram was now stacked up with weeks and months of exhaustion and had started to feel lax-limbed as they drew closer to the comparatively bigger town. He was looking forward to a good meal and some rest for his bones as he felt really famished, tired and was craving for a good substantial meal. He let all the ladies know that a few hotel rooms with toilets and taps with clean running water would be available to them for about four hours; they could wash up, change, eat and brace themselves for the next lap of their journey. He gathered the gentlemen and growing generation (young men led by Prakash) and went to a restaurant, ordering rice and chicken curry for all. The vegetables in the mixed vegetable dish—a mish-mash cooked in mustard oil—were fresh from the fields and, above all, the food was fresh and hot and tasted other-worldly, like a bowl of ambrosia. It goes without saying that their appetites were whetted by a refreshing bath and the smells of cooking from the kitchen. In a while, their full bellies began to make their lids heavy and some of them just snoozed off as soon as they got back to their place in the carts. The younger and able-bodied men followed Goldram and fell in step with the cart's wheels as it moved ahead with groans and screeches. Even Kartarlal, who had known his elder brother from the closest quarters, had awakened to this awe-inspiring aspect of his character. His strength coupled with stamina was not easily bowed or broken under continued mental and physical stress and this three-month long odyssey had been a big enough test of his stamina.

Soon after their overnight sojourn at the small and comfortable township of Karong, they set out on the last and the steepest lap of trudging, while deeply breathing the clear mountain air. They entered the precincts of Kohima sometime around sundown. The mild sunbeams of the setting sun created a beautiful landscape: the mountain tops lit up the valleys in their sleepy deep-indigo shadows. Goldram was glad for having negotiated the most difficult part of their journey without much damage, except for minor illnesses and that jolting mishap of the ox cart slipping into that shallow ditch. Largely carrying themselves well, they all reached the safety of the glorified inn Robin Hood, one of the two hotels in the area. It passed for a modest hotel because the rooms and suites had attached toilets and taps with uninterrupted supply of absolute virgin waters of the Naga Hills. Here, they could rest their deadbeat bones and rejuvenate for the next lap. This would also be the concluding part of their long, onerous, circuitous journey through the foothills of the Arakan to the penultimate big stop at Kohima, culminating at Dimapur.

The road beyond Kohima went winding down through widening valleys with increasing signs of habitation; it was not as thickly forested as other parts of the Naga Hills. In Dimapur, they would arrive at the railway station nestled in the foothills of a region renowned for rainwater pools and rivulets, lush paddy fields and tiny villages. This would be the end; the final destination was not the same for every family of Goldram's party.

And Kohima, too, figuratively, was a place where they would change to horses. Finally, they were going to do away with their bullock carts that had become their second home for about two and a half months. The oxen and the drivers and the passengers they had carried—day and night, sharing in the vicissitudes of uncertain terrain—had more or less become travellers and friends. And now the time had come for their parting. Goldram got the five drivers together and said to them, 'As I observed during our journey, I'm happy to say that you have not taken this job only for the sake of getting paid. You understood the predicament we were in and unstintingly offered your help at every difficult step. No member of our family has anything to complain about on your account. All along our journey you have been like one of us and more. The money that I shall now be paying you is just the amount that your master at Moreh reckoned would cover your labours in roughing out the journey with us and for the maintenance of the oxen. But I know that no amount of money can be enough to equal the kind of care you took of our family through these formidable and adverse conditions, and indeed, it cannot be calculated in terms of commerce. Maybe later, among your own family and in leisure, you will think and recall these days and remember us fondly, as we'll certainly remember you.'

Goldram wound up his parting message to them with a little lump in his throat, which the men were quick to detect. He gave them the settled amount and then gave each one, what he thought was reasonable, a gift for their families. They accepted the gift with a glow in their eyes and walked back sprightly to the cart rank, perhaps waiting a bit and taking whatever passengers they chanced upon and were on their way back home to Moreh and their own lives.

~

There was a bus service between Kohima and Dimapur, but it did not keep to schedule. Its departure and arrival at the terminals depended upon the number of seats occupied, for the conductor continued picking up passengers along the way so long as there were empty seats available. Also these wayside stops depended upon the whims of the driver and passengers regarding the length of time it would take at a stop. Goldram decided that it would be a sheer waste of time to take such a quirky form of public transport. The family group of forty could well be, maybe a few short of, a full small bus. Goldram negotiated the fare for a whole bus (a small one used in the hilly tracks of several sharp hairpin turnings) with a private transporter and settled at a reasonable price, especially going by the price of a single one-way fare of public buses. To engage a private vehicle would also mean a number of advantages, the greatest being the freedom of movement and sitting arrangement inside the bus. Cramped in narrow seats, they would still have room enough to stretch their legs to comfortable postures and would also be able to change seats as and when convenient and could stop wherever they wanted for any flexible duration; all would be in their own control.

Kohima to Dimapur was a sixty-five-kilometre gradual downward climb, and would be covered in around two and a half hours. The road went around the turns of the hills and knolls—none high enough to pierce the sky, nor were there any discernible barefaced steep precipices. The shallow and spreading valleys gave the family a better view of the countryside and the little hamlets with their arable cultivated fields around them (mostly in terraces) as well as of people moving about engaged in chores around their huts and crops under the open skies spangled with clouds that raced across the zigzag horizon.

~

Goldram decided they would give themselves an extra overnight stay at Kohima to relax and feel fresh for the different kind of journey they'd make during the following weeks. It would also give them some time to move about in the market and get the feel of the place and people. Generally, the Nagas were not very different from the Burmese except for their build. The Nagas, in keeping with the characteristics of ethnic hill tribes like the Nepalese Gurkhas, had similar small slits of eyes surrounded by tiny rolls of flesh, which made them look smaller than they actually were. Their culinary preferences, too, were almost the same, except that the Nagas were heavy meat eaters, and their sartorial tastes were almost similar too.

In the markets they saw, like in rural Burma, women as roadside vendors with homemade wares to sell, breast-feeding little ones or with their knitting or sewing in their laps. They sold cane and bamboo baskets, stools, tables and other such items of domestic use. The fabric they used for draping was largely jute, with strands of silk mixed in to give their finished products a characteristic shine. Such yarn was used to weave fabric on looms at home. The craftsmen made sling bags and other items like ladies' and children's dresses in bright reds, greens and blacks, with rows of tiny little cowries strung on them for decoration. The typically striped dresses, stoles and shawls were truly beautiful, but such fine finished products were largely sent to cities in the mainland, where several states had their official outlets—the emporiums that have the elite of the city as their regular clientele and offer better business prospects.

There was a little nip in the morning air as Kohima had experienced a rain shower the night before Goldram's family departed. The day was bright with some spent white clouds tinged with the pink of dawn, floating in the shallow valleys. Since the family had decided upon their departure, Goldram had started getting their bags and bedrolls loaded onto the bus. At the same time, he was telling the ladies to see they didn't forget or leave behind something they might regret and recall only when they'd speeded too far to turn around to go back for their parcels. As soon as they had done the reckoning, they cleared out and got seated in the bus.

According to his estimate, Goldram thought that if they started by ten, they should reach Dimapur by lunch. The driver had been instructed to take the bus straight to Dimapur Railway Station. Goldram was already mentally preoccupied with the priority of getting registered entry for the family as evacuees into India who could then be able to avail facilities and amenities that were provided for the evacuees from Burma.

Once at the station, he left instructions with Dayal Singh to carefully supervise the shifting of their luggage and the members onto the platform, which seemed already overflowing with hundreds of other refugees. All trains at all four platforms were full of evacuees who had completed their transit formalities at Dimapur. Goldram told Dayal Singh to give his full official introduction to the station master and get the permission to use the waiting rooms while Goldram would go to the officials vested with magisterial powers in their office cabins at the far end of the platform to get clearances for other facilities besides seats for the further rail journey towards Lucknow.

23

Lucknow, Goldram had decided, would be their interim stop for a longer while. There they would take care of the sick and the old, especially Mathura Devi, who had been complaining for a few weeks about the pains in her joints. A distance of about two thousand kilometres had to be covered through Guwahati and Siliguri in Assam, Patna in Bihar, to Lucknow in the United Provinces. There onwards, they would be travelling towards the northwestern parts of India—the alluvial plains of Punjab, a land irrigated by the five celebrated rivers. It was here in separate different cities and towns, like Gujranwala, Lyallpur, Lahore and Sialkot, where the families travelling under Goldram's wings were headed to. It was indeed a long wait before they would be able to stretch and relax themselves in homely beds among their own long separated relatives and breathe easy.

~

A yellow card with a seal was made as their identity documents at the terminus in Burmese Territory at Tamu, which helped the local authorities to officially endorse the holders of these cards as Indian evacuees from Burma and rightful recipients of all the sanctioned aids and facilities. Goldram was then further directed to other such temporarily erected kiosks, manned by an official and a few volunteers from schools and hospitals. The stalls, Goldram noticed, had long winding queues in front of their open public windows. Two of these kiosks were doling out full meals packed in banana leaves or old newspapers to the people who inveterately tried jumping the queue and created chaos; some in line had a better sense of discipline and tried to bring some control over the unruly behaviour of the rowdy.

The scenario at the next two cabins was similar except that instead of food, saris and children's dresses were being given away. There was the added cacophony of women's trenchant voices making conversation across the crowd and other lines besides their screaming to bring their naughty and unruly girls to strictly remain by their side in the queue. The chance acquaintances gave them ample opportunity to exchange their stories and experiences of the journey by spicing it up as they went over it in little details of certain wayside mishaps as jokes and sharing a laugh together. It surely took the edge off the congested weight of the collective suffering and grief among some. Others, more philosophically inclined folks, at once found a metaphor for the lifetime in this world in their journeys and therefore, admired those who never dwelt long enough on the shadows in their life to brood and drift into melancholy climes. They just romped along highs and lows of the undulating terrain, humming a tune to the glory of whatever life meant for them.

Goldram had a mind to go and ascertain the timings and the platform number from which they would have to board their train for their journey to Lucknow. He went to the family on the platform a little away from the kiosks to particularly tell Kaushalya that he would be away for a few minutes to make inquiries. But on coming close to the waiting group, he found his two girls sobbing and clinging to their mother, mewling and saying something only she could understand. 'What's it about?' he asked Kaushalya.

'Oh, nothing much. Rajkumari and Tara (Goldram's twin daughters) saw another girl getting a frock with a large red floral design and started to sulk. They want a frock like that with flowers printed across the front. They have enough clothes and don't need more. And isn't it humiliating to stand in the queue and stretch your hands like a beggar?' she replied.

'You're right. But you can't make them understand your views on "need" and the "humiliating" part of it. Try once more. I'm in a hurry. If they're not pacified, get them a frock each from the distribution kiosks and do not let them whine. Remember what Kabir said about the stubbornness of a child, a woman and a king. I won't be long,' he smiled as he assured her and went off.

Wading through the swirling crowd, Goldram went to the information desk manned by two on the platform. He talked to the personnel in charge, learnt about the platform from which the train to Lucknow could be taken and the timings and frequency of its departure. He gave his full official information, showed him his gold and green embossed leather identity card of the Burma Railways and requested the in-charge to somehow manage to get all forty members of his family accommodated in the same compartment. Having done thus, he was given the number NR 4630; the Northern Railway train to Lucknow via Guwahati and Siliguri, he was told, was due to leave in two hours.

Over and above the milling crowds and the general din, the officer said, raising his voice a bit, 'We'll do our best to put you all together in the same compartment and I'll send my man to see that your seats are all together. But I'm sure you can see what the situation is like and things may not turn out to be exactly as you want them to be on the ground.' Both smiled with mutual understanding. Goldram said, 'I appreciate that you're trying your best for me. See you in some time. The world has shrunk because of the railways.' And he left with a wave of his hand and a smile of gratitude.

Goldram got back to the family, and as they ate an early

midday meal, he told them to get ready to move to Platform No. 4 and get into the compartment number NR 4630 as soon as the train arrived on the platform. He also told them to be reasonable and not take up more seats than needed. 'We are all sailing in the same boat and must show care for others,' he told them. 'I know the thought crossing your mind as I say that we're surrounded by grabbers from all around. Well, yes, but by sharing, we have never found ourselves in need either.'

~

There was still half an hour to go before all the members of the family were seated and their luggage were tucked overhead or under the seats. There were some running bench-like seats and some single seats in the corner and they spread sheets or towels across these, like the flags of occupation over conquered territory on the battle ground. The children were already sprawling over them and, as long as they could, jumped and romped across from one seat to the next. Soon, the whole carriage was filled with the din of fresh arrival of passengers until it was at full capacity. The people were literally rubbing shoulders with one another, some getting mauled in the crowd, with their non-stop babbling and screaming children along with the smell of teeming humanity. Some craned their necks out of the windows to get a whiff of fresh air to ease their short breaths.

It was half past three when the train left Dimapur, but they didn't leave completely behind the hilly terrain, the mysterious gorges, umbrageous glens and random chutes piercing down the hillsides and sparsely wooded hilltops. Shepherds could be seen idly slouching after their herds of sheep with a mongrel running along their side to keep the freak straggler or whimsical straying ewes and lambs together in the herd. Natural caves and grottos were hidden in crevices behind the deep verdant growth of tall grass and thick tangled bushes. A grey and lean sadhu was sitting half-hidden and rapt in meditation under a clump of pine trees, inhaling their rich aroma that added to the lazy noonday air. The swaying pines on the mountainside created an intriguing playful design of light and shadow on the grass-patched ground. Wide vistas were changing the topography at every turning of the train as it wound round the hills that lay between Dimapur and Guwahati. Indeed, there was an increasing number of flatlands. Crops of rice could be seen with female bodies bent over to tend to them, the sight stretching to merge with the greying horizon that was streaked with orange strokes of the setting sun. It was only after a journey of around two days and a night that the landscape underwent change again.

Goldram was pleasantly surprised when Nikko said to him, 'Are these carriages not much roomier, Papa, than those in Rangoon, and aren't the railway lines spaced more broadly? We are now travelling in bigger compartments over broadly placed railway lines.' In his joy, Goldram tenderly patted Nikko's back, appreciating his observation. 'You're right, Nikko. Burma Railways have metre gauge all over, except in the high mountainous regions where we use a narrow gauge. In India, too, trains in the hilly terrains of Darjeeling or Simla use narrow gauges. In India we generally have what it's called a "broad gauge" railway.' Goldram was happy that his son showed such promise at his tender age.

Kaushalya looked at the father-son duo engaging in a sort of serious conversation and smiled to herself. She was happy and proud.

~

The woods through the rain belt turned thicker and greener, the sun grew brighter and the air was cool and damp, but the weather could turn muggy if the wind dropped. The sky was without formidable rain clouds—clear and bright. The family observed this scenic change as they drew nearer to Siliguri. Guwahati was comparatively warmer because of its height, but the surrounding areas, like Shillong in Assam and Aizawl in Mizoram, were located on hills and higher sea levels and were pleasantly cool even in the months of May and June. Goldram and family were now travelling through April and so the vales and dales were spring-blessed with verdure in all shades of green with wild flowers strewn across abundantly in all colours of the rainbow. The cattle could also be seen from the train windows, grazing in the meadows or resting in the shade of trees in the warm afternoon.

The breeze was cool and fresh as the train wound its way on its broad gauge rails. The crowded carriages were wrapped in their own vaporous odours of human exudation of every variety—natural and manmade. There was also, mixed with the peculiar smell, the steam and smoke from the hard coke of the engine fuel, which stood out above all other scents. This pungent stench lingers sometimes, long after the train journey, and clings to the sweat and body odour absorbed into the clothing. For Goldram, the ceaseless proceeding cavalcade seemed to be a perfect metaphor for the earth's journey across the infinity of ethereal space. However, his sense of social propriety prevented him from going up to Kaushalya to share the beautiful idea with her. She was the only person with whom he thought he could share the subtle truth of the metaphor. Most others around him, he saw, were engaged with the mundane and the gross—the food packets and the free clothing and discussing how much they had missed and how much the other had gotten. They didn't seem to have the time, inclination or any such urge to look out of the window and savour or reflect upon the gifts of God's plenty.

The music of the cosmos touched the sensibility of a chosen

few. The rest were only concerned about the speed at which the train was going and how long it would take to reach the next junction, where the train would halt for a long enough spell so they could get some more food and clothing meant for the refugees. To the government supplies stocked on the railway platforms were added some goodies and savouries given by local charitable institutions or affluent philanthropic industrialists and merchants. This gesture made evacuees from homes in Burma feel the edge of mortification taken off the gratitude of charity and maybe, their embarrassment was replaced by a sense of warmth of welcome to their homeland. Here Nehru, Gandhi, Patel and others were at the forefront of the fighters for freedom, trying to throw off the yolk of suppression and exploitation. They were confronting the British colonialist rulers with the decisive slogan, 'Quit India', which resonated across the skies of the country. Many others found the time and means to manage relief for the destitute refugees. Of course, there was no dearth of others who took such arrangements and gestures of compassion as their right and coveted more, even lunging forth to obtain their desire.

Goldram knew that he didn't need to spot such doctrine among his family, but he kept quiet and looked the other way, whether he liked it or not. When it came to the conduct of others, he thought that this was entirely their own concern, reflecting their own values and beacons. Besides, he was not going to don the mantle of a social reformer, however much he was impelled to intercede and set things right for the good of the people according to his own understanding of social order and ethics of society. Most people, he had noticed, were averse to outside intercession and considered it an unwanted imposition, even if some sensible part of their mind—while they were stuck in the trials of unravelling a predicament—could find acceptable the random suggestion that came from a stranger in good faith.

Goldram had not as yet attained a stage where he could turn away with a smile without feeling cold disdain towards his effort; it was a waste of breath. He wasn't yet ready to totally forget and abandon his obligations to Kaushalya and his children, and to take to the stony and dusty paths of a life devoted to reform in emulation of the ilk of Ishwar Chandra Vidyasagar and Dayanand. Within himself, he did feel, at times, the tide reaching out to the moon, but his priorities at this stage of life brought the scale of the immediate down in favour of an aged mother, brothers, cousins and related women folk whom he had willingly taken under his wings.

~

At the height of the rough and tumble of the family's earlier journey, all their nervous and mental energy was focused on braving new and strange adversities each new day—if not at every turn—of the muddy roads of the Arakan wilds. Physical discomfort or little problems and ailments had been unattended to or had been brushed aside as trifles in the face of the immediacy of the arduous next steps on the way to where each one thought their ultimate relief lay. Now, as they chug-chugged at a steady pace, the soporific rhythm of the sound of the iron wheels on the iron rails made them stretch their legs in comfort, fully utilizing the leg-space between the seats. They could see, twiddle and examine their toes, see the not-so-little overgrown toenail and how dry and cracked their feet were. Indeed, there was ample time now to think of the constantly itching skin, Mathura Devi's swollen roseate knees and Sheila's constantly irritant throat that caused her to cough and eyes to water. The intermittent fever had left Nikko's body quavering, leaving Kaushalya full of anxious moments. Besides, she herself had been smitten with gripes of having a poor digestive system which made it difficult for her to live on the food cooked and doled out to the homebound travelling refugees. She had to wait for the big station that provided restaurant services so that she could order some soft, almost-fluid khichdi that she could eat without throwing up or causing rumblings inside her abdomen.

The train wound its way into the open vistas of fields in the province of Bihar—some of them arid and fallow, seeming to be struck with drought, but some indeed full of grain where the lean farmers with more than a week's growth on their leathery-lined facial folds, followed their oxen with the sharp endpoint of the iron plough, digging and throwing up the hopeful brown earth gaping for seed, manure and later for rain or irrigation channels. The Indian farmer, over centuries, has left such a mixed trail of history. It is scripted by the vagaries of seasons and weather, but is largely writ in tears of misery of thwarted hopes of fulfilment of the dreams that had sprouted in innocent hearts beating in those mud-cracked homes. Besides, the outstanding strands of grit was the great saga of hapless men pitted against ruthless elements. Such dreams were seen and celebrated by brave sons of the soil and contemporaneous society, like Premchand, who surfaced from the fecundity of the tufts of the crops.

Not only did the family have the occasion to dwell on their ailments, but they also pondered over the medical treatment they needed to get rid of the nagging physical unease. Most voluble in sharing her aches and pains in her stiff ageing joints was Mathura Devi and her easy target was Kaushalya, a patient and sympathetic listener. Even Sheila unburdened her suffering from persistent, fretting tonsillitis and some other troubles on her younger sister. Sheila spent most part of the nights clearing her throat or coughing. The sleeplessness left her exhausted when the day broke, and she had to keep up with everyone else. The occasional engine whistle pierced the still, greyish-pink morning sky. Sounds and movements of the living world merged with the constant rhythmic sound of rolling wheels, rendering the songs of birds that crisscrossed across the sky almost inaudible. If anyone, Sheila was the one who most eagerly waited for relief.

'I don't know, really, when we shall reach the big town of Lucknow, where we can break our journey for a few days—as brother Goldram said—and find a hospital to get treatment from real good doctors. Prakash was telling me that there is a big hospital with a medical college there. Have you noticed that Nikko's intermittent fever over the last few weeks has left him so emaciated, and the other underfed children look just as bad? There is hardly anything nutritive to give them to eat and keep their growing bodies healthy and strong,' said Sheila to Kaushalya.

Dayal Singh and his small coterie, of which Kartarlal was also a part, didn't have much to complain about. Except for having lost some peripheral weight, they had borne the rigours of the journey without any serious damage. They had even found time and cheer to play a game of rummy sometimes. So, too, were the family of Chetsingh. By and large, they were a cheerful lot and had enjoyed one another's company. Prakash and Baldev had once even given a performance with funny humorous skits on stage. They put together some country situations and with the help of Basho, who sang and added folk songs to the situational skits, made the performance livelier. Only their mother, always dressed in the latest fashion and hairdos (as she was fond of proper makeup for outdoor appearances) was sometimes seen fading into a pallor of gloom.

She was the only one who truly understood the pain she had endured from undergoing surgery for a malignant breast tumour just four months ago. In her solitude, she carried the burden of her suffering. However, since the tumour had been detected in its early stages at Civil Hospital, Rangoon, where Prakash was studying to become a doctor, the follow-up treatment began promptly, as did the process of recovery. However, it is up to each individual to nurse their ailment and gather the emotional strength necessary to combat the relentless disease. Despite this personal and intense struggle, the longing for some relief was often expressed and shared with like-minded individuals, creating a sense of solace and understanding. These quiet moments were filled with both anticipation and a subdued eagerness to move forward towards the next stage of their journey.

24

The topography began to change as the train neared the next junction of Patna, the capital city of Bihar. The villages here were larger and were interspersed with smaller towns with larger and better-built houses. The homes had colourful walls, and some children and women were also seen moving around, engaged in activities that seemed to fully engross them. Only some of the children, who were attracted by the distant rumble of the speeding train, stopped short in their sport or chores and shifted a few steps towards the rail lines to let off yells of joy at the passing train and wave at the passengers craning out the windows. The imperceptible joy was mutual and ballooned upon sharing. As the train's last carriage disappeared in the distance with a dot, it left the children in peals of laughter and they returned to their activity which was left halfway. Some of them seemed to be playing a game of counting the number of carriages on the passing train and later compared the tally with one another; they enjoyed the sport every time a train passed by.

Considering the half-hour stop at Patna, Goldram quickly sent word around among the family's ladies, especially the fastidious ones, to go and use the toilet and the bathroom in the railway station's main waiting room. Goldram took the others to the restaurant for a hasty lunchtime meal, different from the run-of-the-mill fare that had been doled by the special kiosks on the railway platform. There were still a good ten minutes left before the departure of the train when Goldram saw his darling boy Nikko, and motioned him to come over to him. Nikko came and eagerly clasped his hand in his father's and fell in step. They began to walk the length of the platform to their compartment.

'Come sweetheart, I'll tell you something interesting about Patna. Not everyone would be interested in this city of Patna beyond the fact that it was the birthplace of Dr Rajendra Prasad, but indeed, it is steeped in some bright moments of our country's ancient history. King Ashoka the Great ruled from here more than two millennia back, when the place was called Pataliputra, the seat of the great monarch's rule. His vast kingdom spanned the majority of the subcontinent of India from north to south, inclusive of the island kingdom of Ceylon, and from Afghanistan down the coastal tip of Kanyakumari. All this was not easy to accomplish. He was a great warrior but he left behind a horrid wake of human bloodshed. The only saving grace was that the human carnage awakened Ashoka to the Buddhist compassion and the path of non-violence—the Buddhist way of life. This then led to the great monarch deploying all means he was master of to spread the Buddhist wisdom as far in the world as he could.

'Furthermore, besides having been a centre and seat of power for King Ashok, Pataliputra remained and still continues to be Buddhism's religious centre. Several vihars or small monasteries were inhabited and run by the monks as dissemination centres of the teachings and philosophies of Buddha. Later, from among the monks who excelled in their several branches of teaching, buttressed with their vision and enterprise, came together and drew up plans to consolidate and unify the several teaching constituents into a faculty. They gave the teaching centre, comprising several different schools of disciplines, a prestigious identity. And indeed, the institution developed into what came to be known as the Nalanda University. The region gained recognition because of the landmark peepul tree at Bodh Gaya, sitting under which, in samadhi, Lord Buddha gained the ultimate enlightenment, or his nirvana. Therefore, Gaya is the holiest of holy places for those of Buddhist faith and it attracts thousands of Buddhist pilgrims from around the world,' he said to Nikko.

The longer stop at the junction gave the passengers enough time for a wash and, if they so chose, a hot fresh meal at the restaurant. Goldram did not waste even a single minute and helped some of the fussier members of the family in the ritual of cleansing and refuelling their appetites, whetted by the aroma emanating from railway restaurant's eating hall. And then, rapidly, as the guard blew his whistle and waved his green flag from the tail end of the train, the milling crowd on the platform began disappearing into the black holes of the carriages and the train started to move out of the Patna station. The scene outside showed tin huts and cabins far and wide along the shunting lines, with provisions for sundry repair and refuelling engines, and the whole picture was blackened with soot and dust. Indeed, it was a shrunken and decadent memory of the many splendored glorious years of Pataliputra of King Ashoka.

~

There wasn't much change in the topography as the train traversed its journey through Bihar into the southern Indo-Gangetic plains of the United Provinces. Compared to Bihar, the air was drier and the sun was warmer with no clouds on the horizon or straying across the skies. The villages, farther or nearer along the tracks, showed similar character as those in Bihar, except—even to the casual observer—there was an increase in the concentration of the populace. The clothes lines were loaded, the space round the huts and cottages were busier with threshing and winnowing of wheat or rice or local produce, and the work was all manually undertaken by the members of the family, especially by the women who didn't venture away from their dwellings. Here and there though could be spotted the chaff-cutting machines in operation or idly standing, like a dwarfed animal skeleton.

The manning of the Persian wells was done by the menfolk, as was manning the sources of water for irrigation, minding the channels into the fields, the ploughing and seeding of fields, and cutting of crops and storing in granaries in due season. As a routine, they went into the fields in the early hours of the day to begin their hard laborious work so that they could finish the day's work and were back before high noon, when the heat of the sun became insufferable on their already tanned neck and shoulders.

The older members of the family had mustered all their strength to wait until the train touched Lucknow. Goldram had told them they would break journey at the capital city of the United Provinces for some days and get the best medical help at the government hospital. But in between that, the train would pass through another big town of the United Provinces called Jaunpur, located in the beautiful natural ambience of the banks of the river Gomati. Goldram learnt about the popular history of the place from a co-traveller, a native Jaunpuri who had ripened in the sun and rain of land. He had a flowing white beard, drenched in henna, and wore a pukhtoon dress and turban. Goldram had met him in the connected carriage and easily fell into a casual conversation, perhaps because he reminded Goldram of his friend, Habib, who was still in Sialkot.

'The city is better known from mid-fourteenth century when it was established by Feroz Tughlaq and built in the memory of his dear cousin brother, Sultan Muhammad, who had met his end at just twenty-three. The still extant mosque at the centre of the town was the first splendid architecture that came up. Malik Sarwar, an aesthetically inclined man, later built several beautiful forts besides the central Royal Fort, and also a number of mosques, tombs and mausoleums in the memory of his ancestors and to commemorate Sufi saints. All these buildings were laid out in well-landscaped rows of pines and streams criss-crossing the manicured lawns dotted with fountains. He called it all by the name of the Sharqui Dynasty. Thus, in the sylvan setting alongside the Gomati, the town and its happy population flourished through centuries and became Jaunpur.'

Many popular savouries originated in Jaunpur, and the two better known were jalebi and fafda. These were served as local breakfast fare, hot and fresh as soon as the train pulled to a stop at the platform of the station. Wheeled along the length of train and meant for passing crowds, the vendors may not have cared much about the quality or the standard of the fare, yet since the wheelbarrows were licensed by the authority of the Indian Railways, the standard of cleanliness and quality were under scrutiny and were also liable to be checked on the spot—and so it was generally quite good, not just passable. The passengers from further north mostly had never had the occasion to taste these varieties; the fafda especially was a delight to indulge in and they went for extra helpings. Most children gorged on the syrup-dripping jalebis. There were no checks on them, except for their yelling parents. But all enjoyed it.

~

From the time of leaving Jaunpur around eleven, when the sun was reaching its zenith and the temperatures were rising, it took about six hours to reach Lucknow. Around half past five in the afternoon, the train entered the railway station area, a steel web of rail lines spread out, criss-crossing all around the slowing train with empty carriages. Goldram got up from his seat and started going around to the family members with instructions. He particularly told the senior women folk to be careful of two things: to see that all members remained together in clusters and that they held hands in the swirling crowd. He smiled and told them to keep count of not only the children but also the pieces luggage to be wheeled out in hand-pushed barrows by coolies.

'Not that there is much of a scare, but it is always good to be alert and be on guard. All along we're going to be surrounded by strangers, although we shall be taken good care of by the workers of one of the oldest religious institutions, the local Arya Samaj. Some employees, according to Dr Dev's arrangements, will be there at the station to meet us and see us through the exit to the tongas that will drive us to the Arya Samaj', Goldram explained.

For a brief layover for distant and outstation visitors, the establishment of the samaj had an annexe of two-storeyed commodious and well-maintained dharmashala or living quarters. It was a sort of lodge with a running kitchen attached to it. During earlier years, the stay and board used to be free of charge and the visitors had to pay maintenance funds of nominal charge. But now, considering the large influx of evacuees from war-stricken Burma which was under Japanese attack, the management had made the payment for their kitchen bill optional too. Those who could not—under strained circumstances—afford it were allowed free meals as well. Dr Dev had given his old friend—a class fellow from the medical college—Chandra Mohan Maheshwari (now a senior doctor and professor of medicine at the UP state medical facility located on the edge of the cantonment area) detailed information regarding the party's arrival. Dr Maheshwari kept the samaj under the care of his hospital. So along with a few workers from the Arya Samaj, he too was promptly at the railway station to meet the arriving family of his friend. He had made all arrangements for the large party on the ground floor of the dharmashala and had ensured that the place was not far from his hospital.

Dr Dev, with a black mole on his plump cheek and his broadened toothbrush moustache, smiled his 'Johnson Baby' smile and rushed to hug his old friend. 'So, brother, the CM himself is here to meet us.' 'CM' was a secret wisecrack between them, referring him to be the chief minister for there had been a chief minister by his namesake. 'I see that you have not brought Kamala along,' and again there was that mischievous smile on his face. 'It would have taken us another half an hour of introductions on the platform. But you must meet my brother-in-law Goldram. He's an engineer and has been like our guardian angel through all the vagaries of the trek.'

Coolies with wheelbarrows were hired and, with the help and guidance of the men from the Arya Samaj, the party began to move out to the waiting tongas that were to drive them to the samaj's premises. The children were especially charmed by the colourful bazaars and streets of the neighbourhood and were turning their heads right and left as the tongas went clippety-clop to their destination. It was already seven by the time they got settled into their quarters and had had a quick cup of hot and refreshing tea. They didn't even get the chance to unpack. In the gathering dusk, they could hardly discern the topography of their location, but they were so comfortably placed that they couldn't ask for more. Summer was almost here and so the ceiling fans were on and the family looked forward to a snug and comfortable sleep.

~

Goldram had decided that a week would be the limit for their sojourn, which was enough to get medical aid for the sick and old members of the family, especially the ones who hadn't still gotten over their coughs and fevers. They would then take another train ride of approximately 500 kilometres. Even the adolescent and the young among them were showing signs of nerves and were running out of endurance by fretting over little things. They seemed exhausted and tired, mentally and physically. All of them secretly desired to get to the places where they would stay put and not be perpetually packing and unpacking their things. With strong and solid muscle and a stronger will and endurance, even Goldram had begun to feel fatigued all over. But he was still able to keep alert and be up and about. He had a job in hand that couldn't be passed on to another.

Yet, after such an arduous journey and considering the pervading lassitude of their volitional limp and accumulated fatigue, Goldram thought they should give themselves a day's complete rest. They could eat and sleep as much as they needed to regain their stamina to push forward with the last ounce of their energy on the road to their destination. They took it easy the next morning and slept until the sun was high up on the horizon, sometime between nine and ten. It was almost eleven before they finished eating their breakfast—their first morning meal from the samaj kitchen—and were quite contented with the fare served: puris with spiced potato curry, curd and some varieties of chutney and pickles. The substantial morning meal brought on a soporific languor and children ran around and played their childish games in the gallery.

Earlier in the morning, Kaushalya and Sheila took a stroll around, bound by the habit of their growing days in Taunggyi. Most of the others slept through the afternoon and were up only by five in the evening. Goldram felt greatly relaxed after his own siesta. Yet, as he confided to Kaushalya, he felt his body had generally shrunk and his ribs were easily discernible as he bathed in the morning. Dr Dev and he went for a stroll up to the La Martiniere College polo grounds, hoping to chance watch an equestrian steeplechase performance. Also, they were mentally preparing for the next day's hospital visit as arranged by Dr Maheshwari. But as they walked leisurely to the polo grounds, Goldram couldn't wait to tell his brother-in-law the very interesting and little-known tale of the tragic and mysterious ending of the reign of Wajid Ali Shah, from the lineage of Nishapuri Kings, who had once ruled Oudh for centuries.

'The history books prepared, written and prescribed as texts for our students don't always carry such tangential tales. They don't suit the doctrinaire of the rulers by means of which they go deeper than physical enslavement. Once they've fulfilled their expansionist designs in one place, they fix their sights on their next convenient victim. For the topical observer and the chronicler, some of these tales would be significant milestones, an important turn of events in the long unending history of the people. Indeed, there was a lot more to Wajid Ali Shah's rule coming to an end when it did.

'But the shrewd and ambitious Lord Dalhousie, the Governor General of British India, precipitated the termination by means of a devious treaty, which he coercively made the Nawab sign in 1856, under which he annexed Oudh. Ignorant of the designs of the British rulers, the Nawab boarded the General Mcleod steamer bound for Calcutta. He thought that after a brief stop there, he would be sailing for London to plead his case of an unjust annexation of Oudh before the queen. I'm sure, brother, as a doctor working with the British officers in the cantonment hospitals, you must have come across several Englishmen who pride themselves for their fair play in all their dealings. No one, Dev, is above being human. It is difficult for one to probe within and pick apart one's own foibles. Picking a moral transgressor, the first thing one does is to eliminate the self and then begin the search among others. It is a presumption, but it is universally true. It is natural, too, to revel in the picture of the ideal that one has created and nourished of oneself. And this can be attributed to a whole race.

'The General Mcleod, on which Wajid Ali left the shores of Gomati for Calcutta, after two days' voyage was docked at Prinsep Ghat, close to the high-end residential area called Garden Reach, which is also close to Metiabruz in western Calcutta. Of the thirteen prestigious bungalows along the banks of the Hooghly—occupied mostly by the rich and famous foreigners—he moved into Number 11. This belonged to the ruler of the small kingdom of Burdwan and Wajid Ali paid a rent of rupees five hundred a month. Eventually, he bought the bungalow and also two other ones when he reconciled with the idea that he had been ousted from his native Lucknow on pretexts and saw no chance of reaching the queen with his plea. So, the last ruler of Oudh spent lavishly and gradually build mosques and imambaras, miniature imitations of the ones he had left back in his beloved city of Lucknow, and tried to create a dream mini-Lucknow around him. And having created the faux bazaars and streets as per his native Lucknow, he began to pass his days of exile luxuriating in his dream world.'

Dr Dev had been listening to the events of this history. Such a miserable end to a king's thriving period of reign, he thought. At the end of Goldram's narration, he heaved a full-throated sigh. 'How the British too could be as brutally callous as the Turks when it came to dealing with someone they considered an adversary!' And not having much else of their interest after a round of the polo grounds, they walked back in the fading light of the sunset towards the western horizon.

~

Tiwari Pandit, the priest in the samaj and keeper of the samaj library, gave the group directions to two particular places they could visit while away for some leisure time if they liked outdoor activity. One was the Wajid Ali Shah Zoological Park and the other was the state's botanical garden; both of these were places of interest and not far at all from the samaj. The family was divided into convenient small parties and they walked out in different directions to enjoy an evening of exploration and adventure. They passed through small bazaar lanes, enjoyed the sights of lighting lamps before they got to their different parks. The children screamed and laughed at the sight of animals, especially at the monkeys at their fantastic antics in their cages. A few monkeys climbed a bole of trees which rose up to foliage and flowers. With the gathering dark of the approaching night, they had to cut short their delightful adventurous outing and deciding to come again, they left reluctantly. Their guardian Kartarlal assured them that he'd bring them again. The ladies, chaperoned by Prakash, too, were seen coming back from the florally rich botanical garden, and the air was laden with a rich mix of the aroma of flowers on their way to samaj.

Besides these parks, there were other places to visit and find amusement. There was this coffee joint, called Cappuccino Blast, with a patio where tables could be set outdoors and an hour of leisure could be spent in its peaceful ambience. For children, particularly, they had a sprawling children's amusement park that came alive with children's voices and screaming laughter. Another inviting little enclosed garden was the Kasturba Gandhi Park, where some ladies of the family went only for Kasturba's name. All these places were in the near vicinity of the samaj. Slightly farther on was the Mall Avenue, another good place to explore and window shop. Biro and Basho, along with the two smaller sisters of Gurbans, Harbhajan and Baby, were game for the adventure. The young ones made full use of the assortment of places to choose from and went there, excited in their congenial company, whenever they could find time. Prakash, a movie buff, located the Pratibha Theatre and went for a late evening show when they were showing *Tom Edison*. Most cinemas known to show foreign movies, mostly English, screened only one show a day. Some elite of the town and other university students came for these shows.

And thus, everyone had several choices of spending their free time as it suited their mood and the week went by in full fun. On Sunday night, the clouds rolled in, rumbling with some lightning and thunder from the eastern skies, and they had a wet Monday. Not suited for any outdoor activity, the packs of cards came out to keep them engaged indoors. They concentrated on the local savouries and tea from the kitchen and the hand of cards to make their moves.

~

Early next morning, as soon as it was time for the workplaces to start their day and when hospitals would be a stir with a new hope among the ailing, Goldram arranged for a tonga. He then went and told Mathura Devi, Sheila and Chetsingh's wife to get ready to go to the hospital. He had talked to Dr Maheshwari before bidding him 'good night' and had fixed an appointment with him first thing in the morning. He told Kaushalya to get Nikko ready too. The delicate boy was still running a temperature and had coughed almost non-stop through the night; this had become a cause of worry for his parents and his grandmother, whose blue-eyed boy he always had been. He told them to pack a few change of clothes, for some of them may have to remain admitted to the hospital for a thorough check-up, tests and intensive treatment for a few days.

By late afternoon, around four, the reports of the tests that had been carried out on the patients began to come in from the pathological department. Bad news, as Goldram thought, was that all of the four patients would have to be admitted for at least four or five days to come. They were not in a fit condition to travel and the doctors could not take chances with their delicate condition, especially in the case of Chetsingh's wife and Sheila. They assured him, though, that under a strict regimen of medication and dietary care (which can only be maintained in the hospital and under the supervision of the matron and the nursing staff) they should recoup to a reasonably healthier condition and be able to continue on the journey. Goldram and Dr Dev were given a list of instructions to be followed even after the patients had left the hospital and were on their own. As a doctor, Dev understood this very well, and reassuring Goldram out of his anxieties, led him to the samaj's premises and asked him to not allow his apprehensions to surface and scare everyone. 'Let's make the news sound routine and casual. Also, somehow prevent them from going and looking at the sick elders in the hospital more than once,' he said wisely.

Everyone in the family seemed to have spent the week of sojourn in the dharmashala of the Arya Samaj quite comfortably and pleasantly. They found something new to explore and interest their fancies every day. From the visits to the state museum to a dip on the ghats of the Gomati, they tried all they could within the area. All in all, although it was a prolonged wayside stop, it was a good enough lay-by for them to get enough relaxation along with some interesting leisure activities including sightseeing and exploring the neighbourhood. Above all, the old and sick returned from the hospice in a smiling condition. Goldram was happy to see them fit to proceed ahead as they were closing in on their destination.

The Calcutta–Golden Temple (now Howrah–Amritsar) Mail would take them into the heartland of Punjab and its terminus at Amritsar—though they could change trains for anywhere in

Punjab from any junction on the way to the terminus. And indeed, soon they would be separated from one another and would leave with shared memories of the vicissitudes of the arduous trek which had been made easier by being together. Yet, they would not only be happy to be back where they belonged but they would also bring joy to those who were waiting for them at home.

25

Goldram's family were from different parts of Punjab, though they were not separated by long distances. Goldram was from Daska in Sialkot. But he and the families of Dayal Singh and Chetsingh had decided that Gujranwala would be their present terminus, and waited to reach Amritsar from where they knew they would have to change trains to reach their destination. At Gujranwala they would get off the train, lock, stock and barrel. Chetsingh had parted company from the family group at the Arya Samaj for some personal interest and came by a different route. He had reached Gujranwala about two weeks earlier than Goldram and had established himself in a rented house in the Nanakpura area on the eastern edge of the town close to Khalsa College on the banks of a well-maintained irrigation canal.

Goldram's old and widowed aunt, too, had a small dwelling in the very heart of the town, in a rather narrow ancient lane off the main Gujranwala bazaar. But not wanting to impose themselves as a burden on their relatives and conscious of the large family that he was immediately responsible for, Goldram had sent a note requesting Chetsingh to arrange for him a place large enough to comfortably house more than a dozen members of his family. And indeed, Chetsingh, driven partially by his desire to shake himself off his beholdenment to Goldram for hosting his children in Gyogon, had willingly seen to the arrangements. He also didn't want his sister's family to face any difficulty while settling down in the new environ. Without Chetsingh's help, as was the case when the Goldram family arrived in Delhi after the vivisection of the country, they would have faced a major predicament.

It was exactly after a week of their arrival on Sunday at Lucknow that the family members were told by Goldram to get their packing done. They were to leave the next Tuesday morning. It was a mail train that they had to take for an overnight journey before they would reach Agra in the United Provinces through Etawah, Shikohabad, and finally, Firozabad. As their mail train chugged onwards, they left behind the fancy tales about Wajid Ali Shah and the cane juice-drenched flavours of the United Provinces behind to enter the ancient historical land of the *Mahabharata*, Kurukshetra. Next they were to breathe the salubrious breezes of the land of golden harvests, the celebrated fertile lands of the five rivers, Punjab, from Ambala onwards.

As the train left a withering smoke trail, it sped along into the vicinity of Ludhiana on the banks of Sutlej. They saw the rich and verdurous green fields and little hamlets with their crops. The sight of the rural abundance of India was a balm to their eyes, elevating their spirits. Waving and bending to the strong early summer winds under the vast and spreading blue sky, the crops would, in time, yield a rich harvest to add to the breadbasket of the country.

It was late in the evening and the large, bright disc of the full moon shone in the sky, surrounded by shimmering stars. Nikko, from his window seat, saw the scene for a few moments with glazed eyes, when the first blazing electric light dazzled him away from the celestial beauty. The train came to a halt by the brightly lit and busy railway platform of Amritsar for an hour-long stop. After the long and tiring journey, Goldram knew they were all too weary to venture out to the station restaurant. Therefore, he ordered food from the dining car for everyone after ascertaining their choice. The young did go out to stretch their legs and hurried to the crowded ice cream vendor. They had all the flavours they wanted, and Kartarlal carried some cones for those who had remained sitting in the carriage. He knew his brother's choice and bought a cream and nut kulfi packet for him and one for their mother. But having lost all her teeth, she picked the nuts and hardened currants out from the soft and sweet cream to be discarded. However, she was fond of sweets and seemed not quite satisfied with just one cup of ice cream, but discomfited, she didn't ask for more and kept quiet. The children and the elders all settled down for the night in their seats and curled up, heavy-lidded, to get some sleep.

They all knew that they'd reach Gujranwala the next morning, where they had to finally disembark. All were in a deep slumber until early the next morning. Goldram was the first to begin his rounds. He slowly got everyone out of their makeshift beds and then lent his helping hand to the elders so they could wrap up and pack their belongings that were spread across overhead seats and under them. They took a count of the bags and were then ready to get down at Gujranwala. But the family of Dr Dev, who were bound for Sialkot, would continue their journey in the same train. Dayal Singh's family, and, of course, Goldram's family, were to get down at Gujranwala. It was 8.20 in the morning when their train steamed with widely placed chugs into Gujranwala station. Goldram, peeping out his of window seat, saw his uncle Chetsingh eagerly walking along the still-moving train until he spotted a waving Goldram leaning out.

Chetsingh had rounded up five coolies to unload the luggage from the carriage on to the platform. He also had five good tongas waiting outside to carry their baggage and all others of the family, who would now stay put in Gujranwala. Mathura Devi was the happiest of them all to again be amidst familiar sights and sounds. In fact, just breathing the air of her native land was enough for her to go into raptures of sheer joy. From the station, the others headed to Nanakpura to Chetsingh's house to wash and have a hearty mouth-watering breakfast of parathas and several favourite Punjabi dishes, while Goldram rode on to unload the luggage in the house that Chetsingh had arranged for them. The plan was to rest for a couple of hours there, and then in the evening around five, go and finally settle down in the house fixed for them on street sixteen of Nanakpura.

1945–1956

In response to his letter to the accounts department of Burma Railways, there was soon an official response for Goldram bearing good news: his gratuity had been transferred to his new account number with the accountant general's office at Gorton Castle in Simla—the summer capital of the British Government in India, from the end of March to the end of October. Henceforth, his pension would be directly transferred into the same account. It was good news for him, except that he would have to make a few trips to Simla to get his identity established and complete the rest of the formalities until he created a bank account in his name and got money transferred from Simla via cheques.

Kaushalya was taken ill then. The diagnosis from the tests revealed that she had typhoid and would have to remain in the hospital for at least two weeks. Even after her discharge, she would need at least two weeks of rest and would have to have a properly supervised diet as her diaphragm had been affected. Even though she was in the midst of the family and a very caring mother-in-law, she said to Goldram out of the blue, 'I can't bear to be alone when you are away in Simla.'

'It is going to be a matter of few such trips and then we shall be fine. I'll have my own bank account and a new number and chequebooks. The funds will be available anywhere we go and finally settle down,' he told her reassuringly. And she felt at rest.

Goldram was not the kind to nurse grudges but was hurt and sore too. He had been superseded at the time of his promotions and financial increments. He thought he amply deserved it after the Sino-Burma cross border railway line he and his team had successfully laid. The worst part was that he felt that the promotion had been given on the parochial grounds of religious bias. Even after coolly pondering over the pros and cons of his decision, his painful conclusion was that he had to turn down his erstwhile benevolent officer, Sir Rolland's offer to return to Rangoon and be promoted as the district engineer. And after having turned down the offer to return to Burma, he was faced with a situation where he had to make provisions for the family. He needed to find a viable vocation for himself soon.

In a couple of long sessions, he discussed and thrashed out the matter with his seasoned and worldly-wise uncle, Chetsingh. The decision, at the end of their confabulations, was to start a small industry—a manufacturing unit for agricultural implements like cane crushers and manually-worked chaff-cutters that were vastly used by farmers all over Punjab. The enterprise was to be financed by drawing upon Goldram's gratuity, and later, perhaps the loan he had applied for would come through. The place decided upon was Lahore; it had a flourishing and renowned industrial area called Badami Bagh, which was almost an extension of the city.

Having been a very competent engineer all his professional life, Goldram planned it out on the drawing board himself. He drew the plans, estimated the cost of materials and set up a team of mechanics and workers under his trusted fried, Habibullah, whom he went and fetched from Daska. The land he had chosen and bought was in the Badami Bagh industrial area, beyond the Minto Park and adjacent to the biggest gurdwara in Lahore. He went house-hunting so that he could bring the family with him. He named his factory 'Allied Factories'. Those were arduous, busy and muggy days during August and September, and at the end of the day, you could see his white shirt all soaked in sweat over a layer of smoky brown dust plastered in patches.

He went knocking from pillar to post before he could conclude the paperwork and get a sanction for a quota of three tons of pig iron and two train carriages of hard coke fuel to fire the cupola once a week for moulding two tons of required denomination of steel from the Tata Iron and Steel Company offices in the town. The pig iron and steel would have to be collected from Jullundur from the company's stockyards there; the carriages of coke would come straight from Calcutta to the shunting yard at the Badami Bagh station with the information and invoice sent to Goldram's workshop and office in the premises of the factory yard, facing the Grand Trunk Road from Ambala in the south and Jullundur in the north.

Goldram found reasonably good living quarters in the residential section of Badami Bagh. Soon, the family arrived from Gujranwala, filled with excitement and anticipation as they moved into the rented apartment that Goldram had diligently prepared for their arrival. Together, they embarked on a new chapter in their lives, hopeful for a brighter future.

Epilogue

With the wheels of progress set in motion, Goldram ensured the smooth functioning of his manufacturing endeavours, overseeing every aspect with precision and dedication. To assist him in his endeavours, he invited his nephew Bhagat Singh to join the business. Despite being an unemployed matriculate, Bhagat Singh proved to be a valuable asset, taking on the role of overall manager and diligently maintaining the accounts in a day-book. In recognition of his contribution, Bhagat Singh was provided with living quarters on the premises, strengthening the familial bond that was crucial to their success.

During his time in Lahore, Goldram's path crossed with Mr L.C. Suri, an accomplished agricultural engineer. Their frequent meetings led to a deep friendship, with Mr Suri becoming not just a well-wisher but a trusted family friend. As time passed, it was Mr Suri who played a significant role in negotiating Nikko's marriage, ensuring a prosperous union for his beloved son when the time came.

As the years unfolded, the entire family flourished. Goldram's manufacturing business prospered, fuelled by his determination and entrepreneurial spirit. Bhagat Singh, entrusted with the responsibility of managing the business, grew in skill and expertise, becoming an integral part of its success. Nikko, now happily married and blessed with a loving partner, embarked on his own journey, his future brimming with promise and possibilities. The entire family, bound by their mutual experiences and unwavering support for one another, found solace and joy in their shared triumphs.

Goldram, looking back and reflecting on his life, couldn't help but marvel at the resilience and strength of his family. He felt grateful for the journey that brought them together and united them. As the sun set, casting a warm glow over his bustling home, Goldram felt hopeful for the days to come; he knew there were uncertainties in the future but he was confident that they would continue to thrive and face the challenges together, as a family.

RUPA
13/4/24